Alley Ciz

POWER PLAY

BTU Alumni Series Book #1

ALLEY CIZ

Also by Alley Ciz

BTU Alumni Series

Power Play (Jake and Jordan)

Musical Mayhem (Sammy and Jamie) BTU Novella

Tap Out (Gage and Rocky)

Sweet Victory (Vince and Holly)

Puck Performance (Jase and Melody)

Writing Dirty (Maddey and Dex)

Scoring Beauty- BTU6 Preorder, Releasing September 2021

#UofJ Series

Cut Above The Rest (Prequel)- Freebie

Looking To Score

Game Changer

Playing For Keeps

Off The Bench- #UofJ4 Preorder, Releasing December 2021

The Royalty Crew (A #UofJ Spin-Off)

Savage Queen- Preorder, Releasing April 2021

Ruthless Noble- Preorder, Releasing June 2021

Hockey players are off limits...especially if they're on your brothers' team.

The last time Jordan did that, it ended in disaster. It was easy to promise her brothers she'd never date another one of their teammates again.
Until she meets Jake.
The spark she feels when she spends time with him makes her promise harder and harder to keep.
Surely her brothers would understand breaking this promise if it means following her heart.
Wouldn't they?

Never sleep with a teammate's sister.

This is the universal rule of athletes everywhere.
Until he meets Jordan.
As soon as Jake sets eyes on her, he wants her.
The goalie's job is to see missed shots and failed opportunities on the ice.
This is one shot he's not going to miss, no matter what obstacles get in his way.

POWER PLAY is a flirty, swoon worthy sexy rom-com and the first book in the BTU Alumni Series and can be read as a standalone. If you like hockey boys, sarcastic friends, matchmaking K9s, too-cute-to-handle kindergartners, fierce heroines and swoony hot as puck Alpha heroes, then you want to get to know this cast of characters. One puck head and an HEA guaranteed.

Power Play (BTU Alumni, Book 1)

Alley Ciz

Digital ISBN: 978-1-950884-00-1

Print ISBN: 978-1-950884-00-1

Cover Designer: Julia Cabrera at Jersey Girl Designs

Editing: Ben Leroy

Proofreading: Gem's Precise Proofreads; Dawn Black

❀ Created with Vellum

For my OG Beta readers Megan and Melanie for pushing me to complete Jake and Jordan's story, regardless for how many years it took.

For my parents for making the dream of being an author possible.

And finally Maria Luis and Renee Linda for giving me the push I needed to take the chance.

Contents

Text Handles

The Coven
    Jordan: MOTHER OF DRAGONS
    Skye: MAKES BOYS CRY
    Maddey: QUEEN OF SMUT
    Sammy: THE SPIN DOCTOR

The Boys
    Jake: THE BRICK WALL
    Tucker: WANNA TUCK

Chapter One

J ake relaxed into his seat in the VIP section of Rookies Sports Bar taking in the atmosphere. Rookies was packed, proving yet again it was the place to be on a Saturday night. Nothing run-of-the-mill about it.

The main floor was comprised of an open dance floor lined with six person bench tables with a U-shaped bar. The access for the VIP area they were sitting in was up a flight of stairs toward the back. It covered half the dance floor providing a great view of the main bar, only surpassed by the DJ's position above all. With its own bar, lounge couches and tables, it was obvious why the guys claimed it. The walls were lined with seventy-inch plasma TV's and one-of-a-kind sports memorabilia, a sports fanatic's ultimate fantasy.

The night started off just like any other Saturday night, with Jake and some of the guys from the hockey team enjoying a night out at Rookies. However, Jake could feel an undercurrent throughout the group.

Two of his friends, Ryan, the captain and star forward of the team, and Jase, a defenseman Jake relied on during the games, caused the change of energy. Jase's twin brother, JD, was supposed to be joining them. It would be the first time he had the opportunity to meet him.

After two long, hard years they had a bond and many fond memories. He was closest with Jase since they were the same year but his friendship with Ryan was not far behind. Those friendships were growing stronger everyday with Ryan and Jase's family moving in next door to Jake's family a few weeks ago.

"When's JD supposed to get here?" Jake asked Jase.

His friend checked the time on his phone. "Any minute now I would think."

Jake couldn't believe that he hadn't met JD in the past two years. It was hard enough to coordinate schedules for one student athlete let alone two, attending different schools didn't help either. He guessed all that would change now that JD was transferring to Brighton Tynes University from NYU.

Thoughts of JD always circled around to the other Donnelly sibling he also had yet to meet, Jordan. Jake knew she also attended NYU, aside from this however he lacked any other details. After seeing pictures of her, drawn by her beauty, he tried to find out more about her through social media but her accounts, like JD's, were private. Her brothers were no help either, they were surprisingly tight-lipped when the topic of their sister came up.

The guys sat in the circle alcove by the bar so they could create their own area in the VIP. They were always able to claim the best spot, close to the bar and overlooking the dance floor.

Jase was sitting next to Jake with his back to the dance floor. He sat up suddenly. "JD's here."

Ryan was sitting across from them and shook his head at his younger brother. "How do you know? You aren't even facing the door."

"I just know. It's a twin thing." He said with a smug look on his face.

Ryan sighed. "You guys and that freaky ESP stuff."

Jake ignored the brothers' discussion over ESP and started looking around the bar and that's when he saw her.

His breath caught as he watched the most beautiful girl he had ever seen hug the bouncer hello and make her way into Rookies. Sure she was beautiful but there was something in his gut that made him unable to look away.

As he continued his gaze, he observed how she walked around hugging some of the employees and he began to wonder how she knew them because there was no doubt he'd never seen her here before, she was not someone you forgot. From this distance there was something familiar about her though he couldn't put his finger on it.

Jake was brought back to reality by Ryan snapping his fingers in his face. "Jake. Hello? Dude, come back to Earth. What are you looking at?"

The realization that there were other people around him struck. "Oh, my bad. Just spaced out for a minute there."

Slowly Jake turned his back to the girl and faced his friends. He took a long pull of his beer trying to take the edge off the feeling in his gut.

He wasn't sure why he didn't tell his friends about her, but a part of him wanted to keep the information to himself. He knew he wasn't successful when Tucker, his best friend from growing up and another teammate, looked over the edge.

"I don't know what he was looking at but I know I see a hot blonde down there that I've never seen before. Who wants to be my wingman?"

Jake's body tensed.

Jake knew most girls thought Tucker was a looker but he was also a big time player. He was cocky and tried to get with anything in a skirt.

"Seriously bro you choose now to give in to your man-whore urges?" Jase rolled his eyes. "JD will be up here any minute. Can't you keep it in your pants for a few more minutes?"

"Plus weren't you trying to seal the deal with Skye again less than ten minutes ago?" Ryan nodded his head toward their pretty bartender.

"She's got plans tonight. So no dice." Tucker said with a frown.

"Come on Jake, be the Goose to my Maverick. You know I'll get this girl to come back up here quick. You know how this works, we've been doing it for over a decade."

Jake followed Tucker down from the VIP area to the main bar. Shaking his head, he watched as Tucker went straight for the blonde he saw.

She was leaning over the bar enjoying a conversation with the bartender, based on the smiles on their faces, as they made their approach.

Tucker broke into a confident stride. His confidence unnerved Jake as he slid next to the girl. "Hey there gorgeous, how about you let me buy you a drink?"

She was almost a foot shorter than them but she had legs that seemed to go on for days, which showed nicely in her short denim skirt and flip-flops. A jeweled belt accentuated her small waist while a long necklace drew attention to the cleavage displayed in her tank. She may have been petite, but it didn't take away from her hourglass shape and dangerous curves. He thought she was attractive from a distance, but up close she was stunning. Long, straight blonde hair framed her face and tumbled down her back. Her hazel eyes were framed by dark lashes and her pink gloss had him zeroing in on her lush lips.

She turned to Tucker. "Um no thanks, I'm good." Jake was pleased to catch her coyly look him up and down and not Tucker.

Her gaze sparked something inside him but he fought to keep his composure.

Tucker was unfazed by her rejection. Jake knew he considered it another hurdle in the cat and mouse game he loved to play with girls. He thought it was all part of his charm. "Come on honey, come with me I'll get you a drink and get you into the VIP. I know people."

She looked annoyed as she turned back to face Tucker. "Oh you know people do you?" She paused to grab a bottle of beer off the bar. "Well I think I'll take my chances. I know people too."

She reached out and took Tucker's hand, turning it palm up. "But here, have this beer on me to help you think of a better approach."

Then with one more look at Jake she turned and went up the stairs to the VIP, stopping to give the bouncer a hug and a kiss on the cheek.

Tucker stood next to the bar, beer in hand, mouth agape at the girl who blew him off. Next to him Jake couldn't help but smile that she didn't fall for his cocky charm.

Along with the satisfaction of Tucker's failure, there was a gut feeling he had to know more about this girl. She was too captivating to be ignored.

JORDAN HUGGED ZEEK the bouncer working the front door of Rookies before she entered. It had been two years since she was there for a night out, which to her was two years too long. The beat of the bass coming through the speakers surrounded her as she let the sense of homecoming settle inside her. It was all the confirmation she needed that she made the right decision.

As she walked around saying hi to any familiar faces, she recalled the fight she had with her brothers over coming back.

"You're transferring to BTU?" Ryan asked. She could tell he was shocked by this.

"Yeah. Skye is too."

"Why? I thought NYU was her dream school."

"It is. Or I guess it was. But BTU is offering a better Public Relations program now. They have courses now that focus on PR for athletes and you know that is what we want to focus on." It took everything in her to keep her voice level. Losing her cool would not help the situation.

"But you're safer in the city."

She rolled her eyes at this. "Now you're being ridiculous."

"But Tommy…"

She cut off that argument immediately. "I'm not going to allow Tommy to be a factor in my decision making any longer. It has been two years and we haven't heard anything from him. I've changed all my social media accounts, you guys moved hockey houses last year, and mom and dad are moving in a month. The only place he would know to look for me is Rookies and Aunt Ei owns it, it's like home ice advantage for us." She wished she was with her brothers in person instead of talking to them on FaceTime.

"Are you one hundred percent sure?" Jase was the one to ask.

"Yes I'm sure. Plus I miss you guys. I hate not seeing you guys all the time and barely being able to come to your games."

"We miss you too but what about swimming?" Jase asked.

"Skye and I both already earned spots on BTU's team based on our times. And they have a diving team we can go out for."

"And you're sure there's no changing your mind?" Ryan turned the camera back to him.

"No. Acceptance and everything are already taken care of," she paused before continuing. "Look school ends in a few weeks, then I head down to Florida for a month for a beach lifeguard training program. I won't be coming home until after that at the end of June, so you have a month and a half to get used to the idea. Now I have to go. I love you both."

Shaking her head at the memory, she made her way over to Erin working the main bar. "Erin," she called out.

"Jordan! Hey girl, long time no see," she greeted Jordan with a face-splitting smile.

"Yeah I know.

"Want a beer?" At Jordan's nod Erin reached into the fridge and uncapped a bottle. "Here you go, love."

"Thanks," she gestured at Erin's shirt. "Taking liberties with the uniform I see."

"Hell yeah. My tips have more than doubled, thank god your aunt is so cool." She pulled at the knot keeping the shirt tied to expose her midriff.

"Not surprised, you look hot."

"Thanks girl. But damn so do you. I'm sure your brothers are going to have something to say about that."

Jordan looked down at her outfit. She wore a sheer, peachy pink cami over a white lace tank, the combination complimented her tan while making the girls look good. It was the short denim skirt she wore that would be the issue for her overprotective brothers. Stopping way before mid-thigh it showed off a lot of leg. At least she was wearing flip-flops and not a killer pair of FMPs.

She kept her makeup light so it wouldn't melt off during her flight home from Florida. Tinted moisturizer, mascara, and lip gloss, simple but effective.

Her conversation with Erin was rudely interrupted by a smug voice. "Hey there gorgeous, how about you let me buy you a drink?"

Confronting the voice, her suspicions were confirmed. Sure the guy was good looking, the quintessential cocky playboy. Most likely an athlete based on his build.

"Um no thanks I'm good." But as she turned away her gaze fell on his dark haired friend.

Oh my God who is that? He's so sexy just standing there all calm and collected. The guy hitting on her was good looking but she wished it was his friend trying to pick her up. It would have been bad though if he did, she was supposed to be meeting her brothers but would gladly be side tracked by that hunk. She quickly turned away so he wouldn't see the mischief in her eyes.

Mr. Arrogant wasn't to be deterred. He tried to entice her with VIP access. Too bad her connections were better than his.

One last look at Mr. Sexy in the background, she said goodbye to Erin to find her brothers and get another beer.

JAKE AND TUCKER entered the VIP section and saw the blonde with her arms wrapped around Ryan's neck in a bear hug so tight she was lifted off the ground.

"Damn, what does Ryan have that I don't?" Tucker complained.

Ryan put the blonde down and turned towards Jake and Tucker, his arm draped over her shoulder. "Hey guys I'd like you to meet my baby sister, JD."

Wait? What?

She looked up at her brother, who towered over her at six four, with a scowl on her face. It was easy to see she did not like to be considered a baby and by the looks of her she was anything but. Dirty thoughts flooded Jake's mind every time he looked at her.

"One, I'm not a baby. Two, we already met." She turned to Jase and was picked up into another bear hug.

"See I told you she was here," Jase announced to his brother in a mocking tone, laughing. He placed her down between him and Ryan facing his friends. "JD, this is Tucker and Jake. Guys meet JD."

Both their mouths hung open in shock.

Tucker was first to recover. "Sup."

Jordan nodded.

"Wait, this is JD? I thought JD was your twin?" He was trying to figure out how he could have missed that JD and Jordan were the same person.

Jake could see the resemblance in their blonde hair and

hazel eyes. The twin factor, more prominent in person than pictures, caused them to have similar features, his strong and masculine to her soft and feminine. The biggest difference though, Jake never wanted to kiss Jase like he did Jordan.

"Seriously how did I miss this?"

"It wasn't intentional," Ryan shrugged.

"Yeah right," Jordan scoffed. "Anyway…" She pushed Ryan's arm from her shoulders. "You guys aren't the only ones I came here to see."

Jake and the guys watched her leave them for the bar. To his amazement, the usual composed and somewhat distant Skye jumped over the bar and embraced her. This must be the friend he heard some stories about.

"I guess Skye is close to your sister?" He asked Jase.

"Yeah her and Jordan have been best friends since kindergarten. You would never know she was a geeky little kid by the babe she's turned into." Jase said about the attractive bartender.

Jake could agree with the babe assessment, her shoulder length strawberry blonde hair and light blue eyes were a striking combination. From what Tucker had mentioned she had an ass that wouldn't quit. Still it was Jordan— he couldn't bring himself to think of her as JD— that held his attention.

Jake used his question as an excuse for his gaze to linger on Jordan without raising suspicion. A moment later he felt like he was punched in the gut as he watched the DJ pick Jordan up and kiss her square on the mouth.

The disappointment and jealousy he felt surprised him. *Of course she has a boyfriend. Look at her.*

He couldn't comprehend why the relationship status of some girl he just met bothered him so much, no matter how hot she was. Luckily he was distracted by Skye's shouting.

"Hey guys get your asses over here and welcome your

sister home right." Skye was filling up glasses from behind the bar as she made her demands.

The four guys made their way over to the bar. Ryan took the lead. "What are we toasting with tonight? Champagne?"

"Irish car bombs brother dear. I need to make sure your friends here can keep up when we party." He saw her wink at Skye as she set the drinks in front of everyone.

So she knew how to party and seemed like she liked being one of the guys. He couldn't wait to learn more about her.

"Well baby sister welcome home this should be interesting," Ryan teased.

The six of them toasted to Jordan's home coming, dropped their shots in their beers, and threw back their drinks.

Tucker grimaced, putting down his drink when he finished. Jake knew he wasn't a fan of Guinness.

"Aw Tucker don't be such a pansy, you're gonna have to learn how to drink the good stuff around us," Jordan gave his arm a nudge. "I would have thought you would have been used to drinking this with Skye being a bartender here."

Jake couldn't contain his laughter after seeing the look on Tucker's face. *How did one respond when your friends' sister calls you a pansy?*

After accepting a fresh round of drinks, they made their way back to where they normally sat, with Skye joining whenever people didn't need a drink.

Jordan sat across from Jake, much to his pleasure.

The guys talked about their plans for the summer and how the season was going to be this year. They discussed what the next movie night flick should be.

Jake felt instant chemistry with Jordan. He had a nagging suspicion that the identity confusion was intentional. But why? It didn't add up.

· · ·

PUSHING FROM BETWEEN her brothers Jordan made her way over to the bar where her best friend in the whole wide world since forever was working.

Skye was pouring out a round of shots when she caught sight of her making her way up to the bar.

"Ohmygodohmygodohmygod! I can't believe you're finally here. I never want to go that long without you again." Skye shouted as she came around the bar to throw her arms around her.

Skye hugged her so hard it felt like she would never let go. Familiar with the feeling, she returned the embraced with equal feeling.

"I know I missed you so much." Jordan pulled her head slightly out of her friend's grip to take a deep breath. "That was the best welcome I've had, but if you don't let go I'm going to suffocate."

She felt Skye loosen her grip from around her neck. Since Skye was half a foot taller, she didn't realize she had Jordan's face buried in her boobs, too caught up in the moment. They missed each other so much. In the month since the end of their sophomore year Jordan was off doing beach lifeguard training in Florida, it was the longest they had ever been apart.

The energy Skye radiated was contagious. She always made Jordan feel loved and was more like a sister than a friend. The two met on the playground in kindergarten when Skye invited Jordan to build bird nests out of dead grass with her. Since then the girls had been inseparable. They attended NYU together and then transferred to Brighton Tynes.

"Seriously, I was completely lost without you," Skye informed her.

Jordan laughed. "The feeling is mutual. Never again."

"Sammy is DJing tonight. Aunt Ei was stoked to land him. Oh my god he is going to be so happy you're back." Skye turned to wave the DJ down to the bar.

Jordan couldn't help the overwhelming feeling that she was finally home. "That's awesome. I missed you guys so much. I was completely beside myself without my best pals to keep me company and to look at the hot guys on the beach with me."

Pausing she looked back at her brothers and their friends, her eyes quickly finding Jake. "Speaking of hot guys, what do you know about this Jake guy?"

She knew Skye had to have some information from bartending at Rookies the last month. The hockey team was known to be regulars.

"Hmm well let's see. He's the definition of tall, dark, and handsome, star goalie for BTU, same year as us, and besides being super hot, he's one of the nicest guys I've ever met. He's pretty close with your brothers too."

Jordan thought that *super hot* was a huge understatement. When Tucker hit on her it was Jake she noticed. Definitely tall, probably had her by a foot. His black t-shirt was snug on his shoulders and chest, showing off his muscles nicely. But it was his eyes that got her full attention. Even the dim lighting of the bar couldn't dull their effect. They were the brightest and softest green she had ever seen and were contrasted nicely by his tan skin. However, it was the heat in them that took her breath away. With his back turned she noticed how nice his butt filled out his jeans. *He looked good enough to eat.*

"Interesting." She observed how the guys interacted.

Too busy ogling Jake, it took her a moment to fully register all Skye said.

"Wait a second," she pointed to Jake. "That's Jake Donovan?" It figured he was a hockey player, they were her Kryptonite. Too bad she promised her brothers she wouldn't date another teammate.

"Yup."

"Damn. It's a shame to cover all that up with goalie gear. The guy is fine."

"I agree. The same could be said for all of them." Skye made her way back to her place behind the bar.

"What about that Tucker guy. He totally hit on me, but the way I turned him down, I think I squashed that problem."

She watched as color crept up Skye's face. "Anything you want to tell me?"

"Tucker is hot too and you don't have to tell him, he knows it. He's got more of that surfer boy appeal to him with that sandy colored hair and brown eyes. He's the cockiest person I've ever met. Kind of a player but he's got the skills in that department to back it up."

She nudged her friend on the shoulder. "Oh my god Skye, you didn't?"

Her friend only nodded her head.

"Lucy you have some 'splaining to do," Jordan teased in her best Ricky Ricardo impression. "I can't believe you didn't tell me about this."

Skye had the good grace to look sorry. "It's a good thing Maddey will be at my house... It's going to be a long night."

"Jordan."

She turned to see a copper haired heartthrob walking purposely toward her.

"Sammy—" The rest of her words were cut off when he lifted her in a twirl and planted a smacking kiss on her lips.

Once back on her feet she continued. "I can't believe you're here. I thought you'd be too busy spinning in the city."

"I gave your aunt a few Saturdays this summer since you two moved out of the city."

"That's awesome."

"It's what I do," he said with a shrug. "Anyway I have to get back to the booth. I'll see you guys later at Skye's."

Sammy was one of her favorite people on Earth, getting to see him now instead of having to wait the extra hours until later made her happy.

"Any ETA on Maddey?" She asked Skye, curious when the final member of their foursome would arrive.

"She should be at my parents sometime after one. I think she's just gonna wait for us to get there since Aunt Ei gave the okay for me to cut out early tonight."

"Gotta love her."

Glancing in the guys' direction again she remembered something that didn't make sense. "So something weird happened earlier."

"What's that?" Skye asked while she mixed a drink for a customer.

"Jake made a comment about Jase having a twin brother and it just seemed odd to me."

Skye's brow crinkled in thought. "You know what? Anytime I heard them talking about you they only ever called you JD. Do you think they would keep your identity a secret?"

"I'm not sure if that's the case because he mentioned something about knowing who I was by name. There's just some stuff that doesn't add up."

"Well knowing your brothers as well as I do, I think the Tommy situation really did a number on them… well all of us really."

Jordan nodded in agreement at the reference of her ex. She was in desperate need of a subject change. "I think it's time for drinks. Let's get the guys over here."

After a round of car bombs, her favorite, she settled in to spend some quality time with her brothers. Originally when she decided to attend NYU with Skye, she'd planned on spending as much time at home as she did in the city. After her drama filled breakup with her ex, it became easier to stay in Manhattan.

From the stories they told and the plans they made it was obvious not much had changed. Now she needed to figure out what the hell they were playing at.

Chapter Two

Jordan loaded her bags into the trunk of her white Corvette Stingray, running her hand along the rear spoiler as she closed the trunk. *Man I love this car.* Going to school in Manhattan didn't provide many opportunities to drive since it was easier to take public transportation where she needed to go, another perk of transferring to BTU.

Unable to stop another yawn from breaking free, she made a mental note to grab coffee before leaving Skye's. A vibration from the back pocket of her daisy dukes distracted her from putting the top down on the car. She frowned at the text.

UNKNOWN: Welcome home.

A trail of unease coursed through her. She was used to getting calls from unknown numbers, but a text message was a different story. *I am so not caffeinated enough to figure this out.*

Once the top was down, she made her way back inside. Navy, her hundred pound black lab, lifted his head from where it rested on Maddey's lap letting out a happy bark in greeting.

"What's with all the noise?" Sammy groaned from the couch he slept on.

Jordan shared a knowing look with Maddey. "Sorry Navy's a bit excited. He missed his mama while she was in Florida. Didn't ya boy." She scratched his ear and placed a kiss on his wet nose.

"Why the hell are you even up this early?"

"It's almost nine thirty."

"You act like that's sleeping late. FYI, it's not when you go to bed around seven in the morning. This baby face needs sleep if it still wants to look good."

"Oh stop complaining Sam." Skye tossed a pillow in his direction.

"But seriously why are we not sleeping until noon?" Sammy pulled the covers over his head.

"Because, drama queen." Jordan headed in the direction of the Keurig. "I haven't been home yet. I took an Uber from the airport to the bar since my car was here. I think it's time to see the new house. Plus I haven't seen my parents or Sean since we all went to the Frozen Four in April."

"Okay I can forgive you for disturbing my sleep since it's for the squirt. Now get the hell out of here so I can go back to sleep," Sammy grumbled and rolled over.

"Love you too."

"Come on, I'll walk you out. I have Navy's stuff in my car." Maddey shifted the dog and got off the couch.

Jordan put her arm around Maddey and called goodbye to her other besties. She whistled for Navy as she opened the door to leave.

Navy, trained well, followed alongside the girls and hopped in the car once the door opened.

"Good boy," she stroked his head.

Maddey leaned in and placed the bag of Navy's belongings in the footwell of the car. "Goodbye my beautiful boy. My bed's gonna be lonely without you."

Jordan laughed as she watched her beast of a dog melt under her best friend's attention. "Thanks again for watching him while I was away. I know it made my mom's life easier with the move and everything."

"No worries. Figured it was an easier transition on him anyway since he's been our fifth roommate the last year."

She pulled Maddey in for a hug. "Love ya girl. See you soon."

"Love you too."

Jake took advantage of the beautiful morning to go for a run, the lack of humidity was surprising for the end of June in Jersey. Being out until three in the morning was no excuse to be lax with his workout regimen. Getting his big break last season after the Titan's previous starting goalie graduated, made him determined to prove himself. He worked his ass off everyday to ensure peak performance each time he stepped on the ice. It paid off when the team won the NCAA Championship.

The Titans were underdogs heading into the Frozen Four. He poured everything he had into those last two games, too exhausted to move after, but it paid off in spades. Earning him .957 save percentage and a finalist nomination for the Mike Richter award.

Thoughts of winning the award played through his head as he sprinted the last few feet to the front door. It was after ten and he was in desperate need of a protein shake and a gallon of water.

On his way to the kitchen to take care of his needs, he was distracted by music coming from a car pulling up outside. *That's odd. Tucker is never early.* Walking toward the window to take a look, his attention turned to the five year old barreling down the stairs and jumping into his arms.

She couldn't contain her excitement. "Jake! Jake! Jake! There's a dog. We have to go see him. Can we? Can we? Will you take me to see him? Please Jake, please."

Of course they could, who could say no to her. Since the day Carlee was born, he had a soft spot for his baby sister, nothing had changed in five years. That fact was driven home when she looked up at him with green eyes so similar to his.

He noticed she was in such a rush to see the dog she put her white sundress on backwards and forgot to put on shoes.

He was in the middle of fixing her dress when he could feel her squirming to break free. "Sure, go put on your shoes and I'll take you outside."

When he opened the front door, his breath caught as he noticed the person in the car was Jordan.

Before he could give the situation any more thought, Carlee shot out the door past him and ran straight for Jordan's car.

As he crossed the front yard, he saw another figure running toward the car. It was Jordan's younger brother Sean.

He laughed at how similar the two little ones were, both missing their shoes. It was cute how eager they could be. Sean, also five, was a smaller version of Ryan with light brown hair and blue eyes.

"Mommy, hurry, Jordan's here."

By the time he reached the bouncing five year olds, Jordan was out of her car and was letting the dog out. "Navy, come."

The big black lab jumped out of the car and sat in front of Jordan waiting for his next command.

"Good boy, Navy." When she bent down to kiss his nose he licked the entire left side of her face with one swoop.

She wiped away the slobber but before she could stand Sean jumped into her arms knocking her over. "Jordy I missed you."

She kissed her brother's cheek. "I missed you, too, buddy." After she put him down she scratched the dog behind the ears. "Plus, Navy loves being around you. With all the food you drop he stays well fed. How could I deprive him of that?"

Sean ran back to the middle of the yard where Carlee was and took her hand. "Jordy this is my friend Carlee, she lives next door. We have swimming lessons together. Can she meet Navy? I told her all about him." Sean was speaking a mile a minute without taking a breath.

Jordan smiled at the kids and spoke with such care and openness. It was a skill you didn't find in a lot of twenty year olds. Jake liked it.

"Of course, buddy. Hello Carlee, it's nice to meet you, I'm Jordan," she turned to pet the dog. "And this is Navy."

Carlee looked at the dog questionably.

It was obvious Carlee was nervous by the sheer size of the dog. Jordan reached out a hand out for Carlee. "Don't worry he's very nice just hold out your hand for him to sniff and if he licks you, you're good to go."

Jake smiled when Carlee took Jordan's hand and cautiously made her way up to the dog. Most guys his age wouldn't think twice about how a girl treated kids, but having a sister so much younger than himself made him appreciate it.

When Navy licked Carlee's hand she laughed and the two kids sandwiched him with hugs. It was an amusing sight and Jake could tell the dog loved the affection.

Carlee ran her hands up and down Navy's back. "Wow your dog is so soft. Thanks for letting me pet him."

"No problem, honey. He loves kids."

"Sean, your sister is so nice."

He nodded. "Yeah she's my favorite. But shh don't tell my brothers." He gave Carlee a little wink, the action not going unnoticed by Jordan.

"Where in the world did you learn to wink at girls? You're five," she asked in disbelief.

"Ry and Jase do it," Sean looked at Jake. "So does Jake."

Unbelievable. Why does it feel like I'm getting played out by a five year old?

"Oh they do, do they," Jordan rolled her eyes. "Do you even know why they do it?"

"No but it makes all the girls happy."

"We are in so much trouble when you get older buddy," Jordan said with a laugh.

Jake had to agree with the sentiment.

"She's pretty too," Carlee added and turned to face her brother. "Jake don't you think Jordan's pretty?"

At Carlee's question Jordan looked at him. "Hey, Jake."

"Hey."

"I can't believe you didn't tell me we were neighbors last night," she scolded.

"I guess in all the excitement I didn't think about it."

"Wow what are the odds." She gestured to Carlee. "I take it she's your sister?"

"Yeah she's my crazy monster." He pulled on one of Carlee's pigtails, smiling as he remembered all the chaos he'd endured since the Donnellys moved in a few weeks ago.

His sister was not one to be ignored and huffed as she moved to where Jake was standing. She pulled his right arm to egg him on.

"Jake, you didn't answer my question. Don't you think Jordan is pretty?"

God how could he not. She was wearing jean shorts and a loose white t-shirt, hair pulled back in a ponytail showing off big hoop earrings, even without makeup she was still a knock out.

He placed a hand on her head. "Yes, Carlee, I think Jordan is very pretty."

His gaze locked with Jordan and he watched her blush.

"You should take her on a date," Carlee announced.

Shocked by his sister's comment he shook his head while running a hand over it. "Excuse me? Since when have you become a little match maker?"

"Since that mean girl Tabby was over last week." Carlee frowned and looked down at the ground.

He heard Jordan giggle in the background.

He couldn't believe his sister's outburst. He didn't necessarily like Tabby in that way either. She was a persistent puck bunny so they went on a few dates but it was nothing serious.

"How do you even remember her?"

Carlee couldn't have spent more than ten minutes with Tabby the one night she was over to watch a movie. That night had been their last date after she tried to get him to have sex in his family's den, with everyone home. Not his style.

"I don't like her, she called me a baby." Carlee's frown deepened.

"Don't worry about Tabby." He pulled her close to his side for a hug. "I'm not sure how Jordan's boyfriend would feel about her going on a date with me though."

But before anyone could say anything else Mr. and Mrs. Donnelly were coming out their front door.

JORDAN COULDN'T BELIEVE her luck. Jake was her new neighbor? How the hell did this not come up the night before? Of all the houses her parents could have moved into, they picked the one next door to temptation itself. If he was just Jake, she would have thanked the stars for her good fortune. But he wasn't. He was Jake Donovan, hockey goalie. AKA her brothers' teammate. *Dammit!*

She cursed ever promising not to date another teammate of theirs. Home not even twenty four hours, she already questioned her decision to transfer to BTU. She thought she built up her resolve while away at NYU. Unfortunately, without the distance school provided, she was more susceptible to temptation than she thought.

It was obvious he recently finished working out based on the sweat soaked tank he wore. Damn if the sight didn't make her knees weak. She tracked a bead of sweat running down the side of his face and had to fight the urge to follow it with her tongue. *Where the hell did that thought come from?*

She was grateful for the distraction Sean and Carlee provided. Jake's sister was adorable and the way he interacted with her was a total turn-on. *Shit. Seriously stop thinking things like that. Nothing more than friendship. Remember?*

It was time to schedule a girl's night out to find a distraction, of the male variety, to get her mind off her sexy new neighbor. A fact driven home by the flutter of excitement she felt learning the attraction was mutual and flash of disappointment over him dating. However, she was confused over why he would think she had a boyfriend.

Unfortunately, before getting clarification, her parents came outside to greet her.

"Jordan, baby, welcome home. I missed you so much." Her mom pulled her into a fierce hug.

Jordan squeezed her mom back as they swung from side to side. "Hi Mom. I missed you too."

"I can't tell you how excited I am that you'll be living at home instead of school. The testosterone in the house is out of hand."

"I bet. I guess it's a good thing Ry and Jase don't live at home."

"You wouldn't think that was the case the way they eat me out of house and home." Her mom let out a loving laugh.

"Not sure if that's gonna get any better. You know Skye will be over all the time. Plus Maddey and Sammy when they have time off from school."

"The more the merrier." Her mom turned her attention to Jake. "Hi Jake, how are you honey?"

"Hi Mrs. D. I'm good. Seeing your boys soon at the rink," Jake said with a smile.

"You boys work too hard."

Jordan turned to hug her father. "Hi Daddy."

"Hi Princess. How are you? Are you hungry? I can make you one of my famous omelets."

"No thanks I'm ok, I just want to get settled in. Is all my stuff here?"

"Yes it is. Your godfather took care of everything." Her dad laughed.

"I'm sure he did." She focused her attention back to her brother. "Sean why don't you take Navy in the house and set him up with food and water while I get the rest of my things from the car. You and Carlee can play with him in the back-yard when he's done. His Frisbee and dishes are in the duffle bag."

The little kid beamed. "Really? Aww man you're the best, Jordy." He gave her a hug before he reached down to drag the bag into the house.

Her parents followed the troops inside. "And while Navy eats, I'll make you two some of my world famous omelets," Jordan heard her father say.

It was the first time she was alone with Jake, not sure what to say an awkward silence followed.

"Sorry about Carlee. She doesn't really have a verbal filter yet," Jake said, sounding embarrassed.

"It's okay. Sean is the same way. He's so nosey, sometimes I swear he's a little spy for my other brothers. When he would visit me at school with my parents, he would ask any guy I talked to if they were my boyfriend," she said on a laugh.

"But I do have one question. What makes you think I have a boyfriend?" She asked with a tilt of the head.

"When I saw you kiss the DJ last night I figured he was

your boyfriend. I didn't think you kissed random guys in front of your brothers. I mean they seem kinda overprotective."

She couldn't stop the bark of laughter that came out in response.

"Did I say something wrong?"

"No, it's just funny," her hand came up to cover her smile. "First off, Sammy is *not* my boyfriend. Neither is anyone else. Let's just say... I'm not his type."

She could see confusion written all over his face. "What do you mean you're not his type? He likes brunettes or something?"

She bit back another grin. "No I'm not a guy. Sammy's gay... Most people wouldn't know it but he is one hundred percent gay." She paused. "He does have great taste in men though."

"I would have never guessed it."

"Yup. It's funny you'd think he was my boyfriend. Gotta love it."

She sighed and looked at her car.

"Well I guess I should finish taking my things out of the car and unpack."

She watched Jake's gaze linger on the convertible, naked appreciation on his face.

"Nice ride." As if drawn by a magnet, he walked closer to the car.

"Thanks, I love 'vettes. It was a high school graduation gift from my godfather."

Jake lifted an eyebrow. "Nice godfather."

"Yeah he likes to spoil me." She shook her head remembering some of the more outrageous gifts she received.

She walked over to where Jake stood and popped the trunk.

"Autobots?" Jake ran a finger over the transformer emblem that replaced the classic flags.

"Yeah. I love the Transformers."

"No shit?" He said with a smile. "You know... I have Optimus Prime on my goalie mask."

"Really?" Her eyes widen in surprise.

"Yeah I was obsessed with the toys when I was younger."

"We had the toys too. It used to drive Jase nuts when I would take the cars and use them for my Barbies. Which only made me do it more."

When her story garnered a laugh from him, she felt ten feet tall. It was shocking how easy he was to get along with.

Jake lifted her carry-on suitcase from the trunk. "When they started making the movies, my parents surprised me one year with the custom artwork."

"That's seriously cool. You've gotta show me sometime."

"You got it."

They were interrupted by a horn honking.

"Yo, loverboy, get a move on. We need to be at the rink in fifteen minutes," Tucker yelled from his car.

"Asshole." Jordan heard Jake mutter under his breath.

"Hey Jordan. Lookin' good." Tucker flirted.

"Hey Tuck," she said with a wave before turning her attention back to Jake. "Guess you gotta go."

"Yeah our team captain is a real slave driver," he said with a wink.

"Guess I'll be seeing you around, since you live fifty feet from me," she said, gesturing to their houses.

"See you later Jordan. Tuck give me a minute I have to get my gear."

As Jake ran to get his gear, she couldn't help but appreciate the flexing of the muscles of his very attractive behind. It really was too bad he was her brothers' teammate.

Chapter Three

Jake slid into the passenger seat of Tucker's Mustang after placing his gear on the backseat. It didn't take long for Tucker to start busting his balls, luckily he was used it.

"*Soooooo*, I see Jordan moved in." Tucker said wiggling his eyebrows.

"What the hell is that supposed to mean?" He tried to be nonchalant. "Of course she moved in, Ry and Jase told us she was moving home since she was transferring to BTU."

Tucker pulled the car away from the curb to drive them to the rink. "Actually they said JD was moving home with the transfer."

"So I'm not the only one who thought JD and Jordan were two different people?" He looked at Tucker, watching his reactions carefully.

"Nah. I thought the same thing. They didn't really talk about Jordan much. I only really remember hearing anything about her after seeing her post on their Facebook and shit. But even then, they didn't say much. I tried to see if I could find out more about her, because she's hot, but her accounts are private."

"Same here. Every now and then she'd post something funny on their walls or trash talk one of their Instagram posts, and I'd want to know more... but nothing."

"Do you think it was intentional?"

"I don't know." Jake shifted in his seat, unsure why the thought made him uncomfortable. "I can't see why. I keep trying to remember if they ever blatantly said JD was a guy. Or a different person from Jordan and I can't recall any."

They pulled into the parking lot of the practice rink and parked next to Ryan's car. As they unloaded their gear Wade and Nick pulled in. Looked like it was going to be drills for Ryan's whole line. Together the four of them walked into the rink.

"So was that her whip?" Tucker asked as they walked down the hallway leading to the locker room.

"Yeah. Sick ride, right?"

Tucker nodded. "Girl has some serious taste."

"She even has an Autobot emblem on her car." Jake smiled at the memory.

"No shit. Damn I thought you were the only grown transformer junkie out there. Marry her."

He popped Tucker in the chest. "Asshole."

"Who you guys talkin' about?" Wade asked pushing the doors to the locker room open.

"Jordan. Ry and Jase's sister." Tucker answered sitting down to put on his skates.

"JD is home?" Nick asked surprised.

"You call her JD too?" Jake asked trying to piece things together.

"Pretty much. Jase was Jay and she was JD anytime they were at the house," Wade confirmed.

"Yeah and I fucking hated it when they called me Jay too. That's why they did it. Thank god they stopped once I was actually on the team." Jase said from in front of his locker.

"You used to hang at the house before you were on the

team?" Jake asked pulling on his leg pads. The other guys didn't need full gear since it was a skills practice, but he did being their target.

"Yeah they used to come by all the time to chill with *Mr. Superstar* over here." Wade waved a hand in Ryan's direction.

Ryan flipped Wade the bird at the dig causing the guys to laugh.

"Why'd she stop coming around? She's a hell of a lot better to look at then your ugly asses," Tucker joked.

An awkward silence descended, making the room feel as if all the oxygen was sucked out of it. Finally Ryan spoke.

"That's why," Ryan pointed his hockey stick at Tucker. "We don't need guys like you hitting on her."

"I wouldn't hit on your sister."

"Says the guy who started hitting on her best friend as soon as she started working at Rookies…" Jase pointed out.

"Hey, Skye isn't your sister."

"Might as well be."

"Whatever," Tucker grumbled.

Jake had to laugh to himself because the moment Tucker saw Jordan he hit on her too, but being the good best friend that he was, he didn't remind their friends of that fact.

"Alright ladies enough chit-chat. Let's get to work." Ryan said with authority only a captain could.

Chapter Four

After spending a few of hours working out with the guys Jake returned home. Between the night out, his run, and practice, he was beat. He stored his gear in the mud room and headed for his room hoping to get a shower and nap in before Carlee returned home from the Donnelly's.

He entered his room and enjoyed the cool breeze he felt on his skin. He'd been taking advantage of the recent lack of humidity by leaving his windows open.

He stripped his t-shirt off and headed for his ensuite bathroom. Before he could reach his destination, he was distracted by the sound of laughter outside. His room was in the back corner of the house and overlooked both his and the Donnelly's backyards. As he looked out the window, he could see Sean and Carlee splashing around in the pool with Jordan.

He was surprised to see Jordan entertaining the kids and not one of her parents. It usually took Carlee time to warm up to new people, instead she played around like she'd known Jordan forever. Shocked by the scene below, he couldn't look away.

Unfortunately, Carlee caught him red handed. "Jake, hey

Jake come down here and play. I wanna show you what Jordan taught me."

He cursed the missed opportunity for a nap. "Sure honey, I'll be right down, just let me put on my suit."

Five minutes later he opened the gate to the Donnelly's.

Carlee waved from her yellow inner tube. "Jake! Jake! You have to watch me, Jordan taught me how to do a front flick."

"It's front flip sweetie but don't do anything until I'm there," Jordan called from the pool.

Jake's heart skipped a beat and his breath caught as he watched her dunk her head in the pool to fix her hair, before she pulled herself up over the ledge of the pool. He couldn't look away from the sight in front of him. Her body was impeccable, all toned muscles and curves. With her bright pink string bikini wet from the pool it clung to her body in all the right places making him think all the wrong things. *Stop it, Jake. She's your best friends' sister. They would kill you if they knew you were picturing their sister naked.*

He watched her help Carlee out of the pool. The bond the two already had made his heart warm. Carlee had never taken to anyone so quickly, if he wasn't there to witness it himself, he would have never believed it.

"Ok, sweetie, watch Sean do it first and just remember what I told you and you'll be great."

Carlee hugged Jordan and ran to join Sean by the diving board.

He watched Jordan flip her head over to shake out her hair, then pull a towel across her shoulders. "Hey Jake." Jordan said as she sat on the lounge chair next to him.

With his mind in the gutter, he was slow to respond to Jordan's greeting. It wasn't until she bumped her shoulder into his, the sudden contact sending a shock through his body and out his toes, did his brain catch up.

"Jake, are you ok?"

When he looked up he could see concern on her face.

"Huh? Oh yeah I'm fine just spaced out. You know how it is when you only get five hours of sleep."

She smiled. "Wow five hours you're lucky. I only got two." She turned her attention back to the pool.

"Why? You and Skye left at least an hour and half before we did."

"Yeah but that's when all the fun began. We hadn't seen each other in over a month and we've never gone that long without seeing each other, that's a lot of time to make up for. Plus our friend Maddey came up to bring me Navy. With our foursome complete we didn't go to bed until around seven and then I was up at nine so I could come here. We're totally insane," she said with a laugh.

Carlee was getting impatient. "Jake you're not watching!"

He looked over at his sister and saw her standing with her hands on her hips and tapping her foot. "Sorry honey. Ok I'm all set show me your stuff."

The excitement radiated off Carlee. When she wanted someone's attention, she always got it. She surely was going to be a heartbreaker.

"Ok but first Sean has to go and then me."

Jake watched the kids do front flips off the diving board, then turned to face Jordan again. "That's amazing," his voice was filled with pride. "How did you get her to learn that so fast?"

She smiled at his compliment. "It was easy. She's a fast learner. Kids their age have no fear and that's usually the biggest obstacle."

Navy raced into the backyard and jumped on Jake. He pushed him onto his back with his front paws and started licking his face.

Jordan tried to push the big dog down without much luck. "Navy, stop that. Get down you big lug."

Jake sat up and used Jordan's towel to wipe the dog drool off his face. "Why is his name Navy?"

Jordan turned her attention back to the kids in the pool. "It's short for Navy SEAL."

His brows went up in confusion. "What? Why Navy SEAL?"

"Because he protects me and nothing's tougher than a Navy SEAL." The dog wagged his tail as she scratched behind his ears.

"It sure is unique."

"Yeah. Maddey had the idea. Her brothers are SEALs and I thought it was perfect."

Their conversation came to an abrupt end when the two were drenched by Navy jumping into the pool. Following his lead, the two joined in.

Jordan spent the morning playing with her younger brother and Carlee. The two reminded her of how she and Skye were at that age. Being a twin, she always had a built in best friend with Jase, but when she met Skye they took an instant liking to each other, much the same way.

After teaching the kids how to flip off the diving board she took a break for another cup of coffee. The tikes had energy to spare, making her grateful for her second wind. A nap would have been in order if she hadn't missed her brother so much.

The lack of sleep was a small price to pay for a night with her three besties. While in Florida, they kept in touch by group text and video chats, but it wasn't the same as hearing their stories in person. The biggest adjustment to the move home was going to be not having her three best friends for roommates anymore.

She spent the night listening to their stories about all the "Mr. Right Nows" they had gone after. She was happy to note her suspicions about Skye and Tucker were spot on. Surprisingly, Sammy was the first of them to find someone more permanent, since he was the biggest flirt of them all.

Coffee finished, she placed her cup on the table, jumped in the pool, and snagged the pizza slice float to lay on.

"So did you guys know I'm going to be your new swim instructor?"

"Really?" Sean asked.

"Yup. Skye gave me our work schedule yesterday and I get your class."

"Awesome!"

"You teach swimming?" Carlee spun in her yellow inner tube.

"Yup. For a long time, too."

"Are you fast?"

"She's the best. She beats Ry and Jase all the time when they race," Sean boasted.

"Really? How? They are so much bigger than you." Carlee asked with wide eyed amazement.

Jordan laughed. "You know how my brothers and Jake are so good at hockey they play for school?"

"Yeah."

"Well I swim for the school."

"Whoa," Carlee's eyes went wide, "you must be really fast. Are you a mermaid?"

"I wish." She sighed.

"Can you teach me to beat Jake?"

"I'll do my best sweetie."

As much fun as she had earlier playing with the kids, it was infinitely more enjoyable now Jake had joined them. When he first walked into the backyard she damn near swallowed her tongue. The way his damp t-shirt clung to his muscles earlier did not do justice to the masterpiece that lay beneath. Her eyes devoured the width of his shoulders and strong pecs, tracing each bump of his defined six pack. His orange and black hibiscus flower board shorts hung off his hips to reveal deep V-cuts. Her fingers itched to trace each bump and groove. Luckily she was able to fight back the urge.

She was grateful for the distraction the kids provided from her lust filled thoughts. *I seriously need to find myself a date.*

She sat on the steps in the shallow end of the pool as she watched Jake toss Sean and Carlee in the air. She was impressed by the stamina he displayed with their repetitive requests for again and again. She guessed he finally needed a break when he swam over to join her on the steps.

"That was more of a workout than earlier. Damn those kids are relentless." She watched his gorgeous chest expand as he took a deep breath.

"You're telling me. I'm kind of jealous actually," she leaned back to rest on her elbows. "So what did my slave driver of a brother have you guys working on today? I know you guys don't officially start practice until school starts."

"He's not that bad," he said with a laugh. "All workouts and drills are optional. Your brother has some serious skills. He's got a ton of pro scouts coming to see him play."

Jordan smiled. She was immensely proud of Ryan. For most of his life he possessed a natural ability on ice. By the time he was in high school, there was no doubt he would play professionally. At the collegiate level he shined but she knew he worked extremely hard.

"Yeah he's had people watching him play since high school. Let me guess… he works in the off season with those he thinks can also go pro."

"How'd you know?" Jake mirrored her posture.

"He did the same thing in high school. His entire line and Jase's line the following year all received full rides to D1 schools. He used to say, just because he was the reason for them coming to the games didn't mean they couldn't also appreciate anyone else who deserved recognition."

"Yup that's the party line," he nodded in agreement.

"What's the focus for you?"

"Glove saves mostly."

Jordan took a moment to think. She knew her older brother's coaching style but goalie training was not his specialty. Jake wasn't aware that she could help, thanks to her godfather. "Have you ever tried playing ping pong or tennis?"

"Huh?" It was clear he couldn't see how they connected.

"Tennis is good because the quickness and movement from side to side is similar to how you move on the ice. Ping pong is good to focus training on your non-dominate hand."

"That's brilliant. How do you know that?"

Before she could answer, her cell phone rang. Based on the ring tone so knew it was one of her besties. She made her way out of the pool to answer.

"Hey, Skye."

"Hey girl. Want any help unpacking?"

"Oh my god, I love you so much."

"I know. I'll be there in a few with a large iced coffee, I just left Dunkin."

"Seriously, I love you. I would turn gay for you."

Skye's laughter was so loud she had to pull the phone away from her ear. "Ditto. Too bad we like guys too much."

In typical Skye fashion she hung up without saying goodbye.

Jordan grabbed a towel, wrapped it around her body, and sat on a lounge chair. She smiled when Jake climbed out of the pool to join her.

"Was your ringtone "Let's Go to the Mall" from *How I Met Your Mother*?"

"You like *How I Met Your Mother*?"

"Love it."

She smiled. It was one of her favorite shows and she could quote most episodes. Knowing her ringtone meant he was equally familiar with the show.

"Hey girl, this house is amazing." Skye said walking into the backyard.

"Wait until you see my new room. I swear half our old apartment could fit in it." She reached to take the iced coffee Skye handed her.

"Nice. Hey Jake, *fancy* seeing you here."

"Hey Skye."

"Skye!" Sean yelled from the pool.

"Hey squirt."

Mrs. Donnelly came out shortly after to watch the kids, allowing Jordan and Skye to head inside and Jake to go home. Jordan looked around her room. The furniture was already setup but tons of boxes waited to be unpacked.

"Give me five minutes to rinse off," she said grabbing clean clothes out of her duffel.

"No worries. I'll start hanging stuff for you." Skye searched for the correct boxes.

Bruno Mars blared through the speakers when Jordan emerged from the bathroom. Skye hung three boxes worth of clothes by the time she finished.

"You are the most efficient person I know. It's one of the things I love about you." Jordan pointed to the clothes stacked on her bed.

"You know I don't like wasting time."

"You mean like you didn't waste any time lining up Tucker as your booty call?" She countered, lifting a shapely brow in question.

"Oh, you mean like you already hanging out with Jake?" Skye tossed back.

"Point taken. However, that wasn't my doing."

"Maybe not but you can't deny the perk. And he's hot."

"Doesn't matter how hot he is. You know I can't be more than friends with him."

"Do you honestly think your brothers will hold you to the promise you made two years ago?"

"You know it's not that simple." She stopped unpacking to focus her undivided attention on her best friend. "The whole Tommy situation almost broke the team. They were terrible that following year. It pulled their focus. Ry and Jase have a serious chance to play in the NHL. I can't be the reason that doesn't happen."

"I get it. I really do." Skye reached out a hand in comfort.

"Do you want to know the worst part of it all?"

"You mean other than what he looks like in a bathing suit?"

She gave Skye her best *don't be stupid* look. "I'm serious."

"Ok, tell me."

"He likes *How I Met Your Mother,* like 'knew your ringtone was from it' likes it."

"Impressive."

"And he told me his hockey mask has Optimus Prime on it."

"Wow, he sounds perfect for you."

"I know."

Chapter Five

C old.

Petrified and shaking.

She was hidden but for how long? She had no idea. The sound of breaking glass could be heard along with his psychotic ranting. She was all alone.

"Jordan, sweetness, where are you? Come out come out wherever you are. I'm gonna find you."

She looked around the closet for anything she could use as a weapon but she didn't have much to work with. She was trying to think of different ways she could escape but just then the closet door swung open and he grabbed her.

Jordan woke with a jolt. Her scream and heavy breathing had Navy lifting his head from his side of her king size bed. *Okay, good, it was just a dream.* She scratched Navy behind the ears. "Good boy. It's okay."

She wasn't sure why the nightmares were back. Months had passed since the last time she'd had one.

Glancing around her new room she smiled to herself. It was perfect and she absolutely loved it. She'd fallen asleep with her balcony doors open. That was her favorite part, the balcony with French doors that opened all the way. She noticed Jake had done the same. Not surprising with the warm summer air.

Of course his room would be across from hers. Their houses weren't on top of each other. But were close enough to have a conversation across the space if you raised your voice slightly, as she discovered earlier.

More thoughts flooded her mind. She loved how good he was with Carlee and Sean. He was so good looking that is was almost unfair for any one human being to look that good. Whenever he was around, her stomach had butterflies. She could immediately feel his presence all around her. But most of all she loved how his eyes made her feel, they had such compassion in them.

"Ugh this is so unfair." *Dear God, why are you doing this to me? It's not funny to dangle him in front of me like this when you know I can't do anything about it.*

With a punch to her pillow and a confused look from Navy she decided to take another shot at sleep.

Chapter Six

The alarm rang, waking Jake from his peaceful slumber. It was eight in the morning and time for his morning workout. *Not today, maybe I'll just skip it.* Oh what a lovely thought but that's all it was, a thought. Grudgingly he got up, he knew the early morning was the best part of his day.

Almost a week had gone by since he had spent time with Jordan. He was a little disappointed she didn't come by the hockey house as much as he thought she would.

The only time he even had a chance to talk to her was when he picked Carlee up from her swim lessons at the community pool. He learned from Carlee that Jordan was her new swim instructor and was impressed with how quickly his sister's technique was improving. But every morning he knew where to find her—in the pool behind her house for her morning swim.

Jordan would swim for an hour and a half but Jake knew before each swim she would warm up and stretch on the patio. He loved watching that particular scene unfold.

Shortly after they finished their respective workouts, Skye would show up and whisk Jordan away for most of the day, giving him no opportunity to spend time with her. All he needed was ten minutes alone with her to see if she felt anything remotely close to how he felt when they were together. With the slightest bit of hope, he would figure a way around the fact she was his friends' sister. Nothing mattered except the connection he felt and he would be damned if anyone tried to break it.

He couldn't stop thinking about her. Luckily it was Friday and movie night at the hockey house. Since he was staying over, there would be no blonde distractions for the night.

Or so he thought.

When Jake pulled up to the hockey house he was relieved to be there. He figured a night with the guys would help take his mind off Jordan.

It wasn't long until that idea was blown to hell. As he got out of his car he saw it, a familiar white Corvette parked across the street. "Shit I can't win, can I?"

"Talking to yourself dude? That's not a good sign." Distracted by the Corvette Jake didn't see Tucker had pulled up behind him.

He regained control of his emotions, he couldn't let anyone know how she affected him. "Just thought I forgot my stuff but it's right here."

For the past week his usual composed demeanor was nowhere to be found and he knew Tucker could tell something was off.

"Come on, dude," Tucker slung an arm around Jake's shoulders. "Let's get inside. We need to get you out of this funk you've been in."

The guys made their way into the hockey house, breathing deeply as they went. The house smelled delicious. The aroma of garlic and spices filled the air. Jake wondered who was cooking. No one on the team cooked for movie night. *Strange.* "Hey guys who's wearing an apron tonight?"

Jake got no response. As he made his way to the breakfast bar in the middle of the kitchen, he saw the seniors and Jase were all crowded around the kitchen.

In the center of all the commotion, giving directions to all the guys, was Jordan.

What is she doing at the hockey house? And cooking dinner?

Jake took in the scene in front of him. The guys each had a station in the kitchen. Ryan handled the pasta, Nick sautéed vegetables, Chris fried chicken, Billy stirred the sauce, Wade cleaned up, Jase set the table, with Jordan giving directions while she moved around to each station.

She had a charisma about her that was captivating. Most of the guys on the team towered around six feet tall. Despite being a foot shorter than most of the guys, she commanded attention.

"I don't know who's more demanding, her or Ryan," Tucker whispered.

He nodded in agreement. "I wouldn't say that too loud. I don't want to know what it would be like for Ry to push us harder."

"True story," Tucker said with a laugh. "Wonder what they're cooking. Smells amazing."

They watched Jordan stop abruptly to glare at Billy. "Billy don't you dare try to add any Tabasco to my sauce. You know I put enough crushed red pepper in it, if you want it spicier you can add more to your own plate but I swear to God if you mess up the whole thing I'll beat you up."

Billy's hand stopped mid-air. He looked like a kid caught with his hand in the cookie jar. "How did you know that's what I was about to do?"

She smiled and shook her head as she walked over to Billy and placed a hand on his back. "Because I've known you for three years and you haven't changed one bit."

The guys all laughed.

Ryan drained the pasta in the sink. "The pasta is ready, now what sis?"

"Now we're ready to eat."

The meal was amazing. Fried bite size pieces of chicken mixed with linguini and fresh veggies topped with a butter sauce loaded with spices. Jake wasn't sure how she came up with it but it was delicious.

Loud chatter and appreciation came from all the guys while they stuffed their faces. Most went for second helpings, him included.

Jordan smiled from her seat. The satisfaction of a job well done showed on her face. "I love how much you guys can eat."

They say the way to a man's heart is through his stomach, if she kept cooking for the team like this, she was sure to capture all of theirs.

"Yeah, well you're one to talk, JD. You can out eat Ryan and everyone knows that's a feat." Billy said as he polished off his plate and shared a pound with Ryan.

"That's the good thing about you hockey players, you can eat. I tried to date this wrestler once but it just wasn't working. I couldn't be with a guy who was more concerned with his weight than I was."

Ryan and Jase both looked up. "When did you date a wrestler? And how come we didn't know about it?" They said in perfect unison.

"Relax, it was for like two weeks."

Jake already guessed his friends were overprotective of their sister, but he was still trying figure out the specifics. He wasn't the only one who could feel the tension between the siblings at the table.

"Sure, out eating Ry is impressive overall, but nothing beats the time she kicked Seth's ass in the wing eating contest we had during the Stanley Cup." Wade tried to distract.

Jordan nodded at the statement. "Oh don't I know it."

"You know Seth Coen?" Tucker asked around a bite of food.

"Yeah Ry's freshman year he was roommates with Seth," Jordan answered.

"You lived in the hockey house as a freshman?" Jake asked. It was unusual for a freshman to move into the house.

"Oh yeah. Ry was the star recruit. The team wanted him bad, so they made the exception as one of the selling points," Nick clarified.

"They even said if Jase came to play for the Titans the following year, he could live in the house as a freshman too," Chris added.

"You guys used to give me so much shit too. Not sure if it was worth it," Ryan stated.

"Hey, they started going easier on you once JD started coming around." Billy stopped laughing when Ryan gave him a death glare.

"Oh yeah. The best thing you ever did for yourself was have the twins visit." Wade waved a hand in the direction of Jase and Jordan.

"Did you hang at the house a lot?" Jake was curious to learn how much she used to come around.

"I guess you could call it a lot," Jordan said with a shrug.

"You guess? You were here all the time. Between visiting your brother and hanging out with your boyfriend, you practically lived there yourself... Ugh... I mean." Nick's statement trailed off as most of the table sucked in a collective breath.

The tension Jake felt was similar to that when Tucker asked why Jordan stopped coming around. The silence stretched on. He looked over at Tucker but his friend looked just as confused as him.

Jake decided to get the rest of the evening started. He looked around the table. "So what movie are we watching tonight?"

Nick was the first to respond. "Well since Jordan's here we decided to watch *The Boondock Saints* because it's one of her favorites." He nodded at her with appreciation.

"Yeah it's one of the few movies that makes me proud to be Irish," Jordan leaned back in her chair smiling. "Ok guys you know the deal, I cook you clean."

Jordan sat in the big, white leather arm chair on the side of the den drinking her beer. To keep with the Irish theme, the guys purchased Smithwicks and Killian's Irish Red to drink along with the classic Miller Lite.

Her phone lit up with a text from Skye.

MAKES BOYS CRY (Skye): How's movie night? So jelly BTW.

Jordan smiled. Skye usually joined Jordan for movie nights and she knew she was disappointed to miss Jordan's first time back in two years. Unfortunately, Aunt Ei needed Skye to fill in for a bartender who called out.

MOTHER OF DRAGONS (Jordan)**:** Putting on the movie now. It's been... good

Skye knew her too well not to pick up on what she wasn't saying and sent back the hands up, questioning face emoji. Jordan smiled as she texted back.

MOTHER OF DRAGONS: It started off great, just like old times

MAKES BOYS CRY: But...

MOTHER OF DRAGONS: The guys were talking about how much I could eat and Jake and Tucker were asking about how I know everyone and how much I used to come around... One thing led to another and Nick let it slip that I used to date one of the guys and things got... awkward

MAKES BOYS CRY: DETAILS NOW!!!

MOTHER OF DRAGONS: Don't yell at me

MAKES BOYS CRY: Then stop stalling. I'm in between customers right now I need to know

She took pity on her friend.

MOTHER OF DRAGONS: Everyone got all quiet. No one would look Ry and Jase in the eye and Jake and Tucker looked so lost. Poor guys

MAKES BOYS CRY: Did they ask anything about it?

MOTHER OF DRAGONS: No. Thank God! But it was weird.

MAKES BOYS CRY: It'll get easier. Ok gotta go

And with a kissy face emoji Skye said bye.

Jordan smiled as she put her phone down.

"Skye?" Jase asked.

She looked at her twin. "How'd you know?"

"Figured she was missing being here tonight. She always came in the past."

"Yup. I told her she wasn't missing anything. You guys are lame."

"Lame?" Nick asked, offended.

"Yeah lame." She tossed back with a smirk.

She watched Nick's eyes narrow before he threw a pillow at her face.

"Hey, you made me spill my beer asshole." She stood to pull her wet t-shirt away from her body.

On her way to the kitchen for a paper towel to dry her shirt, she walked by Nick and tapped the top of his beer bottle with the bottom of hers, causing his beer to spray out. Nick had to act fast to drink his beer before it got all over him.

Ryan pulled her onto the couch to join him and some of the other seniors. They all bent over in laughter.

"Oh my God, Nick, the look on your face. Priceless." She barely got the words out because she was laughing so hard.

Billy patted Nick on the back. "Yeah dude you should know better than to mess with her, she has a thing for revenge."

Laughter finally under control, she got up and made her way back to her chair. "Ok now that that's out of the way lets watch the movie."

As she settled back in, her eyes caught Jake's from across the room and she realized he'd been watching her. He quickly looked away but not before she saw something flash in his eyes. She couldn't figure out what the look meant.

She shook her head trying to derail that train of thought. They couldn't have anything beyond friendship so it shouldn't matter if he was attracted to her or not.

Chapter Seven

After a restless night of sleep, the buzzing of a cell phone woke Jordan. Throwing an arm over her head, her hand searched for the offensive object. Phone in hand, she squinted tired eyes at the unknown number flashing on the screen. She clicked to ignore the call, never answering unknown numbers.

Deciding there was no point trying to go back to sleep, she threw the covers off. She didn't have to workout but needed a way to let off some of the tension she was feeling, luckily she had her backup swim gear in the car.

Swimming laps harder than usual, Jordan executed another flip turn. She should have known Jake would be at the hockey house but when the guys invited her over, she thought it was to hang with the seniors, not their movie night. She figured since Jake didn't live at the house she would be free from seeing him, even if it was only from the distance of her bedroom window, for at least one evening.

So much for that idea.

She was trying to be good. Trying to stay away, even though everything about him drew her in. Apart from his amazing good looks there was also the instant chemistry that seemed to crackle every time he was near. Images from when they met at Rookies filled her head. The sight of him made her breath catch, but coupled with the way he looked at her, like she was something to eat, was enough to make her knees go weak.

Immediately after she shook those images from her mind, ones from the following days would wash over her. Jake in a beater and gym shorts with his hair all disheveled followed by Jake in a bathing suit playing with the kids.

Skye was right, he really was a nice guy. The way he interacted with Sean and Carlee touched a special place in her heart.

Angry with herself for allowing thoughts of how to make things work between them cross her mind, she pushed herself to do more laps than normal. She knew why she could never be with Jake. It was her own fault things had to be this way and maybe one day she would get over him.

Being home for winter break was both a blessing and a curse for Jordan. She let the guilt over the Tommy fallout distance her from her brothers. She was currently curled up on the couch in her favorite NYU Violets Swimming sweats, a mug of hot chocolate in hand, as she binge watched How I Met Your Mother *hiding from them.*

"So you want to explain why you're avoiding me?" Ryan asked joining her on the couch.

"I'm not." She spoke into her mug.

"Bullshit. Jase and I have barely seen you this past semester."

"We've all been busy. Between school and swimming, you know it's hard for me to come home too much."

"Again bullshit. You haven't even come to a game yet, instead you watch them on TV."

She looked up when Ryan touched her arm and sighed. Damn him for calling her out.

"It's too hard," she confessed.

"What's too hard?" The confusion clear was in his voice.

"*Being around you guys and knowing I'm part of the reason you guys suck this season.*"

Her brother laughed at her statement. "*Oh we suck, do we?*"

She sent Ryan her get serious look. "*You know you do. I can see it on the ice. The chemistry isn't there. You guys are missing whatever… I don't know… for lack of a better word, spark that made you gel last year. And I can't help feeling like it's my fault.*"

The silence stretched on. The tension grew so thick, Jordan knew Jase picked up on it when he joined them. He sat on the coffee table, putting himself directly across from her.

"*What's wrong?*" Jase's gaze pinned her in place.

When she didn't answer, her twin turned to their older brother for clarification.

"*I was trying to figure out why our darling sister here has been MIA for the past four months,*" Ryan informed.

"*Well?*" Jase asked as he turned his attention back on her.

When she continued to be silent he again tried Ryan.

"*She blames herself for the team's losing record this season,*" Ryan said.

"*Bullshit.*"

"*That's exactly what I said,*" Ryan smiled.

Her brothers knew how much she hated when they talked about her like she wasn't there. She cursed to herself as their tactic worked to break down her defenses.

"*Are you seriously trying to tell me that what happened with Tommy didn't have any effect on the team?*"

She got blank stares in return.

"*See even you guys can't say that. You know it cost the team one of their star players. And Ry, can you honestly say the juniors and seniors don't hold onto any animosity?*"

Again she was met with silence.

"*See you know I'm right.*" She said, resigned.

"*Wade and the guys ask about you all the time,*" Ryan argued.

"*It's not the same,*" she countered.

"*How so?*"

"Because they're your year. They weren't friends with Tommy first like the older guys. Wade, Nick, and all them got to know Tommy while they got to know me. They didn't have already formed opinions."

"So don't come around the team. Just hang with us," Jase suggested.

"How do you expect that to work?" She waved a hand in exasperation.

"Let us know when you're coming to a game and after we'll do something away from the hockey house," Ryan suggested.

At her hesitation Jase pressed on.

"Come on Jordan, we miss you. Do you have any idea how much it sucks not having you at school with me? Not having you at the games is like not having my hockey stick." She knew he was serious when he called her Jordan. His hazel eyes so like her own implored her to listen.

"I've been to a bunch of games." She admitted in a whisper.

"You have?" They asked in unison.

She nodded. "Yeah. I sat high up instead of close to the boards."

"Why didn't you tell us you were coming?" Jase narrowed his eyes in question.

"You know why. I didn't want to make things any more awkward."

"Ok enough with the past. From now on will you let us know when you're coming to a game? We won't tell any of the guys you're there. We can just meet up after," Ryan offered.

"Fine," she agreed.

Jordan continued to swim laps as memories of the past played through her thoughts. A part of her wished she was home swimming, where the underwater speakers would play music loud enough to drown out her thoughts. Instead the sounds of Aerosmith were muted by the water.

She expelled her frustration in her flip turn. As she pushed off the wall she noticed someone crouched at the end of the pool. Taking off her goggles she noticed the force of her turn had splashed water all over their shirt.

"Aww man, I'm sorry Jake I didn't know you were there."

His smile eased her worry. "It's ok, don't worry about it. I have extra clothes in the house. Ryan told me to tell you the pancakes are done." She watched as he took off his wet shirt to spread out on one of the lounge chairs by the pool.

Even though she saw him without a shirt on in her pool last week, it was still a sight to behold. She watched his biceps bulge as he put his shirt down and turned to face her again.

What was it about this guy that drew her to him? He had some sort of spell about him and she couldn't figure it out. It couldn't be just his looks, she was around good-looking guys on the beach in Florida for the past month and none of them affected her this way. And then there were his eyes, it felt like they could see into her soul. It unnerved her. She realized she was staring, so she took her swim cap off and dunked her head underwater.

She pulled herself over the edge of the pool and tossed her gear by her bag. Using the hair tie she kept on her wrist, she tied her wet hair up in a messy bun.

She pulled on the straps of the one piece she used as a drag suit and breathed a sigh of relief when the pressure from the too tight suit released from her shoulders. She usually wore two one piece suits when she trained, but since she only had her backup gear with her she had to settle on an old Speedo and bikini.

As she stripped she heard Jake call from behind her.

She looked up at Jake with a smile. "Yeah?"

"Here, do you need a towel?" He handed her a towel.

As she grabbed the towel her fingers brushed the back of his hand and the quick contact sent a shock down to her toes. It wasn't the first time she felt it, there was no denying her and Jake shared a connection, but it still didn't make it any less forbidden. Again she cursed the fact he was on the hockey team.

Her gaze never left his. At the contact of their hands she swore she saw his eyes darken in desire. Whenever she was in close proximity to him she could feel her self-resolve weaken. For the past week she had effectively avoided contact with Jake, but he was constantly thrown into her life and she wasn't sure how much longer her self-control was going to last.

"Thanks." She smiled as she admired his sculpted body one last time and wrapped the towel around her. "Come on let's go eat, those pancakes are calling my name."

JAKE AND THE guys woke up to freshly brewed coffee. Lined up on the breakfast bar were mugs, milk, sugar, bacon, and what looked like a tub of already made pancake mix.

Jake was pouring himself a cup of coffee when Ryan came running down the stairs, a worried expression on his face. "Hey guys have you seen Jordan I can't find her anywhere?"

Nick pointed out the glass doors to the patio. "Yeah. JD is out in the pool and, I think, listening to Aerosmith."

Nick yawned as he made his way into the kitchen. Jake passed him the coffee pot, and noticed a note attached to the tub of pancake mix. "Hey Ry, there's a note here for you."

He saw Ryan relax as he took a sip of his coffee. "What's it say?"

"Ry, I started breakfast but you know the deal with pancakes, I make um you bake um. I'll be in the pool if you need me so relax. Come get me when it's ready. Love you."

The guys all started to laugh. "Looks like she knows you pretty well, pal." Billy was the one laughing the loudest.

"Yeah, okay, you guys are a real riot. Now that we've all had a good laugh how about you guys make yourselves useful and help me make breakfast. I don't know about you guys but I'm starving."

The guys busted each others' balls while they worked on getting breakfast made. Once they were done, Jake went outside to let Jordan know it was ready.

Opening the sliding glass doors he thought that it was amazing that she still woke up for her morning swim, even when she wasn't at her house.

He tried to get her attention as he made his way to the pool but she couldn't hear him over the music, so he bent down by the edge to try and get it. It wasn't until after she splashed him from her flip turn that she realized he was there.

She made a face as she took off her goggles. "Aww man, I'm sorry Jake I didn't know you were there."

He smiled to ease her worry. "It's okay, don't worry about it. I have extra clothes in the house. Ryan told me to tell you the pancakes are done." He pulled the wet garment over his head.

After he laid out his wet shirt, he watched Jordan get out of the pool and tie her hair up. With her back facing him he watched as she started to pull down the straps of her purple Speedo. *Oh my god what is she doing? There's a house full of guys in there and she's taking off her bathing suit right next to the pool.* "Umm Jordan…" His voice trailed off as she turned around and he realized she wasn't naked underneath, she actually had on a black string bikini. *Not much better.* It took everything in his power to not take her in his arms and kiss her right there.

She looked up at him and smiled. "Yeah?"

"Here, do you need a towel?" Handing her a towel he tried to play off his insecurity.

"Thanks." She smiled as she wrapped the towel around her. "Come on let's go eat, those pancakes are calling my name."

They made it into the kitchen and saw Skye fighting off Tucker's touchy feely hand as she tried place fresh fruit on the breakfast bar. Jake shook his head at his best friend.

"Tucker stop that!" Skye said as she slapped Tucker's hand away from her ass.

Jordan made her way over to hug her friend. "Skye I didn't think you'd make it for breakfast."

"Please if I know you, and I do, I knew after staying at the hockey house Ryan would be making your pancakes and did you honestly think I'd miss that? And you call yourself my best friend." Sarcasm dripped off Skye's words as she hugged Jordan back.

Everyone settled into their seats around the table.

"So what are you guys up to today that made Skye meet you here?" Jase asked as he stuffed more bacon in his mouth.

Jordan placed half a dozen pancakes onto her plate, the guys weren't kidding when they said she could eat. "Aunt Ei needs help getting Rookies ready for that big party tonight. She also told me to tell you that she wouldn't be offended if you guys don't come tonight since you can't have the VIP."

"Damn no VIP tonight that sucks." Jase whined in mock annoyance and snapped his fingers together for good measure making the guys laugh.

"Yeah well she said she can't let her nephews party for free all the time. Sometimes she has to let paying customers have the VIP area." Jordan stuck out her tongue and waved a piece of bacon at her brother.

"It's no big deal, we can take one week off," Jase stated.

Jake had already decided he was going to spend the night off at home. He figured he'd get Tucker to help him watch Carlee.

"You know what I missed most about the hockey house?" Skye asked the table at large.

"What's that?" Ryan asked.

"How it's a clothing optional establishment." She said pointing to Jake's bare chest.

He looked down and realized he never grabbed a new shirt. "To be fair I put a shirt on when I woke up. But Little Miss Mermaid over here..." He pointed his fork full of pancake at Jordan.

She responded to his comment with a breathtaking smile.

"Hey it's not my fault you were in the splash zone."

"Yeah yeah yeah. Whatever you say Ariel." He could tell she liked the reference to the Disney princess.

"What were you even doing swimming laps? Usually today is a yoga day." Skye asked as she took a piece of bacon off Tucker's plate.

"I got woken up earlier by my phone going off and couldn't fall back to sleep. I had my backup gear in the car so I decided to put it to good use." Jordan answered her friend.

"Who was calling you so early?" Skye asked her.

"No idea. It was an unknown number and I don't answer for people I don't know." Jordan said looking down.

Jake felt the atmosphere around the table change. He noticed a silent exchange between Jase and Ryan and wondered what it was about.

"Do you get calls from unknown numbers a lot?" Ryan finally asked.

Jordan shrugged in response.

"Skye, give me fifteen to wash the chlorine off me and I'll be ready to go." Jordan got up to place her empty plate in the sink.

Jake got the feeling she was leaving to avoid more questions.

Chapter Eight

I t was after four by the time Jordan and Skye returned to Rookies after running around town for Aunt Eileen. Her aunt allowed for booked parties to make special drink requests and it became their job to shop for the necessary requirements.

"Hey babes." Sammy called coming up the steps to the VIP area.

"Sammy what are you doing here so early?" She asked as she emptied the case of beer Skye placed on the bar.

"Wanted to make sure the booth was all set up. Plus I wanted to be here if you guys needed help."

"You are a saint. So happy we got Maddey as our room-mate in college," Skye said.

"Wait… what?" Sammy looked to Jordan for translation.

"What Skye means is, without Maddey as our roommate freshman year we would have never met you. And we love you," Jordan answered. She spoke fluent Skye after fifteen years of friendship.

"So did you have fun at the house last night? I was so bummed I couldn't be there, but I'm sure we'll be spending a lot more time there again," Skye inquired.

Jordan stood up from her crouched position in front of the beer fridge. "Yeah it was so nice. I love hanging out with all of them. I was really worried it would be awkward to be around the guys again but it wasn't."

"Why would things be awkward? We hung out with them all the time Ryan's freshman year." Skye removed the now empty beer box from the bar.

"Because of the whole Tommy situation."

Skye rested a hand on the bar and looked her in the eye. "All the guys that know you, love you. I've been telling you for the past two years no one blamed you for what happened. You can't let one psycho keep you from living your life with the people you love."

She made her way around the bar to sit on the bar stool next to Skye. She put her back against the bar and leaned back on her elbows. "I guess you're right and if last night was any indication of how this year is going to be, I can't wait."

"Do you remember all the pranks we used to play on Nick and Billy? They were suckers for us every time," Skye said with a smile.

Skye's comment caused her to spit the water she just drank out. She laughed hysterically as she tried to speak.

Finally she caught her breath. "Oh my God, you missed it last night." She took another deep breath. "Nick made me spill my beer by throwing a pillow at me. So I got the better of him with the beer bottle tap. I wish you were there to see the look on his face, it was priceless."

Skye nudged her in the arm. "Nice move. Man I'm so jealous you got to be around all those hot ass guys. And Jake and Tucker are perfect additions."

Her groan at the mention of Jake did not go unnoticed.

"Why do you sound like a wounded animal?" Sammy quipped.

"I've actually been able to not think about Jake for a few hours. Not so much now," she answered.

"Why wouldn't you want to think of him? That man is *fine*. If he played on my team I would be all over that," Sammy said.

"Amen." Skye reached out to pound Sammy's outstretched hand.

"So not helping," she turned to rest her forehead on the bar.

"Sorry." She heard her friends murmur.

"It wouldn't be so hard if I didn't think he was attracted to me too," she spoke into the bar.

A memory from the night before crept into her mind. She sat upright suddenly. "Oh my God speaking of Jake, you should have seen him last night when Nick and I were joking around. I could have sworn he was looking at Nick like he was jealous."

Skye lifted an eyebrow. "Really? That's interesting."

"What's interesting?" Sammy asked as he went behind the bar to get them beer.

"Jake's jealous of Nick's relationship with Jordan."

"There is no relationship between Nick and I." Jordan said trying to make a point.

"We know that but Jake doesn't. Come on Jor, to him everything about you is a mystery. He heard about things you and your brothers would do for two years. And when he finally got to meet you, he couldn't believe it because he was expecting to meet a guy not some hot girl."

"And honey, by the way that boy looks at you he's got it bad." Sammy smiled from ear to ear.

Jordan knew exactly what her friends were thinking.

"Oh guys stop imagining things. You two love to play matchmaker so much that you see what you want to see and in this case it's seeing interest in me from a guy you know I think is cute." She paused. "Besides even if he did like me it's not like it would work out anyway. He's on the hockey team and you know I'm not allowed to date anyone on the team so can we just give it a rest?"

She couldn't keep the look of disappointment at the thought from showing on her face. Luckily her aunt was walking toward them, giving her the out she needed from this conversation.

"Hey Aunt Ei." They called in unison.

"Hey girls. Sammy." Her aunt gave them all a kiss on the cheek.

"I'm so happy you girls transferred schools. I love having you guys help me plan and promote any special events. It will be so much better being able to have you guys here to run the events instead of just planning from a distance."

"BTU also gives us college credit for what we do for you unlike NYU," Skye stated.

Jordan looked around Rookies and smiled. The party was a glowing success. The VIPs started showing up around nine and jumped right into the festivities.

"Jordan how are you sweetheart?" Donna Burton from the Garden of Dreams Foundation asked.

"I'm good Donna. How are things at the foundation going?"

Jordan's godfather hooked her and Skye up with positions helping plan events for the Garden of Dreams Foundation. A few members from the GDF were in attendance and had been catching up with the girls most of the night.

"They are going great. Are you and Skye still able to work at the foundation now that you moved out of Manhattan?"

"Yeah we are hoping we can still help out. We will obviously have to cut back on our time but should be able to make it work."

"That's fantastic! You two are miracle workers with the kids. Oh…" Donna reached out for the gentleman next to her. "Ken, come here, there is someone I want to introduce you to.

"Ken this here is Jordan Donnelly, she is Rick Schelios' goddaughter. Jordan this is Ken Oliver, he works for the NHL."

Jordan reached out to shake Ken's hand. "It's nice to meet you."

"Nice to meet you too." Ken paused in thought. "Donnelly? Why does that sound familiar?"

"My aunt owns Rookies?" She pointed around the bar.

Ken shook his head.

"My dad Robert works for ESPN," she supplied.

Another head shake from Ken. A moment later recognition lit his gaze. "Wait, are you related to the Ryan Donnelly who won the Hobey Baker Award this year?"

She couldn't help but smile, beyond proud of her brother's achievement. "Yes he's my older brother."

"He's quite an impressive player. He's certainly gained the attention of a lot of people in the head office."

"Thanks for saying that. I, for one, love watching him play."

After speaking with Ken, Jordan continued to mingle. About an hour later she saw her father making his way up the stairs of the VIP area, carrying what looked like a humungous picture frame.

"Hi, Daddy, I didn't know you were coming tonight." She walked over to give her father a hug.

"Hi, Princess. I wasn't planning on coming but your mother insisted, plus I have something from your godfather for your aunt." He looked around the VIP area. "Where is she anyway?"

"She's just over there." Jordan waved her aunt over. "So what's the present?"

Robert smiled at his daughter. "You'll see in a minute, patience."

When Eileen made it over she hugged her brother. "Nice of you to let me know you were coming," she frowned at him. "It would have saved me a lot a grief if I knew you were going to be here."

"Sorry Ei, I didn't think I was coming tonight but you know Ruth, she wanted me to get out and see the boys." He laughed a very hearty laugh. "To make it up to you, I have a gift from Rick for your bar."

With that he pulled the frame out in front of him. The wide eyes that stared at it made him smile. When Eileen still hadn't said anything he spoke up. "Well do you like it? If not, Rick is going to be offended."

Holy shit! Was her dad serious? How could her aunt not like it?

"Is that what I think it is?" Eileen asked. Shock caused her voice to come out barely above a whisper.

"Yup. Rick is actually disappointed in himself for not thinking of giving it to you sooner," Robert confirmed.

It took a while for reality to sink in. Jordan watched her aunt reach out a hand to touch the framed, signed rookie jersey of one of hockey's most famous goalies, Rick Schelios. Once it all clicked into place, Eileen reached out to hug her brother.

Jordan laughed at her aunt's enthusiastic display. She felt her phone vibrate in her pocket.

UNKNOWN: Looking good

She frowned at the display. To make it easier to be identified, she had worn one of the Rookies' uniform shirts. The tight V-neck referee shirt hugged her curves without being inappropriate and paired nicely with her tight jeans and black and white Chuck Taylors.

She couldn't pinpoint who in the crowd would text her though. Her fingers hovered over the screen as she debated whether or not to respond. The need for more information won out.

JORDAN: Who is this?

No reply ever came.

Chapter Nine

J ake handed Tucker a beer and joined him on the couch. He let out a breath as he relaxed against the cushions. Carlee had them running around the entire night.

"Thanks man," Tucker accepted the beer. "I swear I don't know where that kid gets her energy from."

Jake laughed. "Me either. I swear it's harder to keep up with her than Ryan and his drills."

"Truth." Tucker held out his beer to cheers the sentiment.

"Thanks again for helping me keep her entertained tonight." Jake took a long pull of his beer, draining half in one swallow.

"Hell you know I love the brat. Besides she's a better wingman than you are. At least with her I don't have to worry about the chicks wanting her over me."

He laughed thinking of the last time he was Tuck's wingman and a certain blonde bombshell who did just that. Sure nothing had come of the attraction, but he felt it.

"Hey I'm pretty sure neither of us got the girl." He said on a laugh to make light of his feelings.

"True," Tucker ran a hand through his shaggy hair. "Damn she had to be a sister of not one, but two of our teammates."

"Yup. And I get the feeling they wouldn't take too kindly to any of us sniffing around her either."

"Picked up on that as well did ya?"

He nodded in agreement.

"But what I don't get is she totally dated someone on the team. We've heard them talk about it a few times already," Tucker mused.

"Yeah but have you noticed anytime it's mentioned all the seniors stop talking and change the subject?"

"Yup. Totally weird."

He picked at the label on his beer bottle. "Do you think it's one of the seniors and that's why they get all weird about it?"

"Could be. Something doesn't add up though."

"I agree."

"Damn listen to us gossiping like a bunch of women."

He laughed and drained the rest of his beer. He watched Tucker pull his phone out for the fifth time in just as many minutes.

"Texting Skye?" He asked with a raised eyebrow.

Tucker looked at him surprised. "How'd you know?"

"Dude, you forget I've been watching you hit on girls since puberty. I can always tell when you're trying to spit some game."

"Truth." Tucker held out his fist for a pound.

He didn't leave him hanging. "So what's wrong. Usually you have this cat ate the canary smile on your face by now. Instead you're scowling at your phone."

Tucker blew out a breath in frustration. "I don't know man, I can't figure this chick out. I mean we've hooked up already but now I feel like she's blowing me off."

Jake could only laugh in response.

"Thanks, man. Real helpful," Tucker finished his beer and stood to leave. "Anyway I'm gonna head out."

After Tucker left, he went upstairs to brush his teeth and put on a pair of sweats. He debated calling it a night but decided to take advantage of the nice weather by relaxing in the hammock out back.

Exhausted, Jordan breathed a sigh of relief to finally being home. Her bed beckoned as she pulled on pajamas.

All that was left to do was let Navy out.

The moment she opened the sliding glass doors Navy bolted. He stopped on the patio, sniffed the air and was off again. That's when she saw the open gate and began to panic.

"Navy? Come here, Navy."

Damn it, why is Sean always leaving the gate open?

When she moved toward him, Navy took off again, headed toward Jake's backyard.

When she finally caught up with him, he was standing up on Jake licking his face. "Navy, down! You know better."

At the sound of Jake's laughter she relaxed. "It's okay, as long as he's not trying to eat me for his midnight snack, I'm good."

She quickly walked over to Navy's side to pull him down by his collar. "I'm sorry about that. He's too smart for his own good."

Navy wagged his tail and continued licking Jake.

"It's amazing… I've never seen him take to anyone like this before. He's usually so protective and on edge."

"Maybe I smell like beef jerky or something. By the way he won't stop licking me, you would at least think I tasted like it." He moved over to one side of the hammock and motioned for her to sit. It did look comfy with one of those small mattresses on it. After she was lying down, Navy walked in a circle and made himself comfortable on the patio next to the hammock.

Jake put his arm behind her head. In such a close position she could tell he smelled nothing like beef jerky and more like fresh soap and shaving cream. Instinctively she closed her eyes and breathed his scent in deeply.

Jake looked at her with pure amusement. "So I guess you weren't planning on leaving your house were you?"

"What do you mean?" She looked at him, confused by his question.

"Well seeing as you're in fuzzy pink slippers, minion boxer shorts, and a beater I assumed that wasn't your standard taking the dog for a walk outfit."

She felt her cheeks heat. In her rush after Navy she didn't even realize she was practically half naked. *Thank God I left my bra on.* But Jake wasn't making fun of her, he was smiling.

She looked down at Navy and frowned. "Yeah well when you're busy running after a hundred pound dog you're not really thinking of the fuzzy slippers on your feet, but hey, shit happens," she turned to face him and her eyes trailed over his body. "Well you know my excuse so what's yours?"

Confusion crossed his face. "What do you mean what's my excuse?"

"Well all you're wearing are sweats and a beater. You don't even have slippers, all you have on are socks."

One side of his mouth lifted up in a half smile revealing one of his panty melting dimples. "Well this *is* my backyard."

She realized he was laughing at her. She tried to give him a *how dare you* look but failed. All she could do was laugh at herself when he gave her a small wink with his left eye. Boy he had a good wink, it sent chills down her spine.

"What are you doing home on a Saturday night anyway?" she inquired.

Jake melted deeper into the hammock. "Well since the guys didn't want to go to Rookies, I offered to watch Carlee so my parents could go out."

He just got better and better. It wasn't fair.

"You two do anything fun?"

"Tucker came over and we took her to play mini golf."

It was the last thing she expected to hear.

"*Tucker*, took *your* little sister to play mini golf?" She couldn't keep the disbelief out of her voice.

"Hey, he's not all bad."

She pursed her lips in doubt.

"No seriously, he's great with her. He may be a man-whore but he's an amazing 'big brother' to her." He made air quotes around big brother.

"That's gotta be something to see."

"It is. But I'll give you this, he does love how much of a chick magnet she is."

She barked out a laugh. "Guess she wasn't successful tonight."

"How'd you know?"

She felt his chest rumble under her cheek in laughter. "He was texting Skye tonight."

"She told you?"

"She showed me. He is smooth. Too bad for him Skye is probably the female version of him in a way, so she won't fall for his tricks easily."

She raised her gaze to meet Jake's. His emerald gaze danced with laughter.

"Oh this is going to be fun," he stated.

The hammock caused their bodies to cuddle in a non-platonic way, but she couldn't bring herself to move.

"So how'd everything go there by the way?" Jake asked her after a few beats of comfortable silence.

"It was good, a little hectic but all in all things went well."

"What exactly was it that you guys had to do?"

"Skye and I are public relations majors, so whenever my aunt has special events we usually help her with planning them. This was the first time we were able to be there for the actual event though."

"That's gotta be cool. I've only ever heard good things about any special event she's thrown there."

She smiled with pride. "Thanks. I tried to remind her of all her past success tonight, but she was too stressed for it to sink in."

"Why was she so stressed?"

"Tonight the guest list included a bunch of brass from all the major professional sports. I think she was worried if they didn't like it, it would reflect badly on my dad."

"What does your dad have to do with it?"

"Some of the people are my dad's colleagues through his job with ESPN. He tells a lot of players about Rookies and tells them to check it out when they're in town. So if they didn't like it, it meant the players didn't either, hence making my dad look bad."

"Oh that makes sense, I guess. I wouldn't worry about it though Rookies is awesome. It has a great atmosphere and everyone I know that's been there loves it."

"Yeah that's what I told her. When I left everyone seemed to be having a good time," she sighed and leaned further back into the hammock. "It's really nice out tonight. I'm kind of glad to be outside and not stuck in the bar."

"Yeah my favorite part of summer is that the nights are warm enough to hang out outside. I like to lay out here and relax."

Even though she could feel the heat coming off his body she shivered slightly and it didn't go unnoticed. Jake reached down to the end of the hammock and pulled a light fleece blanket over them to keep her warm. She was touched by how observant and considerate he was of her. It really was peaceful.

NAVY OFFICIALLY BECAME Jake's new best friend. Jake was relaxing in the hammock in his backyard, like he had countless other nights, when Jordan's beast of a dog came barreling towards him. Shortly after Jordan came to retrieve the mutt, hence earning his new best friend status.

Jordan looked surprised to see him with Navy. As she helped remove the dog from his personal space, he took the opportunity to take her in. She was adorable in what he assumed were her pajamas and fuzzy slippers. The way her tiny boxer shorts displayed her legs had him biting back a groan.

He may not be a man-whore like Tucker, but he was no slouch either. Using his considerable charm, he embraced the opportunity to spend some quality alone time.

When she laid down next to him he couldn't stop his smile. But how she snuggled against him as they talked, that was everything.

"So I have a couple questions because there are just some things about you I just can't seem to figure out."

"About me?" She touched a hand to her chest feigning innocence. "What is it that you want to know?"

He took a deep breath before he continued. "So why is it all the seniors on the hockey team not only know you but are really close with you? And why did everyone make it seem like Jordan was another sibling of your brothers and JD was Jase's twin, and brother at that?"

She laughed when she turned to face him. "Well that's an easy and complicated question all in one, so we'll just go down the line. First, when Ryan was a freshman on the team and Jase and I were still in high school, I dated one of the guys on the team so I was around a lot. But things between us ended... kind of... messy. Second, the guys always called me JD... I guess because my brothers always have. But I honestly have no idea why they made it seem like we were two different people. When you told me you thought JD and Jordan were two different people I was surprised. I guess it stems from their overprotective tendencies."

She took a deep breath.

"Now that Skye and I have transferred to BTU I know they are going to drive me crazy with how ridiculously over-protective they are. I even had to promise not to date another teammate of theirs."

Jordan's statement was like a punch in the gut. He figured his friends were protective of their sister, but hearing how she promised not to date a teammate threw a wrench into his plans of asking her out.

"Who'd you date on the team, Nick?"

Maybe if he found out what happened with her past relationship, he could find a loophole for himself. His question earned him a playful smack on the stomach.

"Nick?! Oh my god, are you serious?" She said with a laugh.

"Yeah. I mean besides Wade who has a girlfriend, you seem closest to him and Billy. So I guessed it was either one of them."

"No the guy I dated is no longer on the team. After we broke up he left the team, that's why things were a little messy."

Feeling there was more to the story than she was letting on he decided to push. "Why'd you guys break up? What was so bad that he quit the team because of it?"

She paused so long he wasn't sure if she would answer or not. When she did, she kept her head down and spoke to his chest. "It's complicated. But it created tension between Ryan and the guys in his year and some of the upperclassmen. I swear it's part of the reason the team was so bad the next year."

Jake thought back to his freshman year and first year playing for the Titans. He wasn't a starter but tensions ran high on the team.

"So Wade is still dating Cara?" She asked.

He realized she didn't really answer the question but

thought it better not to push the subject right away. It was the first real one-on-one conversation he'd had with her and he didn't want to spoil it over an ex-boyfriend. "I guess you met her when you hung around the house?"

"Oh yeah. They were the cutest couple."

Jake agreed.

Jordan yawned, the cutest yawn he'd ever heard, kind of squeaky. When she looked up at him a strand of hair fell in front of her face. He reached out to tuck it behind her ear and their eyes met. Something lurked behind her eyes that made his gut clench. In such an intimate moment the electricity between them couldn't be denied. He had to find a way for her to be able to date him.

He watched her bite her lip. The lip biting was going to be his downfall if he wasn't careful. It brought so much attention to her full lips that it took all his self-control to not take her right there.

Trying to mask his emotions he changed the subject. "So what made you go to NYU and not Brighton Tynes? I mean Jase came here, aren't twins supposed to do everything together? You guys even have that crazy ESP stuff so it's weird you guys split up and all."

"How'd you know we have ESP?"

"At Rookies he said he knew you were there without even looking at the door. I thought he was kidding and Ryan was giving him shit about it but I knew he was serious because I was looking right at you when he said you were there." He looked away when he realized what he just admitted to.

"Yeah Ry was always a little jealous of the connection Jase and I have but he'll always be the one I turn to, there's nothing like the bond a girl has with her big brother."

He knew what she meant. Carlee may only be five but he already felt it, even with the age gap.

"I decided to go to NYU because Skye got accepted there and it was her dream school. We've been inseparable since we were five so there was no way I was going to go through four years of college without her."

"So why transfer if it was her dream school?"

"We liked it there, it's a great school and it was nice to put a little distance from my brothers' protectiveness. But we missed Jersey and BTU now offers a better Public Relations program so we decided to transfer. Ultimately we want to open our own firm that focuses on all aspects of an athletes career and BTU added a concentration in sports PR. There's also the added bonus of my parents moving closer to the school."

"I guess that makes sense."

"Why do you go to BTU?"

"They offered me a full athletic scholarship for hockey."

"I've seen you play, they can't have been the only school to offer you a full ride."

A few things rushed through Jake's mind at her statement. Mostly he felt pride she thought he was good enough to assume he had multiple college offers.

"When did you see me play?"

"Mostly I watched the games on TV but I came to the few home games I could. The way you played in the Frozen Four was legend... wait for it... dary."

The *How I Met Your Mother* reference made him smile.

"Yeah that was the best I've *ever* played." The Frozen Four and NCAA Championships garnered him attention from pro scouts.

"I guess I chose BTU for the same reason you originally went to NYU. BTU was the only school whose offers matched for both Tucker and I. We've been on the same team since our Mighty Mites days, didn't see a reason to break up the team."

"You're right. I know the feeling."

The longer the two lay there talking the bolder Jake became. Jordan's long hair tickled his arm around her shoulders. He bent his arm and played with the silky strands.

Curiosity finally got the better of him. It was time to bring the conversation back to what he really wanted to know.

"You know you never did answer my question earlier."

"What question would that be?" She asked from where her face rested on his chest.

"Why you and your ex broke up. Or who he was."

Chapter Ten

J ordan sucked in a startled breath. Her head lifted to look Jake in the eye as a shudder racked her body. She hoped Jake moved on from his earlier questions but he was like a damn dog with a bone.

She must have been silent for too long.

"Hey, it's okay. You can tell me it's none of my damn business."

Jake rubbed her arm that was across his chest. The reassuring touch cracked the wall of her past. Very few people knew what happened with Tommy.

Actually, the only people who knew, outside of those there that night, were Maddey and Sammy.

Something about Jake made her want to bring him into the fold. Before she lost the nerve, she spoke.

"I caught my ex cheating on me at the team's end of summer party."

She felt Jake's chest expand with a deep breath. His silence gave her to courage to continue.

"I may have fudged some of the facts earlier."

"How so?"

"Well when I said he left the team that wasn't necessarily true."

"You mean I play with the jerk?" She liked how he instantly picked her side.

"No, he's not a Titan anymore."

"Okay, still not seeing what you mean."

"He didn't leave the team on his own as I implied. He was kicked off it."

Jake's eyes widen at her revelation. She could see the questions flash in the green depths.

"Who?"

"Tommy Bradford."

Pressed against him as she was, she physically felt the shock rush through his body at the name.

"What aren't you telling me?" He rasped out.

Her brow furrowed in question.

"As messed up as cheating is, it wouldn't get him kicked off the team."

Now came the hard part of the story. She buried her face in his chest.

"After I caught him with another girl, I dumped his sorry ass right then and there. His response was to hit me."

"He did what?!" Jake growled.

Stunned by Jake's reaction, she was unsure of what to say. His entire body coiled tight like a cobra ready to strike.

She needed to diffuse the situation.

Now.

THIS WAS THE absolute last thing Jake expected to hear. The. Absolute. Last. Thing.

Sure, a part of him may have expected the cheating, based on how the guys would clam up when the subject of Jordan's ex came up. But to hear the guy hit her, never entered the realm of possibilities.

And by Tommy Bradford, no less.

"Damn baby, I'm so sorry." The endearment slipped out.

He lifted her face to his, pain clear in her golden gaze.

The tautness of her body released from the soothing of his thumb across her cheek and down her chin.

"So that's my story. I really should get back home now." She moved to get up.

"Don't go."

He tightened his hold when she hesitated. He breathed a sigh of relief when she settled back. He tucked her against him and dropped his chin where her head rested beneath it.

"I just need a minute to process all this." Unconsciously, his hand drew gentle circles on the skin between the hem of her tank and the band of her shorts.

"You know I always wondered what happened to him. Now I know."

"What do you mean?" He felt more than heard her mumble into his chest.

"I researched all the teams that courted me. I tried to find out as much about the players who would potentially be my teammates as I could. I was impressed the Titans were able to land such talented forwards two years in a row. Granted, Tommy's skill was miles away from the level Ryan's is, but the fact that the Titans got him and then your brother the following year proved they were serious in making their program the strongest possible."

Jordan was quiet for moment before she spoke. "It's one of the reasons I blame myself for you guys sucking so bad your freshman year."

He couldn't hold back a laugh. "Yeah the team was pretty awful. But I don't see why you would blame yourself."

"Now you sound like my brothers," she grumbled.

"I take it they don't agree with you?"

"Nope. They got all pissy I wasn't coming around. Cornered me during winter break my freshman year."

"Why didn't you listen to them?" If she did he would have met her earlier.

"I did. I just thought it would be better if I didn't hang around the team though. I knew some of the seniors were upset their last season was ruined. I was the reason one of their star forwards wasn't playing."

"That's bullshit. You didn't hit yourself. I don't care what the reason is, a man *never* puts his hands on a woman." Conviction rang in his voice.

"Thanks... Can we talk about something else now please?"

He pulled the blanket from earlier higher when she snuggled deeper in his arms.

"Sure. What did you have in mind?"

"Don't care. Anything."

He thought for a moment. They needed a light topic.

"So what made your parents have Sean? I know I have a similar age difference with Carlee but you and Jase are so close in age to Ryan, such a big age gap seems odd."

Her laugh confirmed he was successful.

"Yeah... umm... he was a souvenir my parents brought home from their second honeymoon."

"Sounds like a good time." He waggled his eyebrows.

"Eww." She placed a hand over her face as if to ward off the mental images he painted.

"Sorry."

"No worries," her hand dropped from her face to rest on his stomach. "Honestly, I'm surprised it didn't happen sooner. My dad is always grabbing my mom's ass and stuff when he thinks we aren't looking. It'd be gross if they weren't so cute together."

Jake's ab muscles constricted when her thumb started tracing their bumps. He was pretty sure she wasn't aware she was doing it.

"What about Carlee? I can't believe you have the same age gap in your family too."

"Carlee is my mom's little miracle. My parents tried for years after they had me for another baby with no success. Then, poof, Carlee happened."

"Bet they were shocked."

"You have no idea. Now she runs the house. All of us are wrapped around her cute little finger."

"She is cute," she said around another yawn.

Chapter Eleven

J ordan was very warm and comfortable and did not want to wake up. She had such a restful night sleep with no dreams. Her alarm clock hadn't gone off yet but something had woken her up. When she opened her eyes she saw why she was so warm, Jake slept beside her. The guy was like her own personal space heater.

"What are they doing?"

After a few seconds she heard what woke her up, it sounded like whispering. She looked up at Jake when he started to stir.

"It looks like they're sleeping."

"But why?"

When Jake opened his eyes, his emerald depths alight with pleasure, everything else ceased to exist.

"Morning," he said with a lazy smile.

She blinked a few times to clear the fog he created. "Hi," she smiled too. "I can't believe we fell asleep."

"Yeah I guess we stayed up later than we thought."

"Are they boyfriend and girlfriend?"

"That would be so cool."

Again Jordan heard the noise that woke her. "Listen. Do you hear that?"

Jake lifted his head to hear better. "What is that?"

"I'm not sure but that's what woke me up." She sat up in the hammock and saw little feet sticking out from behind the pool shed. "I think I have the answer to that riddle." She paused. "We've been caught red handed."

Jake looked confused. "Huh?"

She pointed over to the shed. "Look at the left side of the pool shed… do you see little feet sticking out?"

He sat up to get a better look. The action caused his body to rub against hers. "Oh yeah now I see them. They are such little sneaks," he said with a lazy half smile that damn near broke her heart.

"You two can come out now, we know you're there," she called.

They watched as Sean and Carlee made their way out from behind the shed, heads down in embarrassment. "Sorry," they said in unison.

They looked so sullen and guilty, there was no way anyone would be able to stay upset with them. "It's ok guys, but why were you hiding?" She asked.

Sean was first to answer. "Well Mom couldn't find you so I went to play with Carlee and to see if Jake would take us to swimming and when we went to find Jake we saw you sleeping out here and we didn't know why so…"

"Crap!" She pushed a hand against Jake's chest. "What time is it?"

She reached for her phone and came up empty.

"Do you have your phone? I guess I left mine at home," she asked Jake.

He pulled his phone out of his pocket. "It's 9:30."

"Crap. I have to be at the pool by 10."

Realization hit that an innocent situation, like accidentally falling asleep with Jake in a hammock, could become a completely disastrous scenario if her other brothers found out about it the wrong way. "Listen you aren't in trouble. But you have to make me one very big promise, okay?"

The little ones looked at each other and nodded. "Okay what?"

"You can't tell Ry or Jase we were sleeping in the hammock. Deal?"

"Deal!" They shouted. She knew they were happy they weren't in trouble.

With that settled she got out of the hammock. "Okay, I'm going to go get my stuff and we can go to the pool. Is Mom picking you guys up after lessons because I have to run practice?"

"I don't know she's not home."

"What do you mean she's not home?"

"After she told me to ask Mrs. D for a ride she went to the store."

Indecision warred within her. She would have to text her brothers to see if one of them could pick the kids up from the pool.

"I can pick them up, it's not a problem," Jake offered.

"You're my savior." She gave him a grateful smile.

"Come on Navy. Time to eat buddy."

Her big lab stood and stretched before following her out of the Donovan backyard.

Moments later she ran through the sliding glass doors of her house into the kitchen. The first thing she did was look for her phone and found it on the kitchen island. As she checked the battery status she noticed a missed call from an unknown number, but no time to figure it out.

In her room she quickly changed out of her pajamas and into her red lifeguard suit and pair of daisy dukes. After confirming her swim duffle had everything she needed, she ran back downstairs to feed Navy.

A glance at the clock confirmed she didn't have time to make coffee. *Dammit.*

JAKE OPENED HIS eyes to what he thought was the best sight in the world, Jordan. She slept with her arm draped across his chest and her leg intertwined with his. He liked that she was drawn to him in her sleep.

He ran a hand up and down her arm when he noticed she was awake. "Morning." He said while a lazy smile spread across his face.

She blinked a few times. "Hi," she smiled too. "I can't believe we fell asleep."

"Yeah I guess we stayed up later than we thought."

He wasn't sure what time they actually fell asleep but it had to be late. They spent hours joking and talking as they learned how much they had in common.

The night could have been described as perfect, with the way Jordan cuddled against him as they talked and the easy chemistry they had. The only exception was having to listen to Jordan explain about her breakup with Tommy Bradford.

Tommy. *Fucking.* Bradford.

He had a feeling there was more to the story than she let on, but he let it go for now.

The bliss from waking up with Jordan was interrupted by two pint-sized troublemakers. He could feel the anxiety roll off her body while she got Sean to promise not to say anything to their brothers. He had to admit he was relieved Sean agreed. The last thing he needed was for his friends to get the wrong impression of his intentions before he had a chance to state them.

"What do you mean she's not home?" Jordan asked her brother, bringing Jake's attention back to the conversation at hand.

"After she told me to ask Mrs. D for a ride she went to the store," Sean answered.

The kids needed to be picked up from practice. Jake saw it as the perfect opportunity to see her again so he offered his assistance. "I can pick them up it's not a problem."

"You're my savior."

When she smiled at him he vowed he would do whatever it took to always keep her that way. The night before only reinforced the instant attraction he felt toward her.

"Come on squirts. Let's get some food."

Jake led the kids into the kitchen. He set them up with Frosted Flakes to eat while he made himself breakfast. He still couldn't believe he'd woken up with Jordan in his arms. It was like his thoughts conjured her up. He'd been dreaming of the two of them together and when he opened his eyes she was really there.

At first he thought he was still dreaming but then he felt her move beside him and knew it was real. You couldn't feel a dream could you?

He was in the middle of scrambling eggs when Sean started talking to him. "Hey, Jake?"

He turned to face Sean. "Yeah, buddy."

"Can I ask you a question?"

"Of course. What's up?"

Sean looked really nervous but still pushed on. "You like my sister, right?"

Jake paused before he answered. He had to tread lightly where Jordan was concerned. He knew how he felt and was pretty sure she felt the same way but also knew it was a complicated situation that involved not only them but also two of his best friends. "Yeah." He decided to keep it simple.

Sean played with his cereal and was still looking down when he started talking again. "So you would never hurt her right?"

Jake wasn't sure how to respond. He was dumbfounded.

Of all the questions he could have been asked, this wasn't one he would have ever anticipated. "No, of course not buddy. Why would you ask that?"

"Just wondering."

Jordan entered the kitchen preventing him from probing any further. "Hey kids, ready to go?"

"Yup!" Sean jumped off his stool and ran over to his sister.

"So what time should I pick them up?" He handed Jordan a travel coffee cup.

"What's this for?"

"I figured you wouldn't take the time to make yourself one, even though I'm sure you need it."

"Thanks." She took a tentative sip before she looked up at him in surprise. "This is perfect. How'd you know how I take it?"

"I remembered how you took it yesterday at the house."

It was obvious she was touched by the comment.

"Anyway lessons are over at 11:30, so any time after that. I can have one of the other lifeguards keep an eye on them until you get there," she turned her attention to the kids. "Are you guys ready to go?"

The kids nodded and grabbed their stuff. Then the three of them were out the door and on their way.

Jake went for a run in the free time before having to pick up the kiddos from swim lessons. He was hoping the exercise would keep his mind off Jordan's revelations. He knew she dated a member of the hockey team and things ended badly. But the truth blew his mind.

Her story was worse than he imagined. Consequently, it created a pact between the Donnelly siblings that Jordan would never date another member of the team.

On top of all that, there was Sean's question if he would

ever hurt his sister. That was the thing that baffled Jake the most.

Was Sean just mature beyond his years and mean emotionally hurt his sister or could he actually mean physically hurt her? The latter tore his stomach up in knots. He hoped Sean didn't see him as anything like Tommy Bradford.

He figured he and Jordan danced around their attraction long enough. It was time to do something about it.

His run took him longer than planned and it was just before noon by the time he arrived at the pool. He found Sean and Carlee playing in the pool with some of the other kids.

Carlee was laughing at something Sean was doing when she noticed him walking their way. "Hey, Jake!"

"Hi, sweetie," he looked around the pool area. "Where's Jordan?"

She pointed towards the deep end of the pool, where the summer team practiced. "Over there."

He followed her finger to where Jordan stood next to the diving blocks and saw her talking to two swimmers, gesturing something with her arms. He'd seen her in pants-tightening bikinis, but in her red one piece boasting Lifeguard across the chest and a white cross beneath, she belonged on the set of *Baywatch*.

A moment later she looked in their direction, waved and motioned she would be there in a minute. After Jake nodded he would wait she turned back to the swimmers she was speaking with.

"Why don't you two dry off and get your stuff? We'll head out after we say goodbye to Jordan."

The kids hurried over to their towels. His attention turned back to Jordan, drawn to her as usual. He watched her remove the whistle and stopwatch from around her neck and hand them to the swimmer at the block she was talking to. Next she donned the goggles wrapped around her wrist and stood on the diving block. She said something to the swimmer in the water while pointing down the lane.

The swimmer in the water swam out a little further before swimming toward the wall with the diving blocks. Jordan waited, bouncing slightly bent over with her arms out. As the swimmer approached the wall, Jordan swung her arms around and launched herself into the pool.

Jake had seen Jordan swim laps in both her pool at home and at the hockey house but neither of those times compared to how she cut through the water now. Her speed and skill were obvious to even a swimming novice such as himself. Quicker than he thought possible she executed a flip turn, he smiled remembering how she soaked him the day before and the adorable look on her face when she noticed.

Finished with her lap, Jordan got out of the pool. She put her whistle and stopwatch back on and grabbed a towel before she made her way over to where he was standing.

"Hey Jake. Thanks again for picking them up."

"Of course. It's no problem at all." He gave her his most charming smile and could tell she was affected.

"Spoiled."

He nodded. "So that was really awesome. I've seen you swim before but that was something else."

She smiled at the compliment and draped the towel around her neck. "Thanks. It's easier to push it in the bigger pools."

"What were you showing them?"

"I'm helping their coach work on their relay starts. It's one of my specialties."

"Looked impressive from over here."

"Thanks."

"Alright kids. How's about we go get us some ice cream?"

Barely two hours later he was regretting the suggestion. Thanks to their sugar rush Carlee and Sean had been non-stop.

Luckily now they entertained each other in his backyard pool. He laid in the same hammock he slept in with Jordan a few hours earlier utterly torn.

His was still wallowing in self-pity when his buddies walked into his backyard. "Yo Donovan, what's goin on?" Ryan asked as he sat down next to him.

"Not much bro. What are you guys doing here?" He reached out to bump knuckles.

Sean noticed his brothers' arrival and called for their attention. Ryan rose from the hammock and made his way over to the pool allowing Jase to take his place. "Well since JD is home now, Sunday night is back to family dinner night. So here we are."

"Oh and Mom wanted us to invite your family over to barbeque with us, but if you ask me it was more of a demand than an invitation." Ryan shouted from by the pool.

Jake couldn't believe his luck. He was being given an opportunity to spend more time with Jordan without raising suspicion. He wondered if it would afford him the opportunity to prove to his friends that he would be a good fit for their sister.

"You know we'll be there. Let me go tell my parents and we can go over there now."

Normally Jordan loved giving swimming lessons and coaching, but today wasn't a normal day. She started her day waking up in Jake's arms and even now couldn't shake the feeling of how good those arms felt around her.

Falling asleep in the hammock was a major tactical error on her part. She should never have sat down to talk to him. Over the past week they started forming a friendship and if she wasn't careful she might let it develop into something she couldn't. Sure, she tried not to be friends with him, because it was too hard with how attracted to him she was, but he was so hard not to like.

He was attractive, witty, sexy, and amazing with kids. Plus anytime they talked she knew he was actually listening. And when he looked at her, it felt like he was seeing all the way into her soul.

Last night she talked more about her past then she did with most people. Sure, she down played what happened, but letting *anyone* know *anything* about Tommy was not an everyday occurrence.

Tommy was her mistake and something she wished she could forget. She learned a valuable lesson from it and the scar above her left eye would always be a reminder. Now every time she was around Jake she just had to keep reminding herself what happened the last time she got involved with one of the hockey players.

If only it were that easy.

Every time she was able to stop thinking about Jake, something else would trigger thoughts about him and it would start all over again.

She decided to take things one step at a time. And if she had to constantly stay busy to keep away from him, so be it.

When she pulled up in front of her house she noticed Ryan's car. At first she was confused to why he was here but then she realized it was Sunday, family dinner night and the thought made her smile. She loved her family and spending time with all of them in the same place at the same time.

She unloaded her bag from the car and made her way into the house. Since it was just her brothers, she went up to take a shower before heading outside. She knew washing the chlorine off her body would be pointless since she would be going into her own pool, but she needed the ten minutes of alone time the shower would allow her to regain control over her emotions toward Jake.

She braced her hands on the wall and let the water beat

the tension from her shoulders. Everything about being with Jake seemed natural and right. She felt comfortable and safe with him. Last night alone was proof of that. With a frustrated sigh she climbed out of the shower and went to her room to get dressed.

As she made her way to the back door she could hear music and laughter and it made her smile. She opened the sliding glass doors to the back patio. Her smile grew bigger when she spotted Jake lounged on a raft talking to her brothers. Sure she spent the past few minutes trying to rein in her growing feelings, but you couldn't blame a girl for wanting to be around him.

"Hi, Princess," her dad said when he saw she was home.

Chapter Twelve

J ake heard Mr. Donnelly greet Jordan. He'd been enjoying the last hour with his friends, but her missing presence was obvious.

Nothing could have prepared him for how he felt when he saw her. She stood on the patio in a purple cami and jean shorts rolled down revealing the bottom of her purple bathing suit. Her wet blonde hair hung around her shoulders. Even without a stitch of make-up she was a total knock out.

"Hey guys," Jordan said as she walked up to the pool.

"Hey sis," Ryan called.

She hooked her thumbs in her front pockets and turned her full attention to Jake. "So what... just because you picked the kids up from swim lessons you think that you can come here and eat all of my dad's good cooking?" She raised an eyebrow in mock challenge.

"No, I was invited but that sounds like a good plan... I'll have to remember that for next time."

He watched Jase approach his sister from behind. Before she noticed, Jase pushed her into the pool and jumped in after her.

"Jase I'm going to get you back for that." Her eyes promised revenge.

Jake watched as she took off her cami and shorts, leaving her in just her bathing suit. She then climbed into the oversized doughnut print inner tube.

"So where's Skye?" Ryan asked.

"Yeah, figured she'd come home with you after coaching. She used to always come to family dinners," Jase added.

"She didn't work today. Sammy stayed at her house after last night. But I'm sure once she hears about people trying to replace her, she'll never miss another one." She pointed to Jake.

"Hey I was invited." He held his hands up in surrender.

"That's what they all say."

"Jake where's Tuck? You guys are joined at the hip as much as JD and Skye," Jase asked.

"I'm sure he's still recovering from helping me babysit Carlee last night."

Understanding laughter met his comment.

"I'm surprised you don't have the guys running drills and stuff today," Jordan said to Ryan.

"Dude, I think I'm going to like having your sister around. She's not afraid to call you out," Jake laughed.

"Shut it Donovan, or I *will* make you do drills," Ryan threatened.

"Whatever you say, *Captain.*"

Jordan paddled her float to where Jake was treading water. "Did you ever try any of the suggestions I gave you?"

He nodded. "Tuck and I played tennis the other day but he sucks."

"What about ping pong?"

"I have to find a table to play on." He folded his arms on top of her raft, taking any opportunity he could be close to her.

"Hey Dad?" Jordan waited until she had her father's attention. "Did you guys keep the old ping pong table when you moved?"

"Of course. It's in the garage. You know your Uncle Rick would kill me if I got rid of it," Mr. D answered.

"Can we take it out?"

"Sure, we have a few hours until we're ready for dinner. Boys come give me a hand."

"You want to play now?" Jake asked looking up at Jordan.

"No time like the present. I'll play lefty too to make it fair."

"What the hell do you have my goalie doing?" Ryan dried off with a towel.

"Jake told me you guys were working on his glove saves. So I gave him some tips."

"Damn, don't tell coach she's here. She's worse with the drills than you Ry," Jase ribbed.

Ryan rolled his eyes. "Please," he turned his attention to his sister. "Where'd you get your brilliant drill ideas, *Oh Great One?*"

Jordan stuck her tongue out at her brother. "You know as well as I do that Uncle Rick swears by ping pong." She tapped Jake on the shoulder, goosebumps spread in its wake. "Give me a tow?"

"You got it."

He swam around the doughnut float to push them both to the pool's edge.

"Okay, I'll give you ping pong. But where'd you come up with tennis?" Ryan asked handing them both towels.

"I learned it from Eddie at a Garden of Dreams event," she stated as she finished drying off.

Jake watched his friends freeze. Ryan's mouth hung open and Jase's eye were as wide as saucers. *What am I missing here?*

"Eddie?" Ryan breathed.

"Yeah," Jordan shrugged.

"Did you seriously just say Eddie?"

"Yeah. You know I've met him a bunch of times through the foundation."

"Yeah but you called him Eddie."

"That *is* his name."

"Guess you can't complain about her source," Jase laughed.

Now I know I'm missing something.

"How can you be so calm when you say that?" Ryan asked his brother.

"What's the big deal? We know she's worked with a bunch of the Storm through the GDF, the hockey team is super active in the foundation. *Dude*, she's sent us selfies with most of them," Jase stated.

"Yeah but she calls him *Eddie*," Ryan said like it was obvious.

"So?"

"*So?*" Ryan threw his hands up in frustration.

"Wait. Hold up. What am I missing here?" Jake asked.

"Nothing," Jase said.

"*Nothing?* God you are just as bad as she is. I blame it on the fact you two used to share a womb," Ryan turned to face Jake. "I don't think it's nothing that my sister here," he pointed back at Jordan, "calls Edvin Ringquist, Eddie."

"Again it *is* his name." Jordan rolled her eyes.

"You've met Edvin Ringquist?" Jake was in awe. Ringquist was one of his favorite goalies.

She shrugged her shoulders. "Yeah. A bunch of times. I've met most of the Storm."

"Damn. I agree with Ry, that's major."

"You just think that because you're a goalie."

"Is he the only NHL goalie you've met?" He was kind of shocked the subject didn't come up the night before. He almost asked her why she didn't but caught himself before he could, still unsure how her brothers would react to their late night chat.

"No."

"Way to bury the lead."

Ryan was helping his dad unfold the ping pong table on the side of the patio. "Yeah, get used to it with her."

"Shut it you," Jordan said to him before turning back to Jake. "I've also met Ryan Miller, Jonathan Quick, and the great Martin Brodeur."

"Holy shit!" Jake looked at her stunned.

"You're forgetting someone," Jase sing-songed.

She's met more?

"You guys never told him?" Jordan asked her twin.

"No why would we?"

"He's your goalie."

"Not our story to tell."

"Also not sure how he would handle it," Ryan joked.

"True. He is his favorite after all," Jase added.

Wait. They couldn't be talking? Could they?

"Wow. Okay." Jordan wore a sheepish expression.

Jake cut her off before she could continue. "Wait... Are you telling me you've met *Rick Schelios*?"

"Umm..."

"Seriously?"

Jake could see Ryan, Jase, and Mr. D trying to hold back their laughter. Shaking his head he turned his attention back to Jordan. She seemed unsure of herself all of sudden.

"Saying I've met him isn't exactly accurate." She wrung her hands together. "He's kind of... my... godfather."

He felt like his eyes were going to pop out of his head in shock.

"Rick Schelios is your godfather? *The* Rick Schelios?" Saying he was Jake's favorite goalie would be like saying pizza is only good.

"He's not *the* anything to me. To me, he's just Uncle Rick."

"I don't know if I can still be friends with you two anymore." He pointed to Ryan and Jase.

"Why?" Jase asked.

"Because. I can't believe you didn't tell me about this. This is epic."

"You'll get over it," Ryan stated.

"Come on let's play." Jordan handed him a ping pong paddle.

"How?" He asked her.

"How what?"

"How did one of the greatest goalies of all time become your godfather?"

"He was roommates with my dad in college when they played for Boston College."

"Damn."

"Let's play. You serve." Jordan tossed a ping pong ball at him.

With family dinner over and the parental units and kids retired for the evening, Jordan sat drinking beer with her brothers and Jake in the Adirondack chairs surrounding the fire pit in her backyard.

She and Jake changed into their pajamas earlier, she in a beater and NYU Violets Swimming sweats, he in a beater and sweats, the same outfit he wore the night before.

Why does he have to have on the same thing as last night? It's hard enough to keep my distance from him around my brothers but does he have to deliberately taunt me with memories of last night? Come on now!

She needed to get her mind out of the gutter and onto something else. "So are you guys staying here tonight?" She asked Jase.

He took a swig of his beer. "Yeah, the team's playing roller hockey at the park near here so we figured it was easier to go from here."

She rubbed her hands together with a scheming look in her eye. "Well now that changes everything." The look she gave her brother was pure evil.

"What are you talking about?" Jase asked with a slight wobble to his voice.

Her smile was all sweet and innocent but he could tell it was anything but. "Unagi." She pressed two fingers to her temple.

"Don't be quoting *Friends* at me."

"Hey it's a great show," Jake agreed. "I think she's trying to tell you to watch your back."

"Oh yeah. You just made it that much easier for me to get you back for throwing me in the pool earlier," she confirmed.

All her twin could do was shake his head and wait for his impending doom. He knew from experience that she loved to get revenge on pranks, no matter how long she waited to act it out.

Ryan took pity on his brother and steered the conversation away from Jase's torture. "Are you gonna come watch us play tomorrow?" He asked her. "You haven't sat close for one of our games in forever and we miss your yelling."

"Hmm, maybe."

"What else do you have to do?"

She toyed with a strand of hair while she debated how to answer. "Well if you *must* know…" She said with mock annoyance. "Maddey is coming up and the two of us are gonna have a girls night with Skye and Sammy."

Ryan's eyebrows lifted. "Girls night huh? But Sammy's a guy, how does he fit in?"

She laughed at her brother. "Gay guys don't count. They like the same topics we do so they get to come." She paused and took a sip of beer. "But no boyfriends, can't talk about someone if they are there."

A few moments passed before she spoke again. "I'll ask them if they want to swing by the park, I'm sure they'll want to."

"Man you underclassmen have no idea what you're up against if you don't play well when JD is around. She can be worse than coach sometimes." Ryan said with a big swallow of beer.

"Aint that the truth," Jase agreed.

"Well bring it on then," Jake encouraged which garnered another laugh from Jordan.

"We should go grab our bags from the car before it gets too late. Game tomorrow and all." Ryan placed his beer bottle on the grass and got out of his chair.

"I suppose you're right. Grab mine while you're out there?" Jase asked.

"I'll do it for twenty bucks."

"Fine, I'll do it myself." Jase followed behind his brother around the house and into the dark.

Jordan enjoyed the moment alone with Jake. She knew she shouldn't but she couldn't help herself.

He was sitting in the chair next to hers so she shifted around to face him, her back rested against the one arm and her legs draped over the other. Her well worn sweats fell over her feet, the hems frayed and small holes on the bottom from walking on the too long material.

"I think it's time you retire these." Jake poked a finger through one of those small holes.

"Yeah I know. I need to get some Titan gear."

"Very true. Can't be reppin' another team."

Jake took a deep breath and focused all his attention on her. "Hey, Jordan, there's something I've been meaning to ask you about."

She could sense the change in his demeanor. "Sure, what's up?"

"Earlier today when I was making Sean and Carlee breakfast, Sean asked me something and I was wondering if you could shed some light onto why he was asking?"

She was a little confused now herself. "Ok. What did he ask you?"

She watched his impressive chest expand with another deep breath. "First he asked me if I liked you, which after last night I can see why he asked me."

Knowing being caught sleeping together in the hammock was the reason for the inquiry, she motioned for him to continue.

"Then he asked me if I would hurt you."

Panic seized her body. *Oh my god, Sean, why would you ask that?* She needed to regain control of what was going on. The last thing she needed was for Jake to question what she told him about Tommy. It was bad enough he knew the general information. She didn't want him to realize there was more to the story.

"He asked you what?" She tried to laugh to lighten the mood.

"If I would ever hurt you, but I'm not sure what he meant by it."

She racked her brain for something to say. "He's probably just being overprotective, he's spends *way* too much time with Ry and Jase. They must have rubbed off on him."

"Are you sure it isn't about Tommy?" He asked bluntly.

This is where things got tricky. "I doubt it. He was only three at the time. I don't think he really understood what happened." Again not the whole truth but it would work.

"Okay, good. I was worried I gave off similar vibes or something."

She did not like him comparing himself to Tommy in any

way. She sat up to reach for his hand, still playing with her sweats. "You are nothing. *Nothing*. Like him at all."

She watched him exhale a breath of relief.

Ryan and Jase came back out into the backyard a minute later which brought a definitive end to the conversation. Using her brothers' arrival as her way of escape she said goodnight.

Chapter Thirteen

J ake held Jordan in his arms as they cuddled in the hammock, it was pure bliss. She couldn't believe how well her brothers took to the idea of them being together. The way they were acting towards her relationship with Jake was like everything with Tommy never happened.

As they talked Jake played with her hair. "You know nights like this are my favorite," he said to her.

She almost missed his comment because she was starting to drift off from him playing with her hair. "Ummm," was the only response she could manage.

Jake smiled at her response and kissed her forehead. Just when she thought the night was one of the best of her life, the impossible happened.

"Jordan, sweetness ,where are you?" She heard someone call.

Her eyes opened wide in shock when she recognized the voice that called her name. TOMMY!!!

"OH MY GOD!" She sat straight up not sure what to do. But before she could do anything Tommy stormed into the backyard.

Tommy spotted them instantly. "Who the hell are you? Get your hands off my girl."

Jake stood and positioned himself between her and Tommy.

"Jordan is not your girl," he shouted back at him. "Now get off my property."

In the blink of an eye Tommy rushed Jake and tackled him to the ground. Catching Jake off-guard put Tommy at an advantage. He grabbed Jake's shoulders and hit his head on the ground to knock him out.

She watched the scene unfold in utter terror. Tommy attacked Jake and was now heading toward her. He moved too fast for her to react and the next thing she knew he had her arm in his vise like grip.

She struggled against him to try to fight him off. She was yelling trying to wake Jake up. "JAKE!!!" She was screaming at the top of her lungs as Tommy dragged her out of the backyard.

Jordan was still screaming when she woke up. She put a hand to her chest and felt it covered in sweat. Navy was growling from the end of the bed. Next thing she knew her brothers were barreling into her room.

"Jordan what happened?" Jase asked.

The look of concern on her brother's face helped pull her out of her daze. "It's nothing, just a bad dream. I'm ok now."

Jase sat down next to her on the bed and ran his hand up and down her back to help calm her nerves. "You know it's not nothing Jor. I could feel something was wrong before we heard you screaming, so come on tell us what this is all about."

She was torn between telling her brothers the truth or making something up. She hated lying to them but she was afraid that if she told them the truth they would become even more overprotective. Taking a fortifying breath she opted with the truth. "Tommy," was the only thing she could manage to get out.

The look of anger that crossed her brothers' features made her doubt her decision in going with the truth. She could only imagine the scenarios racing through their minds at her admission.

"Tommy?" Ryan practically shouted. "Has he been bothering you again? Does he know where we live now, or where the new hockey house is? Jordan why didn't you tell us he's been around again?"

Ryan's anger caught her off guard. Did he really think if Tommy was harassing her again she wouldn't tell them? "No of course not! It was just a bad dream that's all. Nothing more, nothing less."

Her no nonsense tone and steely look convinced them she was telling the truth. They kissed her on the cheek, said goodnight, before going back to the living room where they were bunking for the night.

Chapter Fourteen

Jordan woke up and stretched her arms over her head. As she yawned, Navy made his way up to her side of the bed to give her a good morning kiss. She smiled as she scratched behind his ears. She rolled her shoulders back to help get rid of the after effects from last night's nightmare and climbed out of bed. She grabbed a loose fitting Henley from her dresser, put on her slippers and made her way downstairs with Navy following close behind.

She spotted Jase asleep on the couch and couldn't resist the urge for payback. Grabbing a dog treat out of the pantry she positioned it over her twin's stomach and tempted Navy to jump up onto him.

"Come on boy, come get the treat." She whispered as she waved the treat left and right.

With the instant weight of a hundred pound dog landing on his stomach, Jase sat up with a grunt. Seeing her bent over in a fit of laughter behind the couch he knew Navy's wake-up call wasn't an accident. Once he caught his breath he threw a pillow at her. "At least now we're even."

Still laughing, she stood up and tossed the pillow back at

her twin. "What can I say, I was inspired." She gave him her most charming smile to soften the blow.

Ryan laughed as he got up from the couch he was sleeping on. "See, I told you I was happy not to be the one on her bad side."

Feigning offense, she put her hand on her hip and cocked her head to the side. "Hey I'm just a product of my upbringing. You guys made me the way I am, it's not my fault you can't take what you dish out."

She gave Ryan a pout. He draped an arm around her shoulders, placed a kiss on top of her head, and steered her toward the kitchen. "Oh we can take it Jor, but sometimes you're just evil."

She placed a hand to her chest and looked up at him with puppy-dog eyes. "Who, me?"

Full out laughter was the only response she got from her brothers. She glanced at the clock and saw it was just after nine. Since Maddey would be there soon she opted to just have coffee because the two of them would be going out to breakfast.

Coffee mug in hand, she took Navy outside. *I wonder if Jake is working out this morning since they are playing hockey today. Arggh!! I have to stop thinking about him.*

The doorbell rang announcing Maddey's arrival.

She ran to open the door. "Madz I'm so happy you're here, I feel like I haven't seen you in forever." She threw her arms around her in a giant hug.

Maddey's hug was just as big. "I know I needed me some major girl time, especially with one that knows my pain."

"Tell me about it," she sighed.

"So where's my little boyfriend?"

Jordan smiled at her friend. Maddey had an aura about her that made guys putty in her hands, and Sean was no exception. Ever since Sean met Maddey he was hopelessly in love, it was the cutest thing. "He's in the kitchen with Twee-dledee and Tweedledum."

They made their way into the kitchen where Sean sat on a stool at the breakfast bar talking to his older brothers. "Hey there, handsome," Maddey called to him.

At the sound of her voice Sean looked up cheesing ear-to-ear. "MADDEY!" He shouted as he jumped off the stool and ran into Maddey's open arms.

Maddey laughed at his excitement and returned his enthusiastic hug. She picked him up and carried him back over to where he was eating breakfast. "Did you miss me buddy?" She asked as she tussled his hair.

"Yup! I've been telling Carlee all about you, she can't wait to meet you." He was beaming as he spoke to her.

"Who's Carlee? Am I going to have to be nervous about losing my little boyfriend to another girl?" She put her hand over her heart like she was broken hearted.

Jordan watched Sean blush. "No she's my best friend, she lives next door. You'll meet her soon, she's coming over."

"Good." Maddey said then gave him a kiss on the cheek.

"Madison do you want any coffee?" Ryan asked.

Jordan rolled her eyes. Her brother knew Maddey hated to be called by her full name.

"Ryan, last time I saw you I told you to call me Maddey, but sure, coffee sounds great."

Navy came running back inside and jumped on Maddey. Everyone laughed and Jordan couldn't suppress the smile crossing her own face at the sight. "I guess he missed his adoptive Mama."

JAKE WAS FINISHING packing his hockey gear when Carlee came barreling down the stairs in her usual fashion. "Hey there Speedy Gonzalez, where are you off to?"

Carlee came to a dead stop when she heard him. "I'm going over to play with Sean."

He smiled at his sister, she was too cute for her own good. "Okay. If you give me a minute I'll go over with you because I'm playing hockey with the guys."

"Okay."

He finished zipping up his bag and hauled it onto his shoulder. He grabbed his hockey stick and a bottle of water. "Okay, let's go."

They made their way through their backyard into the Donnelly's. Going over this way had become routine and he loved the casual atmosphere between their families and how much easier it made it to see Jordan.

Carlee ran in ahead of him. As he neared the back door he saw Jordan bent down petting Navy on the stomach, the dog was in heaven. "Hey, Jordan."

She kept petting the dog not answering which was weird. He tried again. "Hey Jordan."

"Hey Jake." She said but it wasn't from in front of him, it was from somewhere inside the kitchen. When he looked up and saw her, she was laughing at him but was talking to someone else. "See Madz? I swear sometimes I think you, me, and Jase were triplets and you were just separated from us at birth."

The girl in front of him was laughing as she stood up. "Yeah one could only dream how nice it would have been to have a sister instead of three crazy brothers."

"Amen," they said in unison.

Jordan made her way over to where he was standing and he was once again blown away by how beautiful she looked when she smiled, she practically glowed. "Jake this is one of my best friends from NYU Maddey. Maddey this is Jake."

When Maddey turned to face him the resemblance between her and Jordan was uncanny. She was an inch or two shorter than Jordan's five foot two height, her blonde hair looked just as long pulled back in a ponytail but curlier. But the biggest difference were the eyes, hers were ice blue surrounded by a think black line, kind of like a husky, where Jordan's were golden and catlike.

"Wow you guys really could be related."

Maddey laughed. "You have no idea." With that she turned on her heel and made her way into the kitchen where the kids were talking. "So this must be my competition, Carlee."

"Competition?" Carlee asked befuddled.

"Yeah ever since I got here all I've heard was *Carlee and I did this and Carlee and I did that.* I should be hurt but I guess I can't be too hurt when the one my little boyfriend is leaving me for is as cute as you." She stuck out her hand. "I'm Maddey."

Carlee placed her hand in Maddey's and shook it. "It's okay I know how to share."

After a few seconds of silence everyone in the kitchen laughed at Carlee's response.

"Jake do you want any coffee?" Jase asked from his place by the coffee pot.

"Sure." Coffee cup in hand, Jake leaned against the breakfast bar across from where Jordan and Maddey sat on the other counter and crossed one ankle in front of the other. He still couldn't get over how much the two of them looked alike.

"I don't know about you Jor, but I'm starving, let's go get breakfast," Maddey suggested.

"Okay let's go." Jordan jumped down from her perch on the counter and placed her coffee cup in the sink.

As they made their way out of the kitchen Jake stopped them. "Wait... are you guys gonna come watch us play today?"

"Oh I totally forgot to ask." Jordan turned to Maddey. "Do you wanna go watch the guys play roller hockey in the park this afternoon, Skye and Sammy said they were down."

"Hmm, watching hot guys getting all sweaty playing hockey." She paused and wicked gleam came into her eyes. "Where do I sign up?"

Jordan full out laughed and threw her arms over her friend's shoulders. "Aww man, what am I going to do with you Madz?"

"I don't know, but let's talk about it over breakfast."

Tucker walked into the kitchen after the girls left. "Who's the babe with Jordan?"

Jake heard Ryan make a noise at Tucker's comment.

"Back off. You've already slept with one of my sister's best friends, you don't need to add another," Ryan barked.

"Noted." Tucker held his hands up in surrender.

"Here Tuck, take this before Ry kills you." Jase handed him a cup of coffee.

"What are you doing here anyway?" Ryan narrowed his eyes at Tucker. "It better not be to hit on my sister. I told you she's off-limits."

Even though the comment wasn't directed at him, Jake's gut clenched at the reminder.

"Relax Cap. I'm here to pick up Jake. When I got to his house, Moms said he was over here."

"Did you hear back from Seth?" Jase asked Ryan.

"Yeah he said him and Pat will be at the game."

"Coen and Taylor are coming?" Tucker asked excitedly.

"Yup. Waiting to hear if any other alumni are coming," Ryan confirmed.

The mention of Seth Coen and Pat Taylor, made Jake think about another from their year, Tommy.

"They aren't still friends with Tommy Bradford are they?" He couldn't resist asking.

"No," Jase answered.

"*Hell* no," Ryan emphasized.

Jake knew Tommy wouldn't be invited to play with the team but it was still unclear where Seth and Pat's loyalties lay. He didn't want drama from Jordan's past to hinder his chances with her future.

Ryan looked at him closely. "Why are you asking?"

Jase dropped his cup against the counter in shock. "She told you, didn't she?"

"Yeah," Jake confirmed.

"Wow," Ryan said.

"Didn't see that coming," Jase added.

"Why would you randomly bring up Tommy Bradford?" Tucker asked.

"He's Jordan's ex," Jake informed his best friend.

"No shit!" Tucker paused with his coffee cup half way to he's mouth.

Jake gave him a nod.

"Why do I sense there's more to the story?" Tucker asked picking up the undercurrents in the room.

"The details of their breakup are why Tommy is no longer a Titan," Ryan stated.

"And those would be?" Tucker prodded.

"Jordan caught Tommy cheating on her," Jake told him.

"Well that's a dick move," Tucker said.

"Agreed," Jake said. For all of Tucker's slutty ways he was always upfront with his intentions.

"Not that I agree with what he did or anything, but what does Tommy being a douchenozzle have to do with him not being a Titan?"

Jake took his cue from the Donnelly boys for how to proceed. At Ryan's nod he spilled the rest.

"When Jordan caught him she dumped his sorry ass... So Tommy hit her."

"The *fuck*?" Tucker's brows disappeared in his hairline.

Jake pretty much had to the same reaction.

"So Coach kicked him off the team. And from what Jordan says, she thinks not everyone was happy with her," Jake informed Tucker.

"Ugh, I can't believe she's still blaming herself. Hopefully after today she'll see how wrong she is," Ryan complained.

The guys finished the rest of their coffee in silence.

"Well that's enough drama for me. Let's head on over to the park," Ryan stated and walked to the door.

Jordan and Maddey looked over the menu for what to order.

"Skye and Sammy are gonna meet us here later so we can all head over to the park together to watch the guys play," Jordan informed Maddey.

After the waitress took their order Maddey focused all of her attention on her. "Okay spill."

She blew out a breath. "All I have to say is I don't know how you do it because I'm so ready to pull my hair out it's not even funny."

Maddey chuckled. "Well have you seen the guy? I mean damn Jordan you really know how to pick 'em, he is smokin' hot. With a capital H-O-T!"

She dropped her head to bang it lightly against the table. "I know."

"I mean come on. The way that boy fills out his t-shirt…" Maddey trailed off to fan her face dramatically.

"I know." She recalled just how good Jake looked in his gray BTU hockey shirt. "He's got dimples Madd," she groaned.

"Dimples are known to make a girl stupid."

"Not helpful. But seriously how do you handle wanting someone who's supposed to be off-limits without going insane?"

Maddey took a sip of her orange juice. "Well my situation is a little different, I only have to see Dex when he's on leave."

"That's true." She paused and let out a sigh. "I don't even know what to do anymore."

Maddey reached across the table and placed her hand on top of her's for comfort. "Well why don't you tell me what changed your mind about avoiding him?"

"It was too hard. I mean he's my damn neighbor."

"And… Come on, I know there's more."

"We have so much in common. He's super easy to talk to." She paused, not quite sure how her friend would react. "I told him about Tommy."

Maddey spit out her juice at the comment. "Shut up. Are you serious?"

"Yup."

"Like everything?"

"No just that I caught Tommy cheating and he hit me. I didn't give him the actual details." She hoped Jake would never have to find out.

"Still you haven't really told anyone about it. Have you?"

"Only you and Sammy."

"Wow."

The waitress came over with their food and conversation stopped for a few as they dug in.

"The thing that sucks the most is even after two years Tommy is still affecting my life," Jordan complained.

"What do you mean? Is he harassing you again?"

She waved her hand and shook her head. "No no no nothing like that, it just seems like my past keeps haunting me."

"You mean like your brothers making you promise not to date another one of their teammates when you told them you were transferring to BTU?"

"Yup."

A sympathetic look crossed Maddey's face. "Well can you blame them?"

"No, not at all."

She looked longingly out the window. "Yeah there's more to the story." She paused. "Oh Skye and Sammy are here. I'll tell you all later tonight."

Chapter Fifteen

The outdoor roller rink the guys used to play in was one of their favorite places to play in the summer. It was covered by a two-story structure to protect them from the elements but was open on all sides. Instead of the usual plexiglass boards, there were chain link fences to protect spectators. On the side of the rink with the team benches were bleachers, currently filled by Wade's girlfriend Cara with a few of her friends and a group of puck bunnies.

The guys had been playing for about half an hour. It had turned out to be a really good game, the alumni that joined them gave it an edge. Jake was starting to get bummed out that Jordan wasn't there yet and was wondering if she was still going to show.

The guys were taking a break when he finally saw Jordan and her friends pull up. The happiness that spread through him at her arrival should have made him nervous but it didn't.

Jordan wore a yellow tube top with blue and white check-ered shorts, Maddey a white tank and rainbow checkered shorts, and Skye a fire-engine red tank and white shorts. One of them on their own caught the eye but together they were guaranteed to make heads turn. Then there was Sammy in his khaki cargo shorts and flip flops with a pale green t-shirt looking like he just stepped off the pages of an Abercrombie catalog. They entered the rink and crossed over to where the guys were standing.

"I thought you guys were supposed to be playing hockey." Jordan said walking onto the rink.

"Just taking a break," Jase said.

Jordan looked around at all the guys. "Yeah I see a lot of old faces, guess they can't hack it anymore."

The guys gasped in mock offense. "JD, baby girl, such harsh words to say about old friends." Seth one of the guys that had graduated two years prior said as he skated over to her picking her up in a hug.

"Oh Seth, you know I love you but you guys have been out of practice for a few years so maybe you just can't keep up."

Seth put his arm around Jordan and put her in a playful chokehold. "Oh JD, you always were a feisty one. You're so lucky you're cute."

Jake watched as Jordan wormed her way out of Seth's grasp and punched him in the arm. She rolled her eyes and laughed at him. The camaraderie between them would seem funny to anyone else, but not Jake, his back teeth clenched irritated by Seth's flirting. *Calm down you don't have any claim on her. You gotta take things slow if you even want to have a chance with things working out.*

Just when he thought smoke would be coming out of his ears, Jordan made her way over to him and instantly his mood brightened. She cocked her hip and hooked the thumb of her left hand through a belt loop. She had a cute smirk on her face and eyed him with purpose. "So Jake, you ready to show me what you got?"

Her doubt of his abilities ignited his competitive nature

and he couldn't help but do a little trash talking of his own. "I was born ready, sweetheart."

Jordan chuckled and he loved it. He was impressed with how she stood her ground, in sneakers her head didn't even reach his shoulders but in skates he practically towered over her. She stood there staring up at him, silently egging him on. He crossed his arms in front of his chest in response.

During their staring contest everyone else broke off on their own. Luckily, Maddey and Skye easily captivated the other players' attention. Jordan moved in closer to his personal space. "You talk a big game but I guess we'll just have to wait and see if you measure up."

He glided toward her to close the last couple of inches that separated them. She had to tilt her head all the way back to see his face and he loved how petite she was. "Jordan, you have no idea just how well I measure up. Because, if given the chance I could totally shake things up for you."

Her cheeks bloomed with color as she blushed. She kept giving off signals that she was as interested in him as he was in her. All he had to do was find a way to get her to admit the way she felt. He had to get her alone so they could talk, he just needed to find his opening.

"Well I guess we'll just have to wait and see." She placed a hand on his chest and pushed him so he rolled backwards.

He called out to Jordan before she could go too far. "Hey still interested in seeing my mask?"

Her face lit up with excitement. "You're using the Optimus Prime one?"

"Always."

"Hell yeah!"

He laughed as she skipped over to join him at the net he rested his mask on. He handed the mask to her holding it so the eyes above the cage faced her. His gut tightened as he watched her stroke her thumb across the intricate detail of the design, imagining what it would feel like if she did it to him.

"This is sick. The detail on this makes it look almost 3D." She said in awe.

"Yeah the artist did an amazing job."

"It is *seriously* badass."

Jordan was still holding his mask when they heard Pat call out to them. "Oh man, I forgot JD was a Transformer geek, too. Now our goalie will never get his mask back. Guess it's time to call the game."

"Ha ha ha. Very funny. Come on let's see if you can still hack it old man. Game on."

Jake watched the sway of her hips as she walked over to join her friends.

WHEN JORDAN AND her friends arrived at the park it was later than they intended. From the look of the guys standing around the edge of the rink, it was obvious they had been playing for a while.

Her gaze automatically homed in on Jake. Being a goalie he had to wear full protective gear but must have taken off his chest pads to get a break from the heat. He still wore the same gray t-shirt as earlier, the color now darkened by sweat. His hair was in disarray from his helmet, he still looked good to her.

As she walked closer to the guys, she noticed a few familiar faces. "Seth? Pat?" She ran up to Ryan's old teammates to hug them. "Oh my god I had no idea you guys were going to be here."

"It's my favorite Donnelly sibling." Seth said returning her hug.

Skye took over introductions and Jordan used the opportunity to talk to Jake. Up close she got a whiff of his clean scent she remembered from the night in the hammock, mixed with sweat from playing. The combination was like catnip to her.

She went to join her friends in the bleachers when it was time for the guys to resume playing. Along the way she passed a group of what looked like puck bunnies, noting the looks they shot her way. Used to dealing with the nasty bitches she ignored them, her focus on the other cluster of girls gathered on the bleachers.

"Jordan, girl, aren't you a sight for sore eyes." Cara, Wade's girlfriend, called to her.

"Cara," she pulled her into a hug. "I can't believe you're still putting up with Wade after all these years."

Cara and Wade were the classic story of jock falling for his non-sports minded tutor. The two started dating around the same time as Jordan and Tommy, so the two grew close. Jordan helped teach Cara all she needed to know about hockey.

"Yeah well like I tell him all the time, he's lucky he's cute," Cara joked. "So we met your old roommates. Man your friend Maddey could be your sister."

"Yeah it's a running joke with us."

"Anyway this is Kim, Michelle, and Beth." Cara pointed to the other girls in her group. "Beth is dating Seth."

"Seth and Beth. Seriously?"

"Yeah I know." Beth confirmed reluctantly.

She spent a few minutes catching up with Cara and getting to know her friends, the whole time she felt the burn of angry stares on her skin. Finally she had enough.

"Puck Bunnies?" She pointed a thumb at the group above.

"Oh yeah. The worst of the bunch too. Usually we just have to deal with them during the season but these few are the most persistent and are around year round," Cara confirmed.

"I know the type."

"Looks like you caught the attention of Tabby and Christine."

"Which one is Tabby?" Jordan asked, curious to check out someone Jake dated.

"The one with the shoulder length brown hair. The chick with the black bob is Christine, she has a thing for your brother."

"Which one?"

"Ryan."

The puck bunnies continued to stare daggers at them. "Can I help you?" Jordan asked, not intimidated at all.

"Yeah. Stay away from our guys," Tabby sneered.

"*Your* guys?" She raised a brow.

"Yeah I saw you hugging all up on Ryan. Back off," Christine said.

Jordan and the girls burst out laughing, their reaction earning more evil looks. "You do know I'm his *sister*, right?"

Her statement shocked them into silence, obviously not what they expected.

"Stay away from Jake, we're dating," Tabby spat.

"That's not what I heard."

"Excuse me!"

"Nothing." Having enough with the drama, she turned her back on the puck bunnies and went to join her friends.

"Puck bunnies?" Skye asked knowingly.

"Puck bunnies," she brushed off.

She settled in to watch the guys play, a sense of peace enveloping her like a blanket.

Ryan scored a goal and she was reminded of how much talent he possessed. Maddey leaned in close to her left ear. "Ryan is really good, he could totally go pro."

The comment made her smile. It was one thing for her to think Ryan could make it in the big leagues but it was completely different when a non-family member thought the same thing. He commanded the rink with natural ease as the captain. Realization dawned on her, this was Ryan's last season and she was lucky enough to be able to witness his possible rise to stardom.

Seth, who had been another forward on the team before he graduated, stole the puck from Jase and was on a breakaway for the net Jake was the goalie of. He got off a very impressive shot but Jake snapped his hand out lighting fast and caught the puck with his glove.

Skye caught her smiling at Jake's save. "So what's going on with you and the hot shot goalie?"

Jordan whipped her head around so fast her neck cracked. "Skye!" She hesitated. "Besides, nothing is going on." She turned to face the game again.

"Bullshit. I've known you since we were five Jor, I know when you're lying and when you're keeping something from me, so spill."

She took a deep breath to calm her down. "Alright I give, but I'll tell you guys later, not here."

"Okay deal."

Jake tried his best to keep his concentration on the game but every now and then his gaze went to where Jordan and her friends sat in the stands. It was easy to see that she loved watching her brothers play hockey and the thought of her limiting the games she attended in the past two years bothered him.

The girls cheered from the stands and occasionally Jordan would yell down and talk some trash if one of the older guys messed up. Her brothers were right when they said she was vicious if the team didn't play well. If she was like this for a pick up game he could only imagine what she was like during a real game. The thought of her tiny self getting in the face of some of the alumni he met made him laugh.

His team was up two to one after Ryan's last goal. Luckily

the other team scored before Jordan arrived. He wanted desperately to show her how good of a goalie he was, almost as badly as proving to her how good they could be together.

The teams were picked randomly but he lucked out that he had Ryan and Jase on his team.

Just then he watched as Seth stole the puck from Jase and headed straight for him. He knew this was the moment of truth for his skills and when he caught the puck in his glove Jordan cheered for him. He noticed she was smiling and looked thoroughly impressed. Good, one obstacle down.

A few minutes after his big save he glanced Jordan's way again and saw her avoiding Skye's gaze. He wondered what they were talking about and that's when it hit him— Skye could be an ally in helping him be with Jordan.

He was such an idiot, why hadn't he thought of it sooner. Jordan told him Skye told her about him. Who knew Tucker's "relationship" with a girl could work out in his favor. He had to find a way to talk to her. He was almost positive she would approve of him dating Jordan so why wouldn't she help in the matchmaking?

After playing for twenty more minutes the guys decided to take another break. Jake was taking off his mask to place it on top of the net to take a sip of Gatorade when Ryan skated over to his side. "Hey bro, nice save." He said with a jab to the shoulder.

Jake smiled. "Thanks, man." He looked at his friend and caught the wistful expression on his face. "Something on your mind?"

Ryan waited so long he was beginning to think he wasn't going to answer. "Yeah... Have you ever wanted someone you weren't supposed to want?"

Jake stood stone still. *Oh no has he figured out I'm interested in Jordan as more than a friend? Crap how should I handle this?* "I'm not quite sure I know what you mean."

"Well you know JD's friend Maddey?" He nodded in the girls' direction.

"Yeah." Confusion laced his tone until it dawned on him. "Oh, you have the hots for her?"

Ryan nodded. "But it's more than that."

"What do you mean?"

"Well the few times Jase and I visited JD at school, Maddey was usually there, and every time we're near something sparks between us."

Jake took a moment to think. How he responded could very well effect how Ryan reacted to his admission of feelings for his sister. "Have you talked to Jordan about it?"

"Yeah and that's what's so weird."

"How so?"

"When I told her I liked Maddey and I thought we had a connection she wasn't mad. Instead she looked like she felt sorry for me and then told me to tread carefully where Maddey was concerned because she's head over heels for one of her older brother's friends. The strangest part was she sounded like she liked the idea of us together but she just didn't see it happening."

Jake took another pause to think. After standing next to each other in comfortable silence he had an idea. "Hey why don't you invite them to the house tomorrow, it's been a while since we've had a party."

Ryan smiled. "You know dude that's a good idea. Thanks." He said as he clamped a hand down on his shoulder.

The guys skated over to where the others were standing. "Hey, JD, what are you guys doing tomorrow night?" Ryan asked.

"Umm no plans right now."

"You guys should come over to the house, we're having a party."

"Sounds like a plan." She turned to Maddey. "You should come too, do you have to be home?"

Jackpot!

"No I could totally stay. You know I always over pack so I have enough clothes and stuff, I'll just call my mom and let her know when we get back to your house later."

Jordan smiled. "Awesome."

Jake caught Ryan's gaze over the heads of everyone else and he understood more than Ryan knew how happy he was the girls would be at the hockey house the upcoming night. The girls said their goodbyes and left and the guys packed their gear to go back to the hockey house.

Chapter Sixteen

Jake pulled into his driveway the same time he saw Skye exit her car. *Perfect.* Now he could see if he could get her to help him out with his Jordan situation.

She pulled two bottles of Patron Silver out of her car as he approached. "Hey Skye." He flashed her his most charming smile, making sure to reveal his dimples.

Skye shut her car door and faced him fully. "Hey Jake, good game today."

His smile deepened at the compliment. "Thanks." He paused and looked in the direction of Jordan's house. "So, hey, listen... I was wondering if I could talk to you about something."

She leaned against her car. "Sure what's up?"

He ran a hand along the back of his neck, unsure how he should proceed. "Um well it's about Jordan."

Skye's eyebrows shot up and her eyes lit up.

Interesting.

"What about Jordan?" She placed the tequila bottles on the ground and crossed her arms over her chest.

It was time to bite the bullet on this one and come out with it. "I like Jordan."

"Of course you like Jordan, everyone does, she's awesome." Skye played dumb.

He made a noise in the back of his throat, she was not making things easy for him. "Skye, you know what I mean."

"Yes I do, it's kind of obvious." She said with a coy smile.

"It is?" *Oh my god I'm a dead man.*

Finally she took pity on him. "Well to someone who pays attention to people it is... I'm a bartender I know how to read people. Sure all the time I've spent around you has been limited to a few interactions when I would work at Rookies, but even *I* was able to pick up on how you act around her and it's different from how you act around other girls." She reached out and put a hand on his arm. "But don't worry, just because I noticed doesn't mean Ry and Jase have, they're not that bright." She said with a wink.

He took a moment to process what Skye said. He sure hoped she was right about Ryan and Jase.

"So why don't you tell me the real reason you're admitting your feelings about my best friend to me."

"Because I need your help," he blurted out.

He could tell his admission piqued Skye's interest. It was one thing for a guy to admit they needed a girl's help but Jordan's history with the hockey team and her brothers made the situation as tricky as a mine field. "Why and how?"

"The reason why is I like her and I think we could be really good together. The how is you can help me get around her not being able to date anyone on the hockey team, all while getting Ry and Jase's approval." He took a deep breath and waited for Skye to hopefully shed some light on Jordan's mystifying situation.

Skye stood there in silence. "You know about that stupid promise they made her make?" She answered his question with a question trying to gauge how much he already knew about the Tommy situation without giving away anything she was sworn to secrecy to keep.

"Yeah she told me it was because of what happened with Tommy Bradford."

"She told you what happened with Tommy?"

"Yeah."

"When?"

"The other night."

Skye had a funny look on her face as she questioned him. "Wow she must really like you."

Happiness bloomed inside him at the revealing statement.

He took another deep breath, the situation seemed more complex than he thought. "Ryan and Jase are two of my closest friends and you've gotten to know me a little over the past month, you all know that I'm a good guy and that I'm not into flings."

"It's not that any of us think you're not a good guy or that we think you're not good for her. Personally, I think you guys would be great together."

He jumped at the admission. "So you'll help me?"

She bent down and picked up the tequila bottles. "I'll think about it." She gave him a wink before she walked away.

He was not happy with that answer. It was time to utilize *his* best friend as well. He pulled out his phone to text Tucker.

Girls night was officially underway. It was going to be a Mexican themed night. Mrs. Donnelly was so excited to have the girls over that she had started setting up for the evening while everyone was out. The tiki torches in the backyard were already lit and all the pickings for fajitas were on the counter. The blender was out with the margarita mix next to it, and she had already prepared five margarita glasses with salt. It was going to be one hell of a night.

Taking in the elaborate spread Jordan was impressed. "Wow, Mom, you really went all out."

Mrs. D turned to face her daughter and her face glowed with pride. "Oh, honey, you haven't seen anything yet, this is just the beginning." She hugged and kissed everyone on the cheek as they made their way into the kitchen.

"Yeah, but, you didn't have to go all out like this."

Mrs. D gestured with her hand. "Pish posh. I haven't had my girls... and guy," she gestured to Sammy, "over in forever, I figured tonight was cause for celebration." She returned to taking things out for dinner. "So how was the game?"

"It was great. Ryan has gotten even better, I didn't think that was possible."

"Yes he most certainly has. Your godfather thinks he has what it takes to go pro when he graduates."

"I was just telling Jordan that at the game, too." Maddey said with a smile.

"Well I'm glad you had a good time today," Mrs. D said.

Skye went over to the counter, took a tortilla chip, dipped it into the salsa and popped it into her mouth. "Yum, Mama D you make the best salsa."

She smiled. "Thanks honey, but come on sit, sit."

Sammy and Maddey took a seat on the stools surrounding the breakfast bar and also started to dig in. "Now all I need is a margarita." Sammy said around a mouthful of chips.

Skye placed the bottles of tequila on the counter. "Coming right up."

"Perfect." Sammy pulled his MacBook Pro out of his bag. "Let me hook this up. I made a special playlist for tonight."

"Let's go out back and I'll start grilling the chicken for dinner," Mrs. D suggested.

"Margaritas," Skye announced.

Maddey went about making the margaritas and passed them out once they were done.

Margaritas in hand, everyone settled into the lounge chairs surrounding the fire pit on the patio while Mrs. D cooked.

"So when I was getting out of my car Jake arrived home... when he saw me he came over to talk to me." She paused. "About Jordan."

Jordan's back instantly straightened, and everything in her went on high alert. Normally Jake talking to Skye wouldn't cause nervousness but by the way Skye was acting their conversation couldn't have been a good one. "What about me?"

"Well he told me he likes you and that he wanted my help in... umm... hooking you guys up."

"Oh my god that's awesome!" Maddey said.

"See I told you he was into you." Sammy said as he cheered his glass with Maddey.

Skye looked at her over the rim of her glass. "Why didn't you tell me you told him about Tommy?"

"You did?" Sammy asked surprised.

Jordan nodded. "Was that all you guys talked about?" She directed the question to Skye.

"No." Skye took a gulp of her margarita for courage. Quickly she rambled off the rest of their conversation. "I may have let it slip that you like him as much as he seems to like you."

She sat completely still. "Damn, maybe I should have just continued to avoid him." Things with Jake were complicated enough he didn't need any encouragement. She wasn't sure her resolve to keep her promise could take much more. After a few tense moments of Skye looking at her for a response she reached out and placed a hand over Skye's. "It's okay, Skye, it's not your fault, we'll figure it out."

"Well I think we should all look on the bright side," Sammy stated. "Jake admitted that he likes you, that's major."

Jordan got up and made her way into the kitchen to pour herself another margarita, downing half of it in one gulp. *Jake likes me. Like openly admitting he likes me to my best friend. And not just likes me, he wants to be with me.* She threw her arms up in the air. "Arggh this is so not fair," she complained as she plopped back down onto a lounge chair.

"Do you wanna talk about it?" Skye asked.

"No... yes... I don't know. This whole situation is so frustrating."

"Chicken is ready," Mrs. D called.

Mrs. D and Maddey set the patio table for dinner. They placed placemats, plates, salad, chips and salsa, and other pickings around the table. "Okay why don't we start with what has happened recently that you haven't been able to tell us about yet," Maddey suggested with a pointed look in Jordan's direction.

"Yeah, maybe like where you were sleeping the other night instead of here." Her mom's statement was like throwing blood in a pool full of piranhas, creating a frenzy between her three friends.

"What?"

"Excuse me?"

"Why haven't we heard about this?"

All at once Jordan was bombarded by questions from her three besties. When she looked at her mom she caught her laughing. *Why I oughta.* She shook her head and walked over to take her place at the table when Sammy carried over the chicken and vegetables for the fajitas.

Everyone else sat down and started to dig in. "So are you going to tell us where you were sleeping the other night or are we going to have to torture it out of you?" Sammy asked.

Swallowing a bite of fajita, Jordan decided to let her friends in on her night in the hammock. "Jake's."

"*WHAT?*" The three of them shouted in unison. Their jaws were practically on the table.

"Come again?" Skye asked.

She took pity on her friends. "I said I was sleeping at Jake's." She took another sip of her margarita. With how crazy, and possibly disastrous this situation was, it was kind of funny to see the look on their faces when she told them where she was.

Skye was still trying to decipher Jordan's comment a few moments later. "Wait so if you're sleeping at his house why is it he's asking me to help hook you guys up? It doesn't make any sense."

Sammy paused in making another fajita. "Wait... are you guys together and you just haven't told anyone because of your brothers?"

The comment almost made Jordan spit out her bite of fajita. She looked Sammy square in the eyes. "Come on. Do you honestly think I would date someone in secret and not even tell my three besties?"

Disappointment washed over the group and Skye's shoulders slumped. "Well that sucks but a girl can dream, can't she?"

Everyone laughed as they finished off their meal.

It was closing in on midnight when Mrs. Donnelly headed up to bed. They had already eaten dinner, done facials, played some games, and were now well into the movie marathon stage of the evening. They had already watched *Clueless* and *Pretty Woman* as their classic favorites and were on the last few minutes of *Twilight*.

Maddey was sitting in front of Jordan on the floor while she let her wrap her hair into twists, her position allowed her to hear Jordan when she sighed. "What's on your mind, Jor?"

"Sometimes I just wish life was like a movie or a book." She continued to wrap Maddey's hair in twists.

"How so?"

"Oh you know where there's always a happy ending no matter what, and the girl always gets the guy." She paused. "Like take Bella and Edward for example, she's human and he's a vampire but they don't let that keep them apart. And look at the books, how many dilemmas and obstacles do they face throughout the whole series and yet they still end up together? I don't have to worry about Jake being a different species, or vampires trying to kill me, or any of the other problems they had to face. I just have to deal with two over-protective, overbearing brothers, and yet I still can't be with Jake."

"Yeah I know what you mean."

Jordan felt guilty for the carelessness of her comment. Being in love with your older brothers' best friend who was a SEAL had to be rough on her friend. "Oh, Madz, I'm so sorry I completely forgot you know exactly how I feel, I didn't even think."

Maddey turned around and placed a hand on her arm. "It's okay, don't worry about it. I know it sucks and I hate that you have to deal with it, too."

"So what do you do to cope?"

Maddey got up from her spot on the floor and made her way into the kitchen. Once there she pulled four bowls out of the cabinets, four spoons out of a drawer, and two gallons of ice cream from the freezer. "First, I veg-out if I get down on myself and then I talk to you guys. But my situation is a little different than yours. I have to deal with not only my brothers but the fact that Dex doesn't reciprocate my feelings and that he's constantly traveling to all parts of the world with his team, it kind of makes things extra difficult." She paused to scoop some chocolate chip cookie dough ice cream into her bowl. "But you on the other hand know that Jake feels the same way about you that you do about him, you just have to figure out a way around this deal you made with your brothers."

While Maddey talked, Jordan scooped a bunch of mint chocolate chip ice cream into her bowl. "Yeah I just wish it was that easy."

The two laughed but the sound wasn't filled with much joy. "So what movie are we watching next?"

Sammy held up a DVD. "I figured a little *Die Hard* action would do you good Maddey, seeing as it's one of your favorites."

Jordan and Maddey made it back over to sit on the couch with their bowls filled to the top with ice cream. "Oh it most certainly is. I love Bruce Willis, he's so badass. Plus he plays a McClane, sure it's spelled different than mine but come on, it's awesome."

"Yeah it's cool," Sammy said as he got up to put the movie on. "So come on Jordan, are you ever going to tell us what happened on your slumber party with Jake? Your mom went to bed a while ago. It's time to spill." He laughed at himself.

"Fine if you guys must know." She feigned annoyance but deep down she knew she would have told them about that night in the hammock eventually.

"Okay, so Saturday night after I got home from helping with the VIP party at Rookies, I went to let Navy out in the backyard."

Hearing his name, Navy got up from his spot on the floor and climbed up on the couch to sit between Jordan and Maddey. "Hey there buddy." Maddey said with a kiss on his nose.

Jordan laughed at the dog. "Anyway… when I opened the backdoor he just took off. Sean must have left the gate open and he got out of the yard and then let himself into Jake's backyard."

"See Jordan, you two have to be fated or something… even your dog tries to get the two of you together." Skye helped point out with her own spin on the situation.

"Yeah I could just see the wedding announcement now, 'Jake and Jordan started their relationship with a meet-cute arranged by her dog.' It would be priceless."

"Oh Sammy shut up!" She moved to get more comfortable

on the couch as she finished the rest of her story, including the abridged version of the Tommy situation.

"I don't know how long we talked, the conversation just flowed, ya know. And next thing I know we were being woken up by Sean and Carlee."

"Oh my god!"

"Are you serious?"

"They didn't?"

The reactions she got from her friends were what she expected. Jordan started laughing and once she started, she couldn't stop. The laughter continued to grow inside her and became contagious around the group. "My thoughts exactly."

"So if Sean and Carlee caught you guys sleeping together in the hammock, how is it that Ry and Jase don't know about it?" Skye asked.

"Because I swore them to secrecy. When they woke us up, they were spying on us from behind the pool shed and I think they were just so happy not to be in trouble that they would have agreed to almost anything."

Jordan got lost in thought. "I think he thinks he's able to convince my brothers that what happened would never happen with him and we could be together."

"Well maybe he's right." Skye tried to offer support. "Your brothers like him and they are closer to him than they ever were with Tommy."

"I think Skye has a point," Sammy supplied. "Like when you started dating Tommy your brothers were getting to know him at the same time you were, but with Jake they have already known him for two years before he even met you, so they know the type of guy he is... maybe they'll have a change of heart."

"I'm not gonna hold my breath." Even though she didn't let her friends know, deep down inside she hoped that they were right. There was something about Jake, she couldn't put her finger on it, but there was this connection between them that made it so she couldn't give up on him.

Jake picked Tucker up and drove them to Rookies to watch the Yankees play the Orioles. They sat at a table which faced the big screen that showed the game. When the waitress came by, they each ordered a beer and decided to split the sampler to start them off.

"So did you guys end up hanging out for a while after the game?" Jake asked Tucker.

"Yeah some of the alumni came back to the house so they were reminiscing about old times with the seniors and telling us stories from way back when."

Jake took a sip of his beer. "Oh yeah? Any good stories about Ryan as a freshman?"

Tucker snorted. "More than you would even believe." He turned to face Jake more fully. "A lot of them were about tricks Jordan and Skye used to pull on the guys."

The waitress dropped off their sampler and when she asked if she could get them anything else, Tucker seized the opportunity to ask her for her phone number in his classic style. He shook his head at his friend, Tucker was constantly on the prowl and watching him in action, he had to admit it was highly entertaining.

Watching Tucker's interaction with the waitress made Jake think of the night when they first met Jordan and he smiled. She saw right through Tucker's cocky charm and was one of the only girls Jake had ever seen turn him down, unlike their waitress who was falling for it hook, line, and sinker.

The happy memory of Jordan turned sour for him when it brought to mind the other obstacles standing in the way of asking her out. He focused his attention back on the game as the Yankees hitter hit a line drive down the third base line to drive in two runs.

After the waitress left they dug into their food. "Something on your mind, bro?" Tucker asked.

He blew out a puff of air, debating how much he should say to his friend. *Screw it. This is why I texted him.* "Yeah... I can't get my mind off Jordan."

"She is hot."

"It's more than that." He went on to tell Tucker about staying up all night and falling asleep with her in the hammock, followed by joining the Donnelly's for dinner the next night.

"So, what, you think Ry and Jase would have a problem with you dating their sister? I mean I know they joke and say she's off limits but you're a good guy. You don't really sleep around or anything, you're more of a relationship guy, they've gotta respect that."

"From what Jordan has mentioned, it's more complicated than that. She said when she told them she was transferring here they made her promise not to date another guy on the hockey team."

"You mean because of what happened with her and Tommy Bradford?"

"Yeah." Jake took a swig of his beer.

"Damn man. Tommy Bradford. Dude was almost as much of a star for the Titans as Ryan."

"I know."

"I'm glad coach kicked him off the team though. Any guy that puts his hands on a woman doesn't deserve to call himself a man."

Jake would never lay a hand on Jordan and the thought of another guy harming even one hair on her head brought out the alpha in him. "I couldn't agree more." The two cheered their glasses.

"So what's our plan?"

Jake smiled. One of the things he loved most about Tucker was he always had his back no matter what. If one of them had a problem, the other instantly considered it their own and was there to tackle the issue.

"Not sure yet. I know I have to get her to want to give us a shot, so that's got to be the first step."

"We got this."

The rest of the evening was uneventful. The Yankees beat the Orioles 4-3 and Tucker went home with the waitress.

Jake was glad to have his best friend on his side. He made a promise to himself that he would talk to Jordan at the party and that they didn't have to let her past, or promise to her brothers, keep them from being together.

Chapter Seventeen

Maddey and Jordan sat on the bed while Maddey finished applying Jordan's make-up. The girls decided to get all dolled up for the night at the hockey house like they would when they went out back at school.

"So are you nervous about seeing Jake tonight?" Maddey asked.

She waited for Maddey to finish applying her eyeliner before she answered. "No… yes… I don't know. I don't think he would say anything to me in front of my brothers, so I'm thinking if I stay around everyone, I should be safe."

To be honest, just the thought of being in close proximity of Jake made her palms sweat. The effect he had on her mind, body, and soul was a little unnerving. Even Tommy hadn't had such an instant and intense effect on her.

Maddey put down the eyeliner and looked at her pointedly. "What are you so afraid of?"

Jordan sighed. "The truth?"

"No, Jor, lie to me… come on now." Exasperated, she placed her hands on her hips.

"I'm afraid he'll ask me just that." She thought back on the night she met Jake at Rookies.

She remembered immediately thinking how attractive he was but it was his confidence and how he was standing calm and collected as he eyed her with appreciation while his friend hit on her that really caught her attention.

If only it was that simple.

Now after spending time with him and getting to know each other, the initial attraction she felt only grew stronger.

Jordan nervously pushed her hair over her shoulder, luckily she had her bangs clipped back so they were out of her face. "I'm so weak where Jake's concerned. I'm afraid if he makes even a semi reasonable argument on how we can be together that I'll crack and throw myself into his arms in front of my brothers and you know how well that would go over."

Maddey went back to finishing her makeup. "Yeah I see your point... but maybe Sammy had a point last night. Maybe your brothers would approve of a relationship with Jake because he is their friend. He's good enough for them so maybe they would think he's good enough for you."

At that the two girls locked eyes and started to laugh. "That's a good one, Madz, but when the alarm clock goes off and you wake up from the dream world then what do you do?"

"Take a sleeping pill and go back to sleep."

The girls erupted in a fit of laughter. "Oh, Madd, you are too much."

Deep down both girls knew that their brothers were more selective about the guys allowed to date their sisters than the guys they were friends with. Someone they deemed good enough to be their friend wasn't necessarily good enough boyfriend material for their sisters.

A few minutes later Maddey finished with Jordan and the girls started getting dressed so they could head over to the hockey house. Jordan paused as she opened a drawer in her dresser. "They have a pool at the house so if you don't feel like wearing a suit, make sure you pack one because whether you want to or not you might end up in the pool," Jordan advised.

Maddey pulled a pair of black shorts and a maroon razor back tank out of her bag, as well as her gray bikini. "I'll wear mine… just in case," she said as she held up the bikini.

"That's exactly how I feel." She said as she pulled her own bikini out of the drawer. She opted to go with her blue mesh bikini to go under her white shorts and royal blue tank top.

Once they were ready, they grabbed a bottle of cherry vodka and a bottle of tequila and were on their way to the hockey house.

Jake sank the ping pong ball in the final cup to win their most recent game of beer pong.

"Nice shot man." Tucker said with a high five.

"Thanks. So who are our next victims?" Jake said as he surveyed the room.

The night was going better than he thought possible. The relaxing fun atmosphere was perfect for what he needed to broach the subject of being together with Jordan when she finally arrived.

Jase started over to the table at Jake's challenge. "We are all-star, this time you've met your match."

"Thought you didn't have a partner?" Tucker asked.

"I didn't… I was just waiting for her to get here so now I do." Jase started setting up his three cups with beer.

Tucker looked around the room. "So where is this mystery person? I don't see anyone."

"I'm right here." Jordan made her way into the dining room from the kitchen. "Sorry I had to make my drink and get extra cups."

"Extra cups for what?" Tucker gestured to the table. "We have everything right here."

"Yeah I know you do but I prefer to play with a mixed drink... beer fills me up too quick and since Jase and I will be running the table from now on I need something I can keep drinking."

At the sound of Jordan's voice Jake's spirits lifted, it was scary how quickly she was becoming part of his life and how much he looked forward to hanging out with her. When he turned to see her approaching the table he was taken aback. He was starting to think he was getting used to her beauty but the way she looked tonight was on a whole other level. Her bangs were pinned back from her face and the rest of her hair fell straight down her back. Her eyelids were dusted with a sparkly powder and lined with light blue liner, combined with her lashes spiked with mascara, her golden eyes looked as if they glowed. Her makeup coupled with her short white shorts, royal blue tank top with a blue and white mesh bikini top that drew attention down her body made his throat dry. She was so beautiful he just wanted to scoop her up, carry her away from everyone else, and spend the night looking at her.

Their gazes locked from across the table and they both smiled. "You really are feisty for such a tiny person," he joked with her. "But I'd be careful about playing with liquor it could be dangerous."

Once Jordan finished setting up her cups with Jase's she walked over to his side of the table and stood directly in front of him. "I wouldn't worry too much, once Jase and I get the balls you won't be getting them back."

He loved her spirited nature and how she was able to joke around like she was one of the guys. Her aura and the way she handled herself around others commanded respect. He looked down at her, a smile pulling at his lips. "Competitive, huh?"

"You have no idea," she said with a knowing smirk.

"Well then," he picked up his beer cup and tipped it in her direction, "bring it on sweetheart."

Jordan walked back over to join Jase on their side of the table. "So Jase, same house rules as the old house?" She asked with a wink.

Jase stared down at his sister slightly confused but a few seconds later he must have understood what she meant. "You bet."

"*Great.*" She responded, a wicked gleam in her eye.

When Jake and Tucker caught her expression they became a little nervous, Jordan had an evil streak in her and they were slightly afraid they were about to become her next victims.

Tucker turned to Jake. "You know how I was telling you about the stories the guys told about Jordan?"

He nodded.

"You don't think she would come after us if we beat her, do you?" Tucker swallowed nervously.

Thinking back on what he already knew about Jordan and on the conversations the two of them had, Jake answered Tucker's concern with as much conviction as he could. "I don't think she's vindictive for no reason... unless... we taunt her too much, then I guess all bets are off."

They finished setting up their own cups and sealed their fate for the night to come.

JORDAN AND MADDEY arrived at the hockey house to the party in full swing. There were people playing beer pong in the dining room, people playing quarters in the kitchen, people in the pool, people playing flip cup in the backyard, and people hanging out in the living room playing cards. They were among the last to arrive and were greeted with open arms. They made their way around the party to say hi to everyone.

"Took you long enough JD. I need a beer pong partner." Jase said as he got up off the couch to hug her. "Jake and Tucker have been running the table for most of the night so someone has to put them in their place."

"Sure sign us up and we'll show them a thing or two." She winked at her brother.

"You know I really hate this twin thing every now and then because you guys always team up for games and then I'm left without a partner," Ryan complained as he made his way from the kitchen to say hi to the girls.

Jordan smiled at her older brother. Even though she and Jase shared a special connection by being twins, she held a sacred place in her heart for him. "Sorry Ry, but we just connect when we team up but I'm sure you'll find someone else to play with." She patted him on the chest in a sympathetic gesture.

He hugged and kissed her on the cheek. When he did the same to Maddey, Jordan noticed the dark looks shot their way by Christine across the room.

Puck bunny drama— just what they needed.

"If you want, I'll be your partner in beer pong… I'm better at flip cup and quarters but I can still hold my own in pong." Maddey said with a bright smile.

"That would be great Maddey. We probably won't be up for a while, so since you're good at quarters, how about we join the game they have going on in the kitchen?" Ryan suggested.

"Sure, bring it on, hotshot."

As Maddey and Ryan made their way to the kitchen, Jordan went with Jase into the dining room to scope out the competition. When she caught sight of Jake her breathing hitched and her heart skipped a beat. He looked so sexy standing there in a pale, sea foam green t-shirt that clung to his muscular physique in a simply mouth-watering way. His long legs were encased in dark denim jeans and with his hair spiked in disarray it took everything in her not to go and mess it up more with her fingers. He had an air of confidence about him and his presence simply commanded a room. *Just like the night we met.*

She watched as he hit the game winning shot and received a high five from Tucker before she went to make her drink.

The game started a few moments later. Tucker shot first and missed and Jake followed by sinking his shot in the front cup. Once it was their turn Jase shot and hit the back middle cup. When Jordan was up she saw Tucker was slow to drink his cup and was holding it out undefended so she decided to aim for the cup in his hand and when she sank her shot she and Jase cheered.

Jake and Tucker looked at them completely perplexed. "See, Jake, I told you once we got the balls you wouldn't be getting them back."

"What are you talking about? There are still five cups left that you have to hit," Tucker said confused.

"No Tuck, we've been had." Jake patted his friend on the shoulder. "When you sink a shot in an active game cup that was already hit but not drank, it's game over," he turned to face her. "But that was playing dirty."

She put her hands up in surrender. "Hey, I clarified house rules first. It's not my fault Tucker doesn't know how to drink his beer."

"HEY!" Tucker looked utterly offended. "It's not my fault you can't win a game playing fair and square," he shot back at her.

"Is that so?" She took a sip of her side drink. "Fine. Let's rematch then, so when we beat you this time you can't say anything about it."

"Deal... and when we beat you don't go crying to your brothers."

"You do realize my partner is one of my brothers."

"Yeah but you get the idea."

"Yes I do… come on Tuck show me what you got."

"Oh I'll show you."

"I bet."

During their exchange Jordan and Tucker inched closer together until they were as close to nose-to-nose as a five foot two girl could get to a six foot plus guy. Jase had moved over to stand by Jake and the two of them laughed as they watched Tucker try and take her on.

"Be careful, Tuck, this kitten's got claws," Jase tried to advise his friend.

She didn't take shit from anybody, growing up with two older, overprotective, hockey playing brothers could do that to a girl.

"Anyway," she said as she made her way back over to her side of the table. "Let's get this show on the road."

She caught Jake's gaze across the table and smiled. She was still nervous about what might happen if she was alone with him, but the way she felt when he was around was worth the risk of her feelings being exposed.

Jake took his place at the end of the table to line up his shot. As he lined up, Jordan placed both hands on her side of the table and leaned over. "Come on all-star, it's shoot till you miss now… if you make this shot we go into overtime."

During the entire game no one let up on their trash talk. He shot her a charming smile, revealing those dimples she loved. "It's in the bag Jor."

People had filtered into the dining room as the game progressed. Jordan didn't miss how Tabby conveniently positioned herself close to Jake. It didn't escape her notice the looks Tabby sent her way.

Determined to ignore her, she gave Jake a smile. "You sound real confident for a goalie... you're used to blocking shots not making them."

Seth came over and put an arm around her shoulders. "Maybe you should go easy on them JD. You're an acquired taste."

She elbowed him in the ribs. "Asshole."

Jake lined up his shot and made it.

"YES! Nice shot man." Tucker congratulated him with a chest bump.

Once the commotion died down, they began setting up three cups for overtime. "Is this still the same game from when you got here?" Ryan asked her.

"No, it's the second." She moved to fill a cup. "In our first game we won on our first turn because I hit Tucker's game cup. We decided to give them a rematch. You were next on the list and since you guys were playing quarters, we figured we could play ten cup."

"Yeah, and now Jordan is about to lose in overtime." Jake threatened from his side of the table.

She turned her full attention back to Jake. "Is that right?" She countered.

"Yeah it is."

Ryan and Maddey laughed at the exchange between her and Jake.

"You know I blame you for your sister's competitive streak," she heard Maddey say to Ryan.

Ryan placed his hand on his chest. "Who me?" He asked like a guilty five-year old that got caught taking a cookie from the cookie jar.

"Yeah you." Maddey poked him in the chest.

Jordan loved that her friend was relaxed enough to flirt a little with her brother.

"Jake, do you remember what I said to you before we started our first game?" She asked with a head tilt.

Sammy and Skye went to stand with Maddey and her brother, the four of them were laughing because they knew Jake had no idea what he was getting himself into.

"Jordan up to her old tricks again?" She heard Sammy ask.

"Yeah... she seems in rare form tonight," Maddey answered. "Remember that first night in the dorms when she took on the guys from the third floor?"

"Excuse me, she what?" Ryan picked up on the comment instantly.

"Relax," Maddey placed a soothing hand on his arm. "I'm just talking about this time Jordan and Skye played these guys that lived on the third floor of our dorm and beat them."

"Yeah they didn't handle losing to a bunch of girls well," Jordan added.

Jake brought her attention back to him. "What are you referring to? How you said once you get the balls we would never get them back?"

She gave him a wicked smile. "Oh good, you remember."

"Yeah but this time I'll make sure Tucker watches his beer cup."

"Oh honey, I don't need to go for a game cup... Jase and I start with the ball and we are going to knock out these last three cups in a row without giving you the opportunity for redemption."

Some of the guys from the team were grunting and commenting in the background. They knew from past experience that she had a nasty competitive streak and once she set her mind to something she almost always succeeded. It helped that she and Jase were reigning beer pong champs at the old hockey house.

Again she caught some of the looks the puck bunnies sent her way. It was obvious they didn't like the attention the guys were giving her. *Tough luck.* She was closer to these guys then they would ever be.

True to her word, she and Jase won in overtime without

giving the guys a chance to shoot. Being a good sport, she carried her and Jase's cups over to Jake and Tucker. She stood directly in front of Jake and offered him one of her cups. She looked him square in the eye. "Drink up," she said with a dazzling smile.

Without breaking eye contact, Jake reached out and wrapped his hand around hers holding the cup to bring it to his lips to drink down.

She blushed and swallowed audibly under Jake's scrutiny. He was purposely taunting her in front of everyone just to get a rise out of her. She watched his Adam's apple rise and fall when he swallowed and had to fight the urge to sink her teeth into his neck. Luckily, Maddey brought her back down to earth.

"So we get to play you guys now, right?"

Damn, it was hard to resist his pull. Thank god the guys didn't think anything about them being close, since they treated her the same.

Slowly, she backed away from Jake and turned to face her friend. "Yeah so let's get set up… maybe you guys will offer us some real competition."

Tucker hooked an arm around her to bring her close to his body. "Hey you only beat us in overtime… you didn't crush us."

"Yeah but it was Jake that carried your team, without him the game would have never gone to overtime," she said while she patted his chest. The guys standing around started to laugh. With the excitement from the game over everyone went back to what they were doing. Ryan and Maddey set up their cups on their side of the table and the game got underway.

Chapter Eighteen

J ake was ready for the party to be over. The puck
    bunnies had been in rare form and he had a feeling it
    had to do with the new additions to their group. Sure
    he couldn't fault the other guys for wanting them
there but he'd had enough.

"Jake, there you are." Tabby walked over cornering him in
the living room.

"Hi Tabby."

"So when are we going out again? It's been like forever,"
she whined as she stroked his arm.

He rolled his arm away from her touch. "Tabby, I already
told you that wasn't going to happen."

"Come on Jake, we have a good time together."

"Not so much," he said under his breath.

He looked around for someone, *anyone*, he could use as a
distraction. This chick seriously needed to get a clue and stop
touching him.

"Look Tabby. I'm just not interested." He took her by the
shoulders gently to move her out of his way.

"It's because of the new girl, huh?" She said narrowing
her eyes.

He paused from walking away and turned back to face Tabby.

"You mean Jordan?" He kept his voice as casual as he could.

"Yeah, I told that bitch at the game to stay away from you," she huffed.

Any kindness he tried to portray fled at Tabby's insult. He straightened up to his full six foot two height and glared down at her.

"Jordan is Ryan and Jase's sister. If you *ever* want any hope of being invited back to this house for a party, I would highly suggest you refrain from calling her a bitch."

Tabby tried to reach for him again. "You know what I meant, Jake—"

"I don't want to hear it," he cut her off.

"She better watch her back." Tabby spoke so low he wasn't sure he heard her correctly.

"What did you just say?"

"Nothing."

He didn't like the vibe he got from Tabby. All night she invaded his personal space, not taking the hint to back off. He didn't like the way the animosity in her voice made him feel.

He saw Tucker across the room. He made his way over to his friend to see if he'd seen Jordan anywhere recently.

"Hey Tuck. Have you seen Jordan lately?"

"I'm pretty sure I saw her outside earlier."

"Thanks man."

"Everything alright man? I saw you talking to Tabby, still not taking the hint, huh?" Tucker gestured to the area where he was just standing with his solo cup.

"You got that right. I don't think I could be any clearer either. Anyway, I'm gonna find Jordan, something Tabby said just isn't sitting right."

"Yo Donovan, get your ass over here." Wade called from the couch.

Tucker gave him a sympathetic look. "Go ahead. I'll go find our girl and make sure she's alright."

Jake knew where his intentions lay so he didn't bother correcting the "our girl" statement. He knew that any girl either of them dated would be considered family to the other.

JORDAN HEADED OVER to the keg for a beer. While she waited for her cup to fill Tucker joined her holding out his own for her to do the same.

"Still upset I beat you at beer pong earlier?" She asked him.

"Nah Blondie, we're cool." Tucker put his arm around her and pulled her into his side.

"Blondie?"

"If the shoe fits," he said with a smile. "So how's it feel to be back?"

"Like home." She looked out over the yard and pool in the distance. "I gotta say this house is a lot nicer than the old one."

"Yeah, I was pumped when they decided to make the move. I have no idea how they were able to afford this place."

"I think I know."

"Care to share with the class, Blondie?"

She took a sip of her beer. "I think my godfather had a hand in helping you guys land it."

"You mean Rick Schelios?"

She let out a laugh, of course he knew. "Why am I not surprised Jake told you?"

"Are you kidding. I don't remember ever seeing him so excited to tell me something before."

Noise by the house drew their attention to a group of puck bunnies coming outside. She tensed at the sight, the movement didn't escape Tucker's notice.

"They giving you any trouble?" He asked nodding a head

in the girls' direction. Tucker's voice took on an edge she wasn't accustomed to hearing. Gone was the playboy, in its place a protector.

She rested her head against his chest. "Nothing I can't handle. Just a little out of practice is all."

"You know we'd choose you every time."

She looked up at him. His face bore an expression similar to ones she had seen on her brothers. His gaze was unflinching.

"You'll let me know if anyone does give you trouble, right? And I mean *anyone*."

"You know, don't you?" Her voice was barely above a whisper.

"Yeah."

"Dammit, Jake."

"Hey, don't blame him. But I'm glad he told me. Gotta have all the facts if I'm gonna keep my little sis safe," he said with a laugh.

"Little sis?"

"Yeah, Jake's my brother in all the ways that count. You're his girl so that makes you my sis."

"I'm not his girl."

"We'll see," he said with a drink of his beer.

Jordan huffed out a breath. "You know, I already have two older brothers."

"Now you have three."

He said it like it was fact so she didn't fight it. "So I guess that makes you my BB3."

Tucker arched a brow in question.

"Big brother three."

At her explanation she was hit with his most charming smile, without a doubt she knew it was what he used on the ladies.

"I like it Blondie."

They finished the rest of their beers in companionable silence before refilling.

"You know they wouldn't be happy," she said referring to how her brothers would feel about her dating Jake.

"We'll figure it out, Blondie."

It was closing in on one a.m. when the party started drawing to an end. Since the guys had everyone over so early most of the people had left, leaving only those that lived in the hockey house and those who were staying over.

Jordan was in the backyard with Skye and Sammy, sitting in the lounge chairs that sat in the corner of the patio.

"So do you want to tell us why you're avoiding Jake like he's the plague?" Skye instigated.

"Especially when that boy is anything but," Sammy interjected.

Jordan twirled a strand of hair and looked down. "I don't know what you guys are talking about. I'm not avoiding him, in fact, I've spent most of the night with him."

Skye looked at her knowingly. "Sure when other people are around."

"But every time that boy tries to get close to you when you're alone, you run in the opposite direction."

"Yeah and you would think you would seize the opportunity of having all these people around to spend some quality time with him without your brothers' knowledge or interference."

She put up her hands in surrender. "Okay okay, you guys are right. I have been avoiding being alone with Jake, but it's only because I'm afraid I'll throw myself at him and that would just open up a can worms I would rather keep closed."

All conversation ceased when Jase came out looking for them.

"Hey, since it's only the crew staying over left, we were gonna play a game. You guys in?"

The three looked at each other and then at Jase. "Of course," they said in unison.

The four made their way into the living room and found places to sit. Ryan sat in the oversize armchair Jordan loved with Maddey on his lap and the sight made her smile. She was happy he finally made a move. She made her way to sit on one of the armrests. Once everyone was settled they decided what to play.

"Why not play chandelier?" Maddey suggested.

"What's chandelier?" Seth asked.

Maddey stood up and grabbed a bunch of solo cups off the counter. As she spoke she arranged the cups in a circle. "It's a lot like quarters. Everyone has a cup and they fill it up to the bottom line with whatever they feel like drinking. Then you set the cups up in a circle and in the middle of the circle you set a cup up that everyone pours some of their beer into, so what makes the middle cup undesirable is that it can be filled with all different kinds of beer."

After she finished setting up the cups, she let everyone fill their cups up with what they were drinking. Once everyone was sitting back down she continued. "Then we take two quarters and everyone takes a turn trying to bounce the quarters into the cups. If the quarter lands in your cup you drink and then you fill it back up. But if the quarter lands in the middle cup everyone has to drink their cup and when they finish they have to place it on their head, the last person to do so has to drink the middle cup."

"You would pick a quarters like game. You killed it earlier," Seth said.

Jordan laughed at Seth's statement. "I guess she didn't tell you guys she's the reigning quarters champion from our old dorm at NYU."

"Nope she neglected to mention it," Wade frowned.

"Yeah, even after we moved out of the dorms and into our apartment she still held onto the title," Skye added.

"Whatever, let's play," Nick said.

TO PLAY CHANDELIER the group had to rearrange their seating to be around the coffee table instead. Jake was pleased to note Jordan chose to sit across from him, in between Maddey and Tucker.

He shared a knowing look with Tucker, recalling how his best friend told him how they bonded.

With Jordan and Maddey next to each other the resemblance between them was even more noticeable and he couldn't help but stare.

"What, do I have something on my face?" Maddey placed a hand to her cheek when she asked.

"No, no it's nothing like that, it's just I can't get over how much you and Jordan look alike… it's kind of scary."

She blushed. "Yeah, we think it's pretty cool especially since we both have three crazy brothers. We like to pretend that we were sisters separated at birth."

"*Ooo* three brothers, you better be careful how close you get to her Ry, you might get your ass kicked," Wade joked.

It was no secret how protective Ryan and Jase were over their own sister. Knowing about what happened with Tommy Bradford it all made sense. One would think Ryan would be cautious of getting close to a girl with three of her own brothers.

"No Ryan should be alright, unless they are super over-protective like him and Jase are." Cara said mirroring his own thoughts.

"Let's find out then," Seth said, always one to cause trouble. He sat up straight in his seat, clasped his hands together on the table and began his inquisition. "Are your brothers older or younger or both?"

"All older," Maddey answered.

"Do they play hockey?"

"No. Two played football and baseball and the other played lacrosse and ran track."

Seth sat back in his seat, folded his hands over his stomach, and smiled like a lawyer that just 'rested his case'. "See Ry, no hockey players, you'll be alright… you could totally take a couple of football and lacrosse guys."

"That's stupid," Jordan chuckled.

"So what do your brothers do?" Beth asked.

"They're in the Navy. They all followed in our father's footsteps, he used to be in the Navy before he retired and became police chief."

"Ooo the Navy… I don't know Ry I'd be careful if I were you," Cara warned.

"Nah, Ryan can handle a couple of sailors," Wade encouraged. "What do they do for the Navy?"

"They're SEALs," Maddey stated matter-of-factly.

Cara and some of the others burst out laughing. "SEALs huh? I don't know Ry, that changes things."

Ryan took a gulp of his beer and Jake bit back a laugh. He hoped his friend learned from hearing of overprotective brothers. Anything to give him an edge.

They played for about a half an hour and everyone seemed to like the game. There was trash talk going around and laughter. Maddey was as good of a shot as promised and every time she bounced the quarter it would land in Ryan's cup.

Jordan was equally as good. She bounced a quarter into Tucker's cup. "Drink up BB3."

"What did you call him?" Jase asked.

"BB3."

"What the hell does that mean?" Ryan asked over Maddey's head.

"Big brother three," Jordan clarified.

"Why does Tuck get a nickname and not us?" Nick complained.

"None of you blatantly declared yourselves as another one of my big brothers." She held up a hand to stop any protests. "Even if you all play the part."

"Careful Blondie, payback's a bitch." Tucker warned as he downed his cup.

"It's okay. So am I."

Jake laughed at the scared look that crossed his best friend's expression. He had a feeling their new found bond would only be beneficial to his plans.

Chapter Nineteen

Jordan laid on the air mattress in Ryan's room next to Maddey, listening to her brother snore. She would have thought she'd be able to fall right asleep after the long night, but no such luck. The one upside to the evening was it finally seemed like Ryan told Maddey how he felt about her. At least somebody could be happy.

Finally giving up on the idea of sleep, she got up and went downstairs. She figured maybe some fresh air would relax her. As she made her way through the dining room to the back doors, she was grateful everyone else was asleep. Once outside she sat on the edge of the pool with her feet and lower legs in the water.

It was beautiful outside, still slightly warm but no humidity to make the air sticky. She leaned back on her hands and let her head drop back taking in the refreshing atmosphere.

Thinking back on the night she couldn't help but smile. All-in-all it was a great night. She was able to spend most of the evening with Jake but avoided any alone time with him. She laughed when she thought back to their beer pong game and how competitive the two of them were.

Too engrossed in her own thoughts she didn't hear the back door opening or closing. She was startled when Jake sat down next to her, as if her thoughts conjured him.

"Couldn't sleep either?" He asked, startling her.

After a few seconds she regained her composure. "Yeah, Ryan is the worst snorer... I don't know how Maddey was able to fall asleep."

Jake let out a laugh at the comment and his smile revealed those amazing dimples. She couldn't help from moving in a little closer to him at the sight, between his dimples and the way his eyes sparkled when he laughed, she was a goner. *Oh man he is perfect.* Her heart broke a little bit at the thought because no matter how right he was for her, she could never have him.

"I know exactly what you mean from rooming with him at away games. I swear sometimes he could wake the dead with his snore."

Being so close to Jake she could feel the heat radiating off his body and it warded off the slight chill in the air. Trying to distract herself from the temptation he created, she started drawing lazy circles in the water with her leg.

They sat in comfortable silence for a few minutes, looking up at the stars. Unfortunately, it brought on memories of their night in the hammock.

"So it looks like you and Tucker bonded," he said without any judgment.

"Yeah, what can I say, he grows on ya."

"That he does."

As conversation between them slowed again she got the feeling her luck was about to run out. All night she felt Jake was waiting to get her alone to convince her they could be together. She was even more sure after her talk with Tucker. Not wanting to give into temptation she quickly got up from her spot on the pool's edge. "Well I'm gonna try and get some sleep now, goodnight, Jake."

He also stood. "Jordan, wait." He reached out a hand to take hers. "I've been trying to get you alone all night to talk to you and when I finally do you're trying to run away from me… again."

Jordan stood there silent, biting her lip.

"I know you've been avoiding me all night and I think it's because you're afraid to admit to yourself that we would be great together because you made this stupid promise with your brothers to not date anyone on the team after you had a really bad breakup with some jackass."

"Jake it's not that simple." She tried to cut off his tirade.

Jake waved a hand stopping her from interrupting him. He still held her one hand in his and with his free hand he reached out to cradle the side of her face. He ran his thumb over her cheek as he spoke. "Wait, let me finish… Now I know why you made it. But I would. Never. Ever. Do *anything* to hurt you. *Ever.*"

She could hear the pure conviction in his voice as he proclaimed his last sentence.

As he spoke he moved in closer. "I also know that when we're together I feel like everything is right. From the moment I saw you at Rookies I felt a connection to you. I swear we are meant to be together, if only you would have the courage to go for it. To hell with what your brothers would say."

Then before she knew what was happening his mouth was on hers.

She was surprised by Jake's outburst but nothing prepared her for his kiss. The utter euphoria that overtook her whole being when his lips came in contact with hers was cataclysmic.

No matter how much she refused to admit the attraction between them was actionable, it was useless once Jake claimed her as his own. She loved the way he held her face as he kissed her. She could feel how much he cared for her in his kiss. Her body instinctively leaned in closer to his as his body wrapped around her like a cocoon.

Abruptly, reality settled back in on her like a dark cloud. Her brothers were inside the house that they were making out in front of. They could be looking out the window at that very moment. As the realization dawned, she quickly pulled away and out of Jake's grasp. Without a word she made a b-line for the backdoor and went inside.

TOO FRUSTRATED TO sleep, Jake laid awake on the couch staring at the ceiling. Most people would think of the evening as a success because he was able to spend a lot of time with Jordan. They drank and played games together. They were able to joke around with each other and enjoy each other's company.

However, no matter how comfortable they were with each other, he felt like she was avoiding him, and that frustrated the hell out of him.

As he lay on the couch festering in his own turmoil, he heard someone open the sliding glass doors in the back. He got up to see who else was up at three thirty in the morning. When he got to the back door he couldn't believe his luck, there was Jordan sitting on the side of the pool.

He watched her from the door for a minute before he went out to join her. She looked so peaceful sitting on the edge of the pool that he almost didn't want to disturb her.

Almost.

"Couldn't sleep either?" He asked.

Clearly surprised to see him it took her a moment to speak. "Yeah, Ryan is the worst snorer... I don't know how Maddey was able to fall asleep."

"I know exactly what you mean from rooming with him at away games. I swear sometimes he could wake the dead with his snore."

Jordan giggled at the comment and when she did, he felt as if she let down some of the guard she constantly kept around her. She ran her fingers through her hair and he noticed she had unclipped her bangs. The way she looked at the moment reminded him of how she looked the night in the hammock. He had to clench his hands into fists to keep from reaching out and doing the same.

Another comfortable silence stretched out between them. The air was crisp, and the wind blew the trees on the property. Sitting on the edge of the pool the scent of chlorine mixed with Jordan's own vanilla essence.

Too soon for his liking she got up to leave. "Well I'm gonna try and get some sleep now, goodnight, Jake."

He was taken aback by her abrupt attempt at departure. She had been avoiding him most of the night and there was no way in hell would he allow this opportunity to slip through his fingers. He too got to his feet. "Jordan, wait." He reached out a hand to take hers.

It was now or never.

"I've been trying to get you alone all night to talk to you and when I finally do you're trying to run away from me... again."

She stood there silent. She was nibbling on her lower lip again and it made Jake burn inside with the desire to kiss her, but he knew he had to get out what he had to say before he did anything like that.

He called her out on avoiding being alone with him throughout the night.

When she tried to interrupt him, he reached out to touch her face intimately. "Wait, let me finish... Now I know why you made it. But I would. Never. Ever. Do *anything* to hurt you. *Ever.*"

As he spoke he moved in toward her. "I also know that when we're together I feel like everything is right. From the moment I saw you at Rookies I felt a connection to you. I swear we are meant to be together, if only you would have the courage to go for it. To hell with what your brothers would say."

At that he closed the rest of the distance between them, he moved his hand behind her neck, and brought his mouth down on hers.

He wasn't exactly sure what he was doing. There were others in the house, including her brothers. The fact that they could be caught at any time was a risk he was willing to take because he could not stand there and watch her take her lower lip between her teeth one more time without acting on the impulses it spurred on.

However, it was the fact that even with all the time they spent together, the conversations they had, and the blatant chemistry he knew they both felt, it made him want to prove something with this kiss.

Yet, all the chemistry he had felt between them didn't even begin to prepare him for what he felt when they kissed.

When she didn't pull away, he moved his hand that was holding hers to cup the other side of her face. He angled her head back to gain better access, intensifying the kiss. He threaded his left hand into her hair and felt the silky weight of it slide right through.

Abruptly she pulled away and silently walked away.

He understood her reaction but still smiled to himself. The memory of their kiss would be enough to sustain him until he could break down the rest of her walls. He knew the night was a major turning point in their relationship because when she kissed him back she was openly admitting, *finally*, that there was something between them. Rubbing the back of his neck he tried to calm down his hormones so he could eventually go back inside for a good night's sleep.

Chapter Twenty

The next morning Jordan was awakened by Ryan.

"So can anyone tell me why there is a pair of socks on my pillow?" Ryan said looking down to where she and Maddey were sleeping.

Slowly she opened her eyes, blinking a few times while they adjusted to the light. "Yeah you were snoring so bad last night that I shoved them in your mouth to shut you up. But it didn't work, you just spit them out," she said around a yawn.

"Why you little..." He trailed off and threw the pair of socks at her, but they bounced off her and hit Maddey in the face.

Maddey opened her eyes and looked at Ryan. "Hey don't throw stuff at me. I let you sleep in peace last night... but I am surprised your neighbors haven't filed a disturbing the peace order against you."

"At least I'm not the only one who feels that way." Jordan shared a knowing look with Maddey before stretching and reaching for her phone. She relaxed when she noticed she still had two hours before she had to be at the pool.

She also noticed an unread text.

UNKNOWN: You're supposed to stay away from him.

A sense of unease overcame her but she tried to shrug it off.

"Well I don't know about you guys, but I could kill for a cup of coffee." With a lingering look at Maddey, Ryan made his way out of his room and down stairs.

Seeing the way her brother looked at her best friend confirmed her suspicions that something had happened between the two. Seizing the opportunity while they were alone she decided to ask Maddey about it. "Okay spill."

"About what?" Maddey tried to play coy but she wasn't having it.

Maddey sat up and crossed her legs in front of her Indian-style. "Umm... well... last night..."

"Yeah?" Jordan prompted. When Maddey still hesitated she pushed on. "Come on Madz, stop stalling. It's obvious that something happened between you and Ryan last night, so don't keep me in the dark here."

"How do you know something happened? Did Jase tell you?" Her voice took on a panicky pitch.

"Jase... what?" She scrunched her face in confusion. "That sounds like a whole other story, but to answer your question so you'll hopefully answer mine, I could tell something happened between you two, by how you guys were sitting together last night. If I didn't think anything then I certainly would now by the way he just looked at you."

Maddey blushed profusely at the comment but her shoulders stiffened. "You're not mad, are you?"

She laughed and placed a reassuring hand on Maddey's arm. "Only if you don't tell me what happened... come on, Madz, I'm dying here."

"Well a little before you guys came inside for the night, I went into the kitchen to make myself another drink." She paused. "And Ryan followed."

When Maddey paused again she almost lost it. "Maddey…" she groaned.

"Well after I made my drink we started talking, and since Ry is so tall I sat on the counter so I wouldn't have to look up at him the whole time… and well… eventually… he kissed me."

She was so excited, she threw her arms around Maddey and caused them to fall to the air mattress.

"Oh my god, Madz, that's great!"

"Really, you aren't mad or anything?"

"Mad? Hell no! It's about damn time he made a move."

Maddey paused at the comment. "What do you mean, it's about time?"

"Oh, Madz, back when we were freshmen Ryan asked me if it would be ok if he asked you out and I told him nothing would make me happier."

"Really?"

"Yes, really."

"Then what the hell took him so long?"

Now it was her turn to not make eye contact. "Jor, what is?"

She let out a sigh as she looked at her friend. "Actually it might be partially my fault."

Maddey couldn't stifle a laugh at the comment. "How could taking two years for your brother to finally grow a set and ask me out have anything to do with you?"

Maddey's bluntness was one of the things Jordan loved most about her. "Oh Maddey, I love you. But what I mean is tha—" She stopped mid-sentence when Maddey's words truly sank in. "Wait a second, he asked you out?" She couldn't stop the joy from showing on her face.

"Yeah well after Jase came into the kitchen and almost caught us making out…"

She laughed and shook her head. "He didn't."

"He did." Maddey laughed at the memory of Jase's face

when he realized he might have interrupted something. "Anyway after Jase left, Ryan asked me out on date for tomorrow night."

She clapped her hands in delight. "So come on tell me why you think it's your fault Ryan took so long to ask me out."

"Okay, but now it's my turn to ask you not to get mad at me." At Maddey's nod she continued. "Well when Ryan came to me and asked if I would be ok if he asked you out, I told him how cool I thought it would be if you two dated." She paused and looked back down at her hands. "But I told him to be careful because I knew how you felt about Dex and I didn't want him to get hurt if he didn't have a chance with you."

Maddey reached out and covered her hand with her own. "Oh, Jordan."

She looked up and met Maddey compassionate gaze. "So you aren't mad right?"

Maddey shook her head in answer. "No. To be honest if he had asked me two years ago I'm not sure what my answer would have been… am I over Dex? No. But eventually I have to grow up and out of my obsession with him and try to move on and be happy with someone else. Your brother is the only other guy that I've ever felt anything toward." She squeezed Jordan's hand. "He gives me butterflies Jor."

The only reaction she could manage was a smile. "Aww, Maddey, that makes me so happy."

"Okay so enough about me and your brother, anything interesting happen between you and Jake last night?" She wagged her eyebrows.

Jordan had gotten up to get dressed and was in the middle of pulling on a pair of jean shorts when she paused at Maddey's question. "What?" Unfortunately she couldn't keep her voice from cracking from nervousness.

"Okay spill."

She knew there was no way out of having this particular conversation. Luckily with Maddey she knew her secret was safe, and if she didn't tell somebody about what happened the night before she might go insane. She finished buttoning her shorts and sat back down on the air mattress next to her friend.

"Fine, don't twist my arm or anything." She paused for dramatic effect. "The whole night I managed to not be alone with Jake. Then when I couldn't sleep last night because of Mr. I Can Wake the Dead with My Snoring, I went outside to relax and Jake followed me out there."

Maddey's eyes lit up with anticipation. "So what did he do when he finally got you alone?"

"At first, all we did was talk, but when I felt things were getting too intimate I got up to leave. Only he didn't let me."

"What did he do?"

"He kissed me." Her confession was barely above a whisper.

"What!" Maddey practically jumped off the air mattress.

"And that's not all. He also told me he likes me and thinks we're meant to be together," she paused to take a deep breath. Thinking about the conviction she heard in his voice sent a shiver of excitement down her spine. "The kicker is he doesn't care about any promise I made to my brothers, he said he'll do whatever he has to for us to be together."

Maddey was silent for a while before she eventually reacted. "Wow."

"Yeah." A sound outside the door caught their attention. "But let's talk about this later, the last thing I need is for someone to walk in while we're talking about Jake."

Maddey nodded in agreement. "Well with that said, I seriously need a cup of coffee. Let's go eat."

The girls finished getting dressed and made their way downstairs.

Jake woke up in need a caffeine fix. He grabbed his phone off the floor and saw a text notification on the screen.

UNKNOWN: Jordan is not yours to kiss. Back off.

What the fuck? Had someone seen them?
He thumbed out a response.

JAKE: Who is this?

When no response came he continued to the kitchen. Coffee cup in hand he went into the dining room to sit and saw Sammy and Skye were also awake.

"You must have had some night last night, huh Jake?" Sammy asked with an amused expression on his face.

His shoulders stiffened as panic seized his body. Did someone see him kissing Jordan and if so what would the repercussions be? Taking in Sammy's facial expressions and body language, he assessed he wasn't referring to the kiss. "Why do you ask?"

Sammy exchanged a knowing look with Skye before turning his attention back to him. "You got your butt handed to you in beer pong last night by Jordan, we were just curious how you were feeling."

The beer pong game that started the night seemed like ancient history compared to the events at the end of the evening.

The confession.

The *kiss*.

He kissed Jordan last night.

He'd been thinking about what it would be like to kiss her since the first time he saw her at Rookies, the reality far surpassed his imagination. The best part was she kissed him back. Eventually she ran away from her feelings for him, literally ran away, but in the heat of the moment she let her true emotions and feelings show through and she kissed him back.

Jake noticed the questioning looks Sammy and Skye sent his way and realized he hadn't answered Sammy's question. "No I'm feeling fine, the only thing hurt from last night is my pride."

Ryan entered the dining room during their conversation about the night before and his sudden bark of laughter brought all the attention onto him instead of Jake. "Yeah your pride may be hurting now from getting beat by Jordan, but don't worry, you get used to it." He clapped him on the back as a show of support.

Jake smiled. The thought of getting used to anything that involved Jordan was a happy one. He ran a hand through his hair to help rid it of some of the bed head he had going on.

Jase came into the dining room with a bag of bagels and all the necessities. He was spreading out butter and different types of cream cheese when Jordan and Maddey joined them. Jordan took the seat across from Jake but quickly looked away when she caught the knowing look in his eye.

Ryan sat at the head of the dining room table and Maddey sat in the seat to his right. The seat must not have been close enough for Ryan's liking because he pulled it over until it was right next to his. Once satisfied with the seating arrangements Ryan leaned back in his chair and placed his arm around the back of Maddey's.

Tucker walked into the kitchen, pausing to take a sip of Skye's coffee. The action earned him the side-eye from her. He made a face. "That's too sweet."

"Well I didn't make it for you." Skye took her mug back.

Tucker placed a hand over his heart. "You wound me, sweetheart."

The table laughed at their antics. Tucker settled into the seat next to Jordan and stole half her bagel. "Do you really not know how to get anything for yourself?" Jordan said on a laugh.

"Have pity on me Blondie. I'm still recovering from last night. I swear you are just as lethal with a quarter as you are with a ping pong ball."

"Aww, my poor BB3," she said as she passed over the rest of her bagel before grabbing a new one for herself.

Everyone else began grabbing bagels and coffee and settled in to eat breakfast. Jake could only hope the growing friendship forming between his best friend and Jordan worked in his favor.

With the text he received earlier still on his mind, he had to wonder if her brothers would be the only obstacle he had to overcome.

Chapter Twenty-One

Jordan stood by Skye's life guard stand while she told her about what transpired between her and Jake the night before.

"Oh my god he just grabbed your face and kissed you?" Skye asked shocked.

"Yeah."

"Wow."

"I know." Just thinking of how Jake commanded her body as he kissed her made her body heat.

"So do you think he meant what he said?" Skye asked from her perch.

"What, that he likes me?"

Skye took her eyes off the pool for a second to look down at her like she grew an extra head. "No, we obviously know he likes you. What I meant was do you think he meant he doesn't care what your brothers have to say?"

Jordan tried to put the conversation preceding the earth-shaking kiss out of her mind. It wasn't the words that made her nervous— okay the words did make her a little nervous— but it was the pure undiluted conviction behind those words that made her anxious. Based on her silence and the look that crossed her face, her friend knew her answer.

The text alert sounded from her bag, she tensed recalling this morning's cryptic text message. She relaxed when she saw it was Sammy.

THE SPIN DOCTOR (Sammy): Lucy you have some 'splaining to do

She let out a laugh. She and her friends were so much alike.

"What's so funny?" Skye asked

Jordan showed her the screen.

"Maddey must have told him about your kiss with Jake."

MOTHER OF DRAGONS: Maddey knows the details

"There we go. That'll buy me some time with him," she said.

As if all the talk about Jake conjured him up, she saw him walking toward the pool behind Sean and Carlee.

Sean ran up to her and hugged her around the legs. "Hi, Jordy!"

She smiled down at her brother. "Hey there, buddy."

When she looked up her gaze fell directly on Jake like a missile seeking its target. Unfortunately, she couldn't tell what he was thinking because of his aviator sunglasses. She quickly averted her eyes to the kids to help break the tension that always seemed to flow between them when they were together.

Jordan looked at the ground, Sean, Carlee, the pool, anywhere except Jake. She was scared if she looked him in the eye he would see the longing in hers. Blessedly her phone started to ring from her bag again, the tone indicated a phone call this time. She bent down to retrieve it but didn't recognize the number on the display and ignored it.

Skye watched her replace her phone without answering. "Everything alright, Jor?"

She rose to stand next to Skye. "Yeah, didn't recognize the number. You know I always let it go to voicemail when that happens."

"Are you sure? You seem a little tense."

"Yeah, I'm sure. I've been getting a bunch of calls and texts from unknown numbers lately. My number must be on some list or something."

She knew that could be the case for the phone calls but it didn't explain the texts, they were too personal. She couldn't bring herself to tell anyone about those yet. She spent too much time having people hover around her after the incident with Tommy, she wasn't looking to repeat it anytime soon.

Jake gave her a funny look as she described the phone calls but she brushed it off.

She watched Jake say his goodbyes to their siblings. He gave Sean a pound and Carlee and Skye a kiss on the cheek to say goodbye. When it came time to say goodbye to her, he hesitated before doing the same.

She sucked in a startled breath when his lips came in contact with her cheek. His kiss was extremely close to the edge of her lips and flashes of the night before passed through her mind.

She caught his knowing smirk as he pulled away. He knew exactly how he affected her. *Bastard.*

She told herself not to look at his ass as he walked away but failed miserably.

After Jordan returned home from teaching swim lessons, she decided to treat herself to a nice bubble bath in her Jacuzzi tub. She set up calming, scented candles around the bathroom and filled the tub with bubbles. Before she eased into the warm water, she placed her phone and book on the tub's ledge.

Once she was settled into her version of porcelain heaven, she rested her head against the folded towel she placed on the edge like a pillow. She let the warm water sooth her aching muscles and hoped her mind would follow but as she settled into her bath images of the night before invaded her thoughts.

She needed to escape. The whole night she spent carefully avoiding alone time with Jake but now that she had a moment to relax the night was starting to take its toll. As she lay there next to Maddey, sleep eluded her.

The temptation Jake presented was becoming too great. Sure she promised her brothers she wouldn't date another member of the team after what happened with Tommy, but would they really hold her to it?

She shook her head to rid herself of the thought. She got herself into this mess, she could deal with the consequences. Having enough of Ryan's snoring she got up and went outside for some fresh air. As she sat down on the edge of the pool, she placed her legs in the water and leaned back on her hands to look up at the night sky. Her peaceful haven didn't last long, after a few moments she was joined by Jake.

It was becoming more difficult to deny the chemistry between them every time they saw each other. She was trying her hardest to keep her promise to her brothers but it seemed no matter how hard she tried to keep him at an arm's distance Jake was that much more determined to get close.

After one last attempt to keep her distance, Jake stopped her from leaving and confessed his feelings and his intentions. She was rendered speechless by his confession and when he kissed her the rest of her resolve melted away.

Jake's kiss was perfect. Not too hard or demanding, but enough pressure to show his alpha side. The tingles of pleasure she felt from it had her head ringing even a day later.

But the ringing kept going.

It was after a few seconds that she realized the ringing wasn't in her head but her phone. Wiping her hand on a towel she reached over to answer the phone.

"Hello."

"Hi, Jordan, it's Tyler, Maddey's brother."

"Hi Tyler. I was expecting your call."

"Okay, good, you got my message. I didn't think you would answer before because Maddey mentioned you don't answer your phone when you don't know the number."

She settled back against the tub to make herself more comfortable. "No worries. So what's up? It's not every day I get a call from one of the famous McClain brothers."

Tyler's deep laugh reverberated through the phone. "Well I don't know about famous."

She laughed at Tyler's good humor. As the middle of the three McClain boys, he was the one Maddey was closest with. "So what's up?"

"It's Maddey."

She shot up in the tub, sloshing water over the edge. "What happened?"

Tyler could hear the anxiety in her voice and blew out a breath. "Nothing's wrong, why would you think that?"

She let out the breath she didn't realize she was holding. "Well let's see... the older brother of my best friend, who's in the Navy and is barely around by the way, calls me out of the blue to talk about her... forgive me for thinking the worst," she said sarcastically.

Tyler laughed hard at the comment and it took a moment before he composed himself enough to respond. "Wow you really are a lot like my sister."

She couldn't help but laugh in return as she settled back into the tub. "I'll take that as a compliment."

"As you should. But anyway… the reason I'm calling is to talk about Maddey's birthday next month."

"Okay, shoot."

"So Justin, Connor, and I all arranged to take leave to be home for her birthday and we want to surprise her."

She played with the bubbles floating around the tub. "So I'm guessing you need my help?"

"Yes."

"Okay what do you need me to do?"

"I'll be stateside next Thursday and I was wondering if you were available to help me make the plans and everything and possibly get Skye to get Maddey out of the house."

She smiled. "On Thursdays I only teach one swim lesson in the morning so I'll be free after noon. Does that work?"

"Yeah that sounds perfect."

By the time the two of them finished hammering out the rest of the details, her bath had gone cold. She climbed out and wrapped herself with a fuzzy towel. After being up late the night before she decided to make it an early night.

Chapter Twenty-Two

J ake watched his Yoshi get hit with a shell as Maddey cheered in delight next to him. She'd been spending a lot of time at the house the past week much to Ryan's pleasure. The bonus for him was Jordan would also come around.

"Sorry Jake, but you're in my way," Maddey taunted while her Princess Peach passed him on the screen.

"Ry you may need to reconsider having her around," Jake said.

"Yeah she totally cheats." Tucker complained as Maddey's driver hit his out of the way.

"I do not cheat. You guys just don't like losing to a girl." She bumped Tucker with her shoulder.

"I swear these girls are taking over the house." Nick said, handing out beers.

The sound of the front door opening and closing could be heard in the room before a familiar female's voice followed. "Nobody better be naked. I don't need to see all that." Jordan said as she walked into the house.

"See what I mean. Coming in here like they own the damn place," Nick pointed out.

"Shut it Nick." Jordan said as she took his beer.

Jake patted the armrest of his chair motioning for her to sit before returning his attention back to the TV, he had a princess to catch after all.

"Let me guess. Maddey's kicking your ass?" Jordan asked as she laid against the top of the chair, the position had their bodies touching a little. Since the night of the party the week before things had shifted between them. Unfortunately there were no repeat performances of their kiss.

"Oh yeah. No one's even come close to beating her," he confirmed.

"I guess she didn't tell you that back when we lived in the dorms freshman year, we had Mario Kart night every Wednesday." Jordan said with a laugh.

"Nope she neglected to mention that." Jase said as his Bowser spun out on a banana peel.

A few minutes later the race ended with Maddey once again the winner. The guys passed off their controllers to the next challengers. With his attention now free he was able to focus it on Jordan.

"Where's Skye? She's usually with you," he pointed out.

"She should be here soon. We've been trying to find a yoga studio around here but haven't had much luck."

"You know where you guys should go?" Jase said from his spot on the floor.

"Where?"

"The Steele Maker. It's a gym in town. I know they offer a bunch of different yoga classes there."

"Is that Rocky's dad's gym?" Jake asked thinking of the pretty physical trainer major that sometimes worked with the team.

"Yeah," Jase said.

"I thought her dad trained fighters?" Tucker asked.

"He does but he owns a full size gym. They have the usual gym equipment and a room they offer classes in." Jase turned back to face his sister. "If you want, I'll go with you guys to take a class. I can even introduce you guys to Rocky, she's pretty cool."

"That sound great. Are you free tomorrow?" Jordan asked.

"Sure I can make that work. Let me text Rocky and see what the class schedule is like."

Jordan pushed Jake by the shoulder. "You should come too."

"For yoga?" He asked, confused.

"Yeah."

"You want Jake to get all bendy, Blondie?" Tucker said around his beer.

"Why not? Jase does it. Plus it's good for his butterfly style playing. Gotta keep up the flexibility for those straddle split saves."

Jake knew she had a point. Anything that aided in his training he would try. Plus it was another way to spend more time with her so there was no way he would say no.

"The pro scouts love that sort of stuff too. Anytime they hear of unorthodox training they take notice," Ryan added.

Jake nodded. Ryan constantly used the attention he garnered from the pros to help those with potential on the team who dreamed of going pro. It was something else that could be affected by dating Jordan. Besides the possibility of ruining his friendship with the Donnelly brothers, he feared his chances of playing professionally could be at stake.

In the end she was worth any fallout to his potential hockey career.

"Sure, I'll come. Tucker you're coming too," he announced.

"Bro," Tucker complained.

"Come on BB3. It'll be fun."

"Ok, fine. But you owe me Blondie." Jake loved how much of a push over his best friend was when it came to Jordan. It was another tool he had in his arsenal in convincing her to take a chance on them being together.

JORDAN PARKED HER car across the street from the hockey house, not at all surprised to see Maddey's car parked nearby. Her friend had been spending quite a bit of time at the house since Ryan asked her on their first date.

She also caught sight of Jake's Jeep and couldn't stop the bloom of happiness it caused her to feel. Ever since Jake made his intentions known the week before, he was constantly around. It was like the universe was pushing them together.

She deserved a medal for not giving into her urges where he was concerned. Everyday she cursed her brothers for making her promise not to date another teammate.

She did however take every opportunity available to be close to him. She was only human after all.

Luckily she'd always been friendly with the guys so it wasn't suspicious when she sat close to him or had casual touches.

He was quickly becoming one of her closest friends on the team. Surprisingly enough, so was Tucker, even if he was a man-whore. Proving it once again by how he started hitting on Skye the moment she arrived.

"Seriously. Can anyone beat her?" Billy complained as Maddey won yet another race.

"What can I say? I have skills." Maddey charmed him with a smile.

From somewhere in the room a phone went off. Wade grabbed it and held it up for the room. "Whose phone is this?"

Jordan was closest and recognized the cartoon frogs on the case as Maddey's.

"Hey, Madz, looks like you're getting a Skype call," she said to her friend.

Maddey jumped up from the couch to reach for the phone. "Oh my god it must be one of my brothers."

Maddey sat down next to Jordan as she answered the call. When the call connected Maddey's brother Connor filled the screen.

"Connor!"

"Hey, sis."

"How are you? Are you okay? Where are you calling from?" Maddey's rapid fire questioning made Jordan laugh.

"Are you with Jordan? I thought she and Skye moved out?"

Maddey adjusted the phone so the two of them filled the screen. Jordan waved when Connor turned his pale green eyes on her. They were nice but didn't compare to the emerald ones Jake had. "Hey, Con."

"Hey, Jor."

"So what's up bro? Didn't realize you missed me so much." Maddey joked with her brother.

"Can't a brother call his sister?"

"Is that Tink?" They could hear a voice call in the background.

"What's Dex doing there?" Maddey asked, sounding concerned.

They watched Dex move his way into the picture to wave.

"Seriously Con, is something wrong? Did someone get hurt? Is it Ty? Is that why Dex is with you? Your teams usually don't get stationed together." Maddey's voice started to take on a panic quality. Jordan reached out a hand to calm her down.

"Nothing's wrong Tink. Ty's with our LPO," Dex said.

"Yeah he's gonna be pissed when he finds out he missed a call with you," Connor added.

"Who needs a beer?" Billy called out to the group.

A chorus of mostly male voices sounded through the living room.

"Madison Belle where the hell are you?" Connor demanded after hearing the guys.

"Don't you Madison Belle me, Connor Matthew."

Jordan laughed at the badass look on her friend's face. The two of them had bonded over the ridiculousness of their older brothers' protectiveness.

"Ooo she told you McClain." Dex clapped Connor on the back as he laughed.

"Anyway… Not that it's any of your business, I'm at the hockey house with Ryan."

"Ryan? Is he the guy Mom told us you were dating?" Connor asked.

"Ahh… so *that's* the real reason you called. To check up on me." Maddey looked to Jordan, the two sharing a knowing look.

"What, it's our duty to make sure he's not a total asshat."

"I'm pretty sure Babs and Jack are my parents, not you idiots." Maddey's comment earned a laugh from their listening audience.

"Don't worry he's not an asshat," Jordan informed them.

"You know I can hear you right?" Ryan said from his seat on the couch.

The girls ignored him.

"And how would you know?" Connor directed his question to Jordan.

"Because he's my brother. And as much as he annoys me, he's a good guy."

"Not really feeling the love JD," Ryan grumbled.

"Quiet you," she said to him.

"I can't believe you wasted a phone call to check up on my dating life," Maddey complained.

"You know you love us," Connor stated. "Now come on, we want to meet this guy."

Jordan caught the worried look on her older brother's face. It was about time he got a taste of his own medicine.

Maybe dealing with Maddey's overprotective brothers would make him ease up on how he treated her.

"Okay, but be nice. If not, I'll shoot you myself," Maddey warned.

"You know how to shoot?" Nick asked.

"Of course, I come from a family of SEALs."

Maddey's tiny stature and gorgeous appearance were deceiving. Underneath she was tough as nails.

"Wait is your dad's name really Jack McClain?" Jake asked.

"Yup," Maddey said with a smile. Her dad's name was one of the biggest jokes in their group.

"So your dad's legal name is John McClain?" Jase asked.

"Yeah so don't get any funny ideas with my sister. He's a lot like the other John McClane," they could hear come from phone.

With Maddey now back in her seat next to Ryan, Jordan leaned back to her original position on the chair, bringing her body back in contact with Jake's.

"I take it you know Maddey's brothers pretty well?" Jake asked.

She watched as Ryan and Maddey talked to Conner and Dex. Her usually calm and confident brother looked a little green around the gills and she couldn't suppress her laughter.

"Yeah, I guess. I've only met them a few times between deployments. They all Skype pretty regularly with her, so living with her, Skye and I have been around for most of their calls and have gotten to know them more that way."

"I take it they're close?" Jake's hand reached out and started tracing circles on her knee.

She stiffened at his touch, but relaxed after a quick survey of the room showed everyone else occupied with either the video game or harassing Ryan while he got grilled.

"Yeah. One of the first things we bonded over was how

much we *love* and *hate* our overprotective brothers," she said with a smile.

"You know," Jake continued to trace the bumps of her knee cap as he spoke. "If Ryan can convince a bunch of Navy SEALs to approve of him as boyfriend material, how hard can it be to do the same with a bunch of hockey players?"

He shot her one of his smiles that revealed the dimples she loved so much. She wasn't surprised at all that he was pushing the envelope about them, even in the presence of their friends. He was as fearless in his pursuit as he was between the pipes. Just another thing to add to his attractiveness. *Damn him.*

She really hoped Ryan's relationship with Maddey would make him okay with her breaking her promise. Because her resolve to stay away from Jake was paper thin.   •

Chapter Twenty-Three

Shortly after returning home from teaching swim lessons, Jordan was showered and changed to go out and help Tyler plan Maddey's birthday celebration. She sat at the kitchen table with her mother telling her about her plans for the day when the doorbell rang.

Before anyone else could get up to answer it, Sean was out of his seat and running to answer the door himself. A few moments later he returned with Tyler in tow.

Sean stood in front of Tyler, his own head barely reaching Tyler's hips, and looked up at him in wonder. It wasn't surprising that he was fascinated. Standing at six feet four inches, Tyler's height was intimidating but with his broad shoulders and military stance he looked down right menacing.

However, Sean didn't relent in his perusal. He looked Tyler over from head-to-toe trying to assess who the strange guy was.

Tyler looked slightly uncomfortable under Sean's scrutiny so she jumped in to save him.

She reached out and picked Sean up by the waist and

placed him on her chair while she got up to hug Tyler hello. After that she made introductions with her parents.

She heard Tyler's big exhale. For a guy who faced down terrorists in the dark of night, it was funny how rattled he was by a little five year old staring him down.

"So how'd you manage to get Maddey away from home?" Tyler asked.

With the tension in the room now broken Jordan settled into the chair next to Sean and looked up at Tyler. The family resemblance between him and Maddey was striking. His overall size was impressive and the way he filled out a pair of well worn jeans and gray Navy t-shirt could only be described as mouth watering. So why was it that Tyler didn't pique her interest?

Because you idiot, you only have eyes for a certain dark haired guy with killer green eyes. She cursed her inner voice and shook off the aggravation at her constant thoughts of Jake.

"Promise not to go all big brother on me?" She asked remembering how Connor reacted on the phone the other day.

Tyler quirked a brow at the question but nodded.

She wasn't fully confident Tyler wouldn't freak out but she decided the truth would come out eventually. "She's spending the day with Skye getting ready for her date with Ryan tonight."

Now Tyler looked utterly lost. "Ryan? As in your brother?"

"The one and the same." She shared a look with her mother.

"How'd that happen?"

"Wait you mean Connor and Dex didn't tell you?"

"I haven't been with Dex and our team for a few days. I was running a training stateside."

"Do they know you're here?"

"Of course. This is all part of our plan."

"So they were lying when they called her last night."

"They called her?"

"It's a long story. I'll tell you about it later." She got up and placed her coffee cup in the sink. She made her way over to the stairs, picked up a small duffle bag, before bringing it into the kitchen and handing it to her mom. "My skates are in here along with a few other things for Maddey. Ryan is going to come by later and pick this up."

Her mom leaned up to give her a kiss on the cheek goodbye. "Will do honey, have fun." Then she turned her attention on Tyler. "It was nice to meet you, Tyler."

"Nice to meet you too, Mrs. Donnelly." He reached out and shook her dad's hand.

After saying goodbye they made their way out the door. "So, what's the plan for the day?" She asked as they walked toward Tyler's car.

Tyler opened the driver's side door and leaned on the roof as he slipped on his sunglasses. "I figured we swing by my parents first and then go see if there's a couple of places that we can try and get a private party reserved."

She put on her own sunglasses to combat the strong summer sun. "Okay sounds like a plan." She checked her watch on her left wrist. "We'll be in the clear by the time we get there because she should be getting to Skye's as we speak." As she made to get into the car she saw two runners making their way up the street. They slowed as they neared the car and she noticed one of the runners was Jake and a little thrill shot through her. She waved hello before she got into the car. As Tyler pulled out, she noticed Jake and Tucker sharing a bewildered looked.

JAKE JOINED TUCKER for a late morning run. The run was the perfect outlet for the extra tension that had been building inside him since the hockey house party. The only consolation was even though Jordan denied her feelings with words, the way she reacted to his kiss revealed the truth.

He just had to be patient.

Yeah, easier said than done.

The three mile run he and Tucker were finishing up helped to distract him a little, but as they got closer to home, he couldn't squelch the excitement that the possibility of seeing Jordan brought on.

As they rounded the corner of his block, he noticed an unfamiliar coupe parked in front of the Donnelly's home. His heart skipped a beat when he saw Jordan standing by the passenger side of the vehicle.

She turned in their direction and waved when she saw them approaching. He smiled as he returned the greeting but it quickly faded as he saw that the driver of the car was a guy. The sight caused his stride to stumble.

"Who do you think that was?" Tucker asked from beside him.

He was so far gone with his emotions that he completely forgot Tucker was with him. "I have no idea."

The two watched Jordan and the mystery guy get in the car and drive off.

"You don't suppose—" Tucker's question trailed off.

Jake's chest rose and fell with deep breaths, both from his run and from the tension he could feel coiling through his body. His gaze cut to Tuck, stopping the question he didn't even want to think about himself.

"I don't think I want to know," he answered truthfully.

He knew she was hellbent on trying to keep her promise to her brothers but he hoped with time he would be able to prove it wouldn't be an issue. Now he wasn't so sure.

Could it be... Was she so determined to keep her word, she would date other guys instead? Did he really not have a chance?

Shaking off those dark thoughts Jake sprinted the last couple of yards to his front door.

Before they went inside they saw Ryan park in his parents' driveway. They changed direction to see their friends.

Ryan and Jase got out the car as they all exchanged greetings and bumped fists.

Jase laughed when Ryan dropped his keys on the ground. "Man, I can't remember the last time I've seen you this nervous. And over a date, too." His toothpaste ad smile spread across his face.

"I don't know why I let you tag along. You are *so* not helping," Ryan complained.

Jase laughed louder. "And that's what makes this so much fun for me," he said as he slapped Ryan on the back.

"He's right Cap, I don't think I've *ever* seen you like this," Tucker added, earning him another fist bump from Jase.

"It's not like it's your first date with Maddey," Jase said.

"Tonight's special okay. I'm going for official status," Ryan said.

The group made their way through the front door of the Donnelly home. Immediately they were enveloped by the scents of Mr. D's cooking and knew they could find everyone in the kitchen.

"So Dad, what's for dinner?" Jase asked making their presence known.

Mr. Donnelly looked up from chopping vegetables to greet them. "Chicken Marsala, my specialty." He said the last part with a flourish.

"Yum," Jase rubbed his stomach. "Maybe I'll stay for dinner."

"Oh, that would be wonderful," Mrs. Donnelly said as she made her way over to hug the boys hello.

"Do you have any extra?" Jake asked.

"For you dear, absolutely," Mrs. D said. "Tucker you're more than welcome to join too."

"Sweet. Thanks Mrs. D." Tucker turned to Ryan and Jase. "I don't know why you guys live at the house. If I had cooking like this at my house I sure as hell would live at home."

Ryan looked around the kitchen. "Is Jordan around?"

"She went out with a boy!" Sean shouted from his seat.

Both Ryan and Jase snapped to attention at their younger brother's words. "WHAT?" They asked in unison.

Jake and Tucker didn't react since they saw her drive off with said boy.

Mrs. D looked her three sons over. "She went out on a date."

Ryan and Jase looked like they swallowed a lemon. Sure Jake wasn't happy with the revelation but he managed to keep his cool.

"And who did she go out with?" Ryan asked.

"A guy she met while she attended NYU," she said as she went back to chopping vegetables.

"And what exactly do you know about this guy?" Jase asked.

"Not much," she said with a shrug. "But he is very handsome."

Ryan's mouth all but gaped open. "And you were okay with this? Letting *your* daughter go out with a guy you know absolutely *nothing* about?"

Mr. Donnelly looked to his wife and shrugged. "He seemed nice."

"Your sister is big girl and she can take care of herself. I swear, it's about time you boys learned that."

Jase moved to sit next to Sean at the kitchen table and gestured for Jake and Tucker to join them.

"Anyway… if you are done *interrogating* us on your sister's love life, there is a bag in the front hall by the stairs. Jordan put her skates along with some other things she thought *you*," she pointed her finger directly at her oldest son, "might need to help on your date with *her* best friend."

Ryan slumped in his chair after being chastised by his mom. "Thanks, Mom."

The warm air blowing in through the car window was soothing. Jordan relaxed in the front seat enjoying the ride down the Parkway. She and Tyler worked over their plan for Maddey's birthday surprise and had it pretty much settled.

Tyler parked his car behind his father's police cruiser in the driveway. He told her earlier his parents were each taking a half-day from work since he would be home. They entered the house and found both his parents on the back deck, his father was grilling while his mother read a book in a lounge chair nearby. When Babs and Jack McClain heard the back door open, they both looked up and grinned ear-to-ear.

Babs came over and enveloped first Tyler then Jordan in a backbreaking hug, before her husband did the same. Tyler went over to the cooler next to the house and pulled out a beer for him and his father.

Jordan settled onto the lounge chair next to Mrs. McClain and they started chatting away, catching up on all things. Since she and Skye were the first girls Maddey had ever become close friends with, Barbara took the girls in as her own.

She studied the McClain family dynamics. Jack McClain was career Navy until he retired and became police chief when Maddey was a child. Their family was just as close as her own and it was nice to be around them. Spending time with the McClains with Tyler around, it was easy to see where each child got their looks. Maddey and Tyler clearly got their looks from their father, with light hair and blue eyes, whereas their other brothers, Justin and Connor, took after their mother with dark hair and green eyes.

"So what's the plan for Maddey's birthday?" Mrs. McClain asked.

"Well, we all arranged to take leave from the day before her birthday till two days after. The only one who hasn't gotten approval yet is Dex," Tyler supplied.

"So I'm going to have Maddey stay over my house the night before her birthday and Skye, Sammy, and I are going to plan stuff for her," she added.

"Then Jordan, Skye, Sammy, and now maybe even Ryan will all come down here to have family birthday dinner and we'll all be here to surprise her."

"And if that's not enough, after dinner we are all going to go out to a bar around here and the rest of our friends that she's made from the hockey team and some friends we know from NYU will be there to surprise her again."

Wow, was the only response they received about their plans.

"Is that a good wow or a bad wow?" Jordan asked. She was a little nervous about how Maddey might react to the surprises.

"It's a great wow." Babs looked like she was trying to hold back tears. "I am so happy you were Maddey's roommate at school, she is so lucky to have a friend like you in her life."

She reached out to place a hand on Mrs. McClain's. "I feel the same way about Maddey."

With the emotional part over, the four finished planning out the rest of the details and were confident they could pull it off.

Chapter Twenty-Four

ookies was bumpin' even though the night was
still young. Jordan sat on the bar in the VIP area
looking down at the dance floor below. It had been
a few days since she'd seen Jake, having traveled to a meet
with the pool's club team she helped coach. She couldn't get
the look on his face when he saw her with Tyler out of her
mind. It wasn't so much he looked jealous, more like he was
hurt. That was the last thing she wanted.

She blew out a frustrated breath and tightened her ponytail with more force than necessary. "Here, you look like you
need it," Skye said as she held out a bottle of beer for her to
take.

She smiled down at Skye, grateful her friend could read
her so well. "Thanks."

"Penny for your thoughts?"

Before answering she picked up the beer bottle and took a
long swallow from it. "You know exactly what my thoughts
are." She inhaled a deep breath. "I've been thinking about the
exact same thing for days now and it's driving me crazy."

She paused to take another pull from her beer and looked
over the dance floor down below again. "The last time I saw

Jake I was getting in the car with Tyler so who knows what he thinks about that. Then I remind myself it shouldn't matter what he thinks because I'm only supposed to be friends with him."

Skye rested her elbows on the bar to lean beside her. "So what are you going to do about it?"

"I have no idea. I feel like a wire ready to snap."

She looked up at Sammy in the DJ booth and waved when he looked down. Always knowing what to do to make her smile, he played an old school Spice Girls song. If it weren't for her amazing friends she would be completely lost.

As she observed the bar and dance floor below, she hoped that the chaos would be enough to distract her from her feelings. Things had been weird at home with Sean's unpleasant attitude.

As the Spice Girls song ended and gave way to a current rock hit, she watched as her brothers, and most of the hockey team, made their way into Rookies. Her gaze skimmed over the group to see if Jake arrived yet. She all but jumped off the bar when she saw Maddey enter next to Ryan.

"Oh my god, did you know Maddey was coming?" She asked Skye.

Skye leaned over the edge of the bar to see the dance floor below until she was able to see Maddey's head of crazy blonde curls. "No." She paused surveying the scene below some more. "Oh look how cute, Ryan is walking with his arm around her shoulders."

She took a few moments to study her brother. Having girls with him wasn't new but bringing a girl to Rookies, especially one he was staking claim on for all to see was. She looked over her shoulder at Skye and shared a knowing look.

The night should be interesting.

As the guys made their way across the dance floor to the stairs of the VIP section, she finally saw Jake enter the bar. She kept her perch on the bar as everyone made their way over but jumped off to give Maddey a big hug.

"Maddey, I had no idea you were coming tonight."

Maddey returned her fierce hug with one of her own, a blush staining her cheeks. "Well I wasn't sure what the plan was. I was up here to spend time with Ryan again and we decided to come here tonight."

She wondered how long it would take before Maddey was comfortable with the fact that she was dating her best friend's brother.

All around greetings were exchanged and the atmosphere became charged with excitement. She resumed her perch on the bar as the team settled in around the VIP area.

She couldn't help but smile as she watched Tucker give Maddey a tour. It was nice to see that even though Maddey seemed hesitant on how she would feel about her growing relationship with Ryan, she wasn't afraid to show her true colors. Tonight she was being classic Maddey in her hot pink baby t-shirt, dark washed skinny jeans rolled up at the ankles, and hot pink peep-toe heels. Eventually, they settled into one of the lounge couches that faced the flat screen playing the Yankees game.

Jordan couldn't stop the laugh that bubbled up inside her. "Relax Ry, no one is gonna make a move on your girl." She nudged his arm for good measure.

The tension in Ryan's shoulders eased as he turned to face her.

"Speaking of making moves, what is this we hear about you going out on a date with some guy no one knows?"

Her mouth fell open at Ryan's sudden interrogation. She wasn't sure what emotion was more prominent, confusion or frustration. Confusion because she wasn't exactly sure what he was talking about and frustration at the attack she was receiving. Even if she did go out with a guy it was none of their business. It's not like it was Jake or anything.

"Excuse me what are you talking about?" She held up a hand to cut off Ryan's tirade.

"I'm talking about the guy you were out with when I came over to pick up the stuff you left me for my date with Maddey."

Ryan and Jase watched as realization crossed her face then watched as it transformed into anger.

Not good.

Her eyes narrowed. "Did Jake tell you that?"

Jake stood a few feet away so he was able to hear when she said his name. He excused himself from Skye and headed over to where she stood with her brothers.

"What's up, guys?" Jake said as he looked between the Donnelly siblings.

"What does Jake have to do with anything?" Jase asked not sure where Jake fit in to the scenario.

She heaved an irritated sigh, this whole situation was getting old real fast. "What… are you saying he's not the one who told you about Tyler?"

"What are you talking about?" Jake asked confused.

"Why would Jake have anything to do with this?" Jase asked ignoring Jake's question.

"Because he and Tucker saw me leaving with him." She paused. "I don't know how else you would know?"

"You think I spy on you for your brothers?" Jake said, offended.

"Sean told us," Ryan answered.

"And Mom elaborated," Jase added.

She looked between the three guys, all of them radiating some form of ire. She could understand why her brothers were upset, their baby sister has a bad breakup with their friend and is now dating a guy they don't know about, but Jake's didn't fit.

She took a deep breath and rolled her shoulders back to

ease some of the tension. She still wasn't clear on what was going on but it would get sorted out soon enough.

"Okay, okay, hold on a second." She waved her hands in front of her for emphasis. "Back up here let's start from the beginning. How did you find out I went out with Tyler?" She sent a pointed look at Jake.

Jase caught the look she sent Jake. "Wait, why do you keep looking at Jake in all this?"

"Isn't he how you found out I went out with Tyler?"

"And why would I do that?"

"Why would you think that?"

Jake and Jase asked simultaneously.

The whole situation was getting ridiculous and she still didn't have the answers she wanted. "Because Jake and Tucker saw me as I was leaving the house, that's why," she added on for good measure.

Ryan realized they were getting nowhere with this line of questioning. "We found out about this Tyler guy from Sean."

"Sean?" Now she was totally lost.

"Yeah when we showed up at the house and you weren't there we asked where you were and Sean said, 'She's out with a boy.'"

It was finally clear to her why Sean had been in a bad mood recently, he was so much like his older brothers it was scary. "Okay, that explains how you know I went out with Tyler but it doesn't explain why you think I went out on a date with him."

"After we recovered from Sean's revelation, Mom told us how you were out on a date with this guy you met at NYU."

As Ryan's explanation sunk in she burst into laughter. Now everything made sense. Her parents knew exactly who Tyler was and them going out together was completely platonic. Good ol' Mom must have decided to give her sons a taste of their own medicine. She had to remember to thank her when she saw her.

"Do you want to clue the rest of us in on the joke?" Jase asked.

Once she composed herself, she decided to put her brothers out of their misery, besides she had to keep seeing Tyler under wraps.

"Okay… well first off Tyler and I were not on a date, Mom was just having a little fun at your expense. Second off, Tyler is Maddey's brother and we have to keep me going out with him a secret."

"Why? Maddey can date your brother but you can't date hers?" Jake asked.

"It wasn't a date, Mom was just trying to goad you guys, now get serious for a minute." She looked at her brothers. "We have to keep me seeing Tyler a secret because he's supposed to be in some corner of the world no one knows about, not here in the state of New Jersey."

"So if he's supposed to be out fighting some war somewhere what was he doing going out with you?" Ryan asked clearly trying to understand what was really going on.

"He was unexpectedly stateside so he wanted my help in planning some sort of surprise for Maddey's birthday. He and his brothers are all arranging to take leave for her birthday and plan on surprising her, hence the need for secrecy."

The guys all looked at each other while they took in her explanation. She knew for the most part it made sense.

"Okay you got a deal, but we are so getting Mom back for this," Ryan said as he left to head over to where Maddey was sitting.

As Jase also made his way to the other side of the VIP section she released a sigh of relief. She ran a hand over her ponytail and took another long swallow from her beer.

"You and I have to talk." Jake moved closer to where she sat on the bar.

She saw the fire in his eyes as he approached her. She quickly hopped off the bar and moved toward the railing that overlooked the dance floor below. Grabbing the railing, she tried to control the urge to throw her arms around his neck to pull him close for another one of those mind blowing kisses. As she sat there arguing with her brothers, she couldn't help but notice how nice he looked in dark jeans and a light gray t-shirt. Or the way his muscles bunched under said t-shirt when he crossed his arms when he got mad.

"What, Jake?"

"Now I know you said that you going out with Tyler was purely platonic, which for that I'm glad, but did you honestly think I would rat you out to your brothers if I saw you with some guy?"

She could feel the heat from his touch burn through the fabric of her jeans at her hip and liked it. She turned to face him and instinctively looked into his eyes, getting lost in the bright green depths like always. "Honestly, I have no idea."

"I wouldn't betray your trust like that." Jake reached up to stroke a hand across her cheek, resting it along the side of her throat. "But I will tell you this, I'm really glad you weren't out on a date with him."

She couldn't stop from leaning into his touch. "And why's that?"

Jake's mouth hitched up in a sexy smirk. "Because now I know that there's no competition and all I have to worry about is getting around this stupid promise you made your brothers. Piece of cake."

Her breath hitched at his comment. "Why aren't you mad at me?"

"Why would I be mad?"

"I pretty much just accused you of ratting me out to my brothers."

"It was an obvious conclusion. Besides how can I be mad when I know it's me you really want?"

She rolled her eyes but before she could comment her

phone vibrated in her pocket. When she saw it was another unknown number she sent the call to voicemail.

Jake moved to join their group while she was distracted by her phone.

JAKE SAW THE guys from the team walking into Rookies as he parked his Jeep. It had been two days since he saw Jordan go off with another guy. He was determined to talk to her about it because the facts he had didn't add up.

Tucker was already giving Maddey the grand tour by the time he made it up to the VIP section. He knew his best friend would never come between Ryan and his relationship with Maddey. However that didn't stop Tucker from flirting with Maddey, especially when he knew how much it got under the captain's skin.

He made his way over to Skye for a beer. They spent some time chatting when he heard someone say his name. If it were anyone else calling his name he would have ignored them, but the voice he heard was Jordan's, he would know it anywhere. He excused himself from Skye and headed over to where Jordan and her brothers were and stood next to Ryan.

Based on the look on her face this wasn't going to be a friendly conversation.

As Jordan explained the whole story about Tyler he had to force himself not to laugh. He was mildly annoyed she would assume he would run to her brother's with information about her but she was so cute when she was all worked up amusement overrode his annoyance.

After Ryan and Jase went off to join the rest of the team, he knew it was time to have his own talk with Jordan.

Jake watched her regain her composure. She was safe from her brother's interrogation but things between them weren't even close to being settled. "You and I have to talk." He moved in closer to where she sat on the bar.

"What Jake?" She said moving over the railing.

With Jordan facing away from him, he took a moment to take her in without interruption. Her white tube top revealed her tan shoulders and hugged the curves down to the top of her stone washed, low-ride jeans. The gentle swell of her hips was accented by a wide silver sparkle belt and her long legs were encased in her tight ripped jeans all the way down to her purple Chucks.

Glancing back, he checked to make sure her brothers were occupied before he moved in closer. Seeing the coast was clear he made his move. He placed a hand on her hip to get her attention before he spoke.

"Now, I know you said that you going out with Tyler was purely platonic, which for that I'm glad, but did you honestly think that I would rat you out to your brothers if I saw you with some guy?"

He couldn't help but smirk when she revealed she was more concerned with upsetting him than anything else. He could tell she tried to keep things purely in the friend zone with them but every so often, like now, she showed how much she really cared.

When her phone rang he left to join their friends to give her some privacy.

He sat on the couch next to Ryan and propped his feet up on the table in the middle. "So Maddey, what do you think of Rookies?"

Jordan sat next to Tucker on the couch and smiled at how much he had grown on her since the first night they met.

"Beer Blondie." Tucker held out a beer from the bucket.

"Thanks BB3." She accepted the beer to take a long drag.

Her eyes once again found their way back to Jake's sitting across from them. When he caught sight of her looking, he winked. *Always the charmer.* She responded with an eye roll.

"Hey all you party people out there, here is a dance mix for my special ladies, so I want to see your sexy asses on that dance floor now!" Sammy's voice came over the speakers.

Jordan and Maddey simultaneously looked up at Sammy in the DJ booth and saw him looking down in their direction and burst out laughing.

"Well as much as he wants every girl in this place to think they are his special ladies, if we don't get down there to dance, he'll kill us," Maddey announced as she got to her feet.

Jordan looked back up at Sammy. "Yeah I think you're right, come on let's go."

The girls got up and walked down the stairs holding hands and laughing the whole way. They found a prime spot in the middle of all the action but also in perfect position to still see the Yankee game playing on the TVs above the main bar.

The place was in full swing with bodies moving to and fro. Jordan had forgotten how much fun Rookies could be when she had a dancing partner. Skye was always bartending when they came, so it was nice to be able to go down to the main level, away from her brothers' constant presence.

They danced with abandon and sang along to the Britney Spears song playing. Sammy was playing a mix full of their favorites. Maddey was always Jordan's dance partner when they would go out in college and it was nice to have her back. Another bonus from Maddey dating her brother.

By dancing together, it kept strange people from coming in between them.

"So, I see you're not wasting any time with showing Ryan your love for heels," she said.

Maddey was the biggest shoe whore she knew, she was a virtual Carrie Bradshaw, almost always wearing heels.

"Yeah, well, you know I love my shoes, plus the heels give me a little more height when I stand next to him."

"Yeah he does have a way of making a person feel like a midget… So how was your date last night?"

Maddey let out a happy sigh. "It was amazing."

"Details please."

"When I met him at the hockey house I wasn't sure what our plans were. I didn't know where we were going until he was parking in the lot of the hockey arena."

"The place is impressive, isn't it?"

"Oh yeah. Huge… Anyway he showed me where they displayed all the team's past awards and stuff and I got to see the Championship Trophy from this past year."

"Did they have his Hobey Baker award there, too?"

Maddey looked confused by the question. "What's that?"

"It's an award the NCAA gives out to the top player each year."

"He's that good?" Maddey said impressed.

"Oh yeah. It's not talked about a lot but I've heard some people compare him to Gretzky, which is like top praise. But that's not what's important here. Keep telling me about the date."

"So he gave me a tour of the arena, even the locker room, which stunk by the way. Then he had me put on a pair of skates. Not sure where he found them in my size."

"They were mine. I put together a whole bag full of stuff for you." Her comment made Maddey smile, she knew it helped ease any residual doubts Maddey had about how'd she feel about her friend dating her brother. "But the locker room, really Ryan?"

"No it was super sweet. He said he wanted to make sure I was familiar with the whole arena because he was hoping I'd be spending a lot of time there. And when I asked him what he meant by that he asked me to be his girlfriend."

"Oh my god, really? That's amazing." She reached out and pulled Maddey in for a hug.

"Then if that wasn't awesome enough, he took me out to the ice where he had a picnic set up."

"So romantic."

"I know and if I wasn't already a pile of goo, I was after I asked him why he did it. His answer was that the rink was a special place for him and he wanted it to be special for me too."

"Wow... I didn't know Ryan had it in him."

The girls danced a little longer before Maddey leaned in closer to her. "Hottie behind you is checking you out," she said with a smirk.

She raised an eyebrow. "Really? Which one?"

"Blondie in the bright blue shirt."

The girls rotated while dancing, trying not to be obvious. Sure enough when she looked over Maddey's shoulder the cutie in the blue shirt was looking right at her. She quickly averted her gaze to the TV above the bar. She smiled, flattered by being checked out by someone that attractive. *But he's no Jake.* She groaned at the thought.

Maddey watch her closely. "What's wrong? He's a total babe."

Instinctively she tightened her ponytail, at the rate she was going she felt like she was going to end up ripping her hair out. "It's not that... it's just... I can't get Jake out of my head."

"Aww, babe." Maddey slung her arm around her shoulders. "Come on, let's get away from here then." She pointed toward the TV above the bar. "Come on, let's go watch the game, the Yankees have two men on with Matthews up. If he gets on and Johnson does good, we have a chance to win our game this week."

"Okay."

They made their way over to the bar and watched as

Matthews worked his bat to a full count and in the end walked to load the bases. Maddey checked how far behind they were in their fantasy baseball game for the week. "Okay, we are down by nine points, if Johnson steps it up we have a shot at winning."

Jordan rubbed her hands together. "Okay come on Johnson, bring it home."

Maddey laughed beside her. The hairs on the back of Jordan's neck stood up, a sense of unease trickled down her spine. She turned around to look at those around her and saw nothing out of the ordinary, but the discomfort she felt didn't dissolve.

She jerked when her phone vibrated in her pocket again with an unknown number.

"What's wrong?" Maddey asked.

Jordan worried her bottom lip between her teeth, a clear sign something was bothering her. "I don't know, I just feel like somebody is watching me."

Maddey's protective instincts took over. She scanned the crowd for anyone paying special attention to them but nothing seemed amiss. As her gaze scanned over the crowd one more time, she saw Ryan and the guys looking down at them from up in the VIP section.

"Well there's the cause for you feeling watched." She pointed up to where the guys were standing.

She followed Maddey's hand and saw her brothers, Jake, and Tucker standing by the railing watching them. When they noticed the girls saw them the jerks waved.

She turned her attention back to the Yankee game and away from her annoyingly overprotective brothers. However, even knowing they were looking down on them, the prickles at the back of her neck did not ease.

The atmosphere in the bar changed completely when the Yankees loaded the bases. The energy was almost palpable, it seemed like everyone in the bar now had their attention on the TVs to see what would happen, Sammy even lowered the music. When Johnson hit a long foul ball deep into left field the whole place groaned in unison. Four pitches later, Johnson was pitched a high fast ball over the middle of the plate and hit a rocket straight out to center field for a deep grand slam. The bar cheered, thanks to Johnson's home run the Yankees now had the lead.

"Oh my god, wait, did we just win our game?" Jordan asked.

Maddey pulled her phone back out to see if the scores updated. "Let's see we get a point for the hit."

"Three points for the homerun."

"A point for each RBI so that's four points there."

"And a point for the run scored."

They went back and forth ticking off ways to earn points on their fingers.

"So what we're tied?" Maddey asked.

"Wait… no we won because in our league you get a bonus point for the grand slam."

"Nice!" They bumped fists and headed up to gloat.

THE GUYS STOOD sentry over the dance floor.

"They are quite the showstoppers aren't they?" Tucker said from his perch next to Ryan.

Ryan looked over at his friend. "What do you mean?"

"I mean," he pointed out to the dance floor below, "look at how every guy around them is angling themselves towards them and watching them like the bright blonde beacons that they are."

Jake scrutinized the people around where the girls were dancing, and sure enough they had the attention of every guy within a ten foot radius.

He observed Ryan's tense shoulders and white knuckled

grip on the railing. "Do you want to go down there?" He asked Ryan.

Ryan seemed to mull over his question and shook his head. "No they seem to be okay, if there's any trouble we're close enough."

Jake watched as the guys down below drooled over the girl he was starting to think of as his own and wished he could make it known to the world.

"We could go down there if you want. It wouldn't be suspicious if we both danced with her," Tucker offered.

"Nah man, it's cool. But thanks." He clapped his friend on the back. Tuck always had his back, time wouldn't change that.

The girls made their way over to the bar to watch the excitement taking place in the Yankee game. Maddey pointed in their direction and Jordan sent them all a glare that could turn a person to stone.

"Umm, I think we should go sit down unless we want to suffer the wrath of Jordan when they come back up," Jase stated after Jordan's death stare.

"I think you're right," Ryan agreed.

The guys made their way over to the couches by the railing and settled in. A few moments later they were joined by a few puck bunnies and Tucker fell into full flirt mode.

"Nice, the Yanks look like they have a chance to take the lead," Jake said pointing to the game.

Just than Matthews drew a walk to load the bases. "Aww, man," Ryan complained.

"What's wrong? That's awesome, bases loaded with Johnson coming up and only one out, it's like the ideal situation," Jake said.

Ryan watched the game feeling torn between what he wanted to happen. "It's not that... it's just who I'm playing in our fantasy league has Johnson and I'm only up by a few points."

"Well if he just hits two runs in they will tie the game and you'll still win."

"Yeah, that's true."

Then Johnson hit a grand slam, putting the Yankees up by two runs and costing Ryan is fantasy baseball game. Jase burst out laughing and all Ryan could do was hang his head in shame.

Chapter Twenty-Five

J
ordan and Maddey made their way up the stairs to
the VIP section. As they got to the top Jordan made
sure she introduced Maddey to Don, the bouncer that
usually worked the VIP section, she didn't want
Maddey having any issues getting in on her own.

As they made their way past where the guys were sitting,
Jordan cringed at the company that the guys kept. Her reaction didn't go unnoticed. Maddey looked over to see that girls
were practically hanging off the guys and her own hackles
rose.

"Who are they?" Maddey asked, she was so unfamiliar
with most of Ryan's friends she didn't want to get defensive
for no reason.

Jordan rolled her eyes. "Puck bunnies."

Maddey almost gave herself whiplash as she turned back
to look at the girls. They were scantily dressed in dresses so
short they could have passed as t-shirts and hung all over the
guys like vines on a trellis.

"Do I have anything to worry about?"

She stopped walking and went to put her arm around
Maddey's waist in comfort. "No, there's nothing to worry

about. When it comes to puck bunnies it's more of an annoyance than a problem." She paused and looked the girls over. "I've seen them around before but you probably wouldn't have paid much attention to them. I've been dealing with their kind for years so I can pick them out of a crowd. Don't worry we can handle them."

They approached the bar and Skye was grinning at them. "Great game right?" She said pointing to the TV.

"Yup, we won our fantasy game too," Maddey replied.

Skye paused mid pour of the drink she was making. "Wait," she held up a hand for emphasis, "weren't you guys playing Ryan this week?"

"Yup," Jordan answered.

"Oh that's rough." Skye reached down and pulled a beer from the cooler. "Here he's going to need this."

The girls shared a laugh. "Make it six would ya? We'll bring all the guys one."

Skye placed five more beers on the bar and went to go help actual customers. She and Maddey each picked up three of the beers and made their way over to where the guys were sitting.

The VIP section was almost full for the night. Most of the hockey team was scattered throughout as well as other people with VIP wristbands. The lounge couches where their guys sat were the largest of all the couches and surrounded a long coffee table. But looking at how the puck bunnies were sitting in reference to the guys one would have thought they were sitting at the smallest of the couches because they left no personal space between themselves and the guys.

As they made their approach, they received glares from the puck bunnies. She rolled her eyes and cast a quick glance to Maddey, she was used to how the puck bunnies acted but Maddey wasn't, she just hoped her friend didn't let them get to her.

She went to sit on the arm of the couch next to Jase and

handed both him and Jake a beer. When Jake reached out to take his beer his fingers brushed hers. She felt a jolt of heat from his unintentional touch but his wink proved it was deliberate.

After Maddey handed Tucker and Ryan a beer she remained standing. Jordan caught the look she sent Christine who sat obnoxiously close to Ryan.

"What's this all about?" Ryan asked.

"We figured you might need one," Maddey said with a smile.

"Oh yeah and why's that?"

Jordan answered. "You did just lose your fantasy game to your sister and your girlfriend, so we thought you could use a drink." She tipped her beer in his direction trying to goad him.

Beside her, Jase burst out laughing and clicked his beer with hers. They nudged each other and shared a silent conversation.

"Damn that's gotta hurt man," Tucker said around the puck bunny in his lap, barely keeping his own laughter in check.

"Yeah yeah yeah. Laugh it up." Ryan noticed how Maddey still stood while she watched the girls with trepidation. He reached out and grabbed her gently by the wrist. "Come here." He pulled her onto his lap and she settled in with a giggle. The action pushed Christine away.

"You're in more than one league Ry?" Jake asked. He was surprisingly impressed by Jordan and Maddey's baseball knowledge to not only be in a fantasy league but to also win.

"No just the one." Ryan mumbled from where he nuzzled Maddey's neck.

"Come on just because I'm ok with you dating my best friend doesn't mean I want to be subjected to your PDA," Jordan groaned.

Tucker looked completely lost in the fantasy baseball

conversation. "Wait so that would mean you guys are in our fantasy league?"

"Yeah and you've all played us," Jordan supplied.

"So what team are you guys?"

"The Virginia Jays."

"Why would you pick Virginia?" Jake asked.

"Because if you shorten it, it's the V.A. Jays."

"As in vajays," Maddey added.

The guys just looked completely lost. "As in vajay jay because we are girls… come on it's not that difficult to put together." She shook her head for emphasis.

"Wait that's what it stands for?" Ryan asked.

Maddey laughed and patted Ryan's cheek. "You are so lucky you're cute." Sometimes guys could be so clueless.

AS SOON AS the guys settled into their usual couches, they were joined by a group of puck bunnies. Unfortunately for Jake the group included Tabby.

The chick was like a damn cold sore always popping up. He wasn't the only one brushing off advances, Ryan was also the recipient of unwanted attention with Christine trying to sit practically in his lap.

When Jordan and Maddey rejoined them, the atmosphere charged with hostility. The guys shifted their attention to them, their closeness evident.

"Wait a second, I lost to you guys two weeks ago." Tucker said looking up from his phone.

Jordan let out a laugh. "It's okay BB3. The only team we haven't beaten is Jake's." She looked over in Jake's direction.

Jake made eye contact with Jordan at her comment and electricity sparked between them. He made sure he smiled big enough to reveal his dimples, he could tell they affected her.

"I guess I'm the only one man enough not to lose to a couple of girls." He took a long swallow of his beer.

Tabby ran her hand over his bicep. "I'll say you're man enough alright."

He visibly flinched at Tabby's touch. "Thanks, Tabby." He reached over and removed her hand from where she was feeling him up.

Tabby was a cute girl and they had gone on two dates, however there was no spark for him. He told her so the week before at the party at the hockey house. She was always touchy feely but she seemed to turn it up a notch when Jordan and Maddey arrived. Normally he could brush it off as an annoyance but now he didn't want Jordan to get the wrong impression. Like things weren't complicated enough already.

As much as it pained him to miss out on an opportunity to spend time with Jordan, he got up to hang with some of the guys across the room.

Jordan watched, with growing irritation, the girl Tabby, who if she remembered correctly Jake had dated, constantly put her hands on him. To his credit he tried to avoid her as much as possible. But now she had *officially* reached her limit.

It was bad enough being around him and her brothers, especially with him looking like a Greek God spread out on the couch, but having to watch some girl hang all over him without her being able to do anything about it was downright cruel.

She needed a break. She got up and went to see Skye at the bar. Skye caught the pained look on her face. "What's wrong?"

"Puck bunnies," she answered on a sigh.

Skye breathed out a sigh of relief, she knew she was used

to dealing with puck bunnies. "Is that it? Geez you had me worried for a sec. You've been dealing with puck bunnies for years I'm sure you can handle these bitches."

She laughed, leave it to Skye to make her smile. "Yeah the only difference is the last time I had to deal with an obnoxious puck bunny, I had a right to stake my claim and say back off but now I can't do that."

"You're referring to Jake, aren't you?"

"Bingo!"

"So what are you going to do?"

"I have no idea." She shook her head for emphasis. "But for now I'm going downstairs, I just have to get away from all this for awhile."

She made her way away from the bar and toward the stairs leading to the main level. Before she could make it down a step Jase called out to her.

"JD, where ya going?"

"Just downstairs for a little while."

"Do you want me to come with you?" Maddey offered.

She could tell Maddey still wasn't sure how to handle the puck bunnies, as much as she would like the company she couldn't create stress for her friend.

"No. I'm gonna see if Aunt Ei needs help with anything. I'll be back soon."

As she turned to face the stairs, she instinctively looked in Jake's direction and instantly regretted it. Tabby followed him when he moved earlier and was trying to trail her hand down his chest. She steeled her expression against the boiling jealousy she felt and practically fled down the stairs.

Aunt Ei was easy to find, with her short black hair spiked in funky angles, and her referee style staff shirt, one could say she stood out.

"Hey Aunt Ei," she yelled over the increasing music.

"Hi Sweetheart." Her aunt enveloped her in a huge hug. "What's up?"

She leaned against the bar next to her aunt. "Oh nothing, just getting away from Tweedledee and Tweedledum for a while."

Eileen nodded knowingly. "I have some stuff I have to get done in the office, so I'll see you later."

"Okay, bye." They kissed each other on the cheek and Aunt Eileen set out toward the back of the bar where her office was located.

She looked over the dance floor and the people that filled it. When she caught sight of the hottie in the blue shirt, she let out an inward groan. Her feelings and attraction for Jake clouded everything else, normally she would go over and flirt with him but all she wanted was Jake. It was infuriating.

Still not sure how she was going to handle things, she made her way to the restrooms to splash water on her face. On her way there she walked past a couple making out, jealous of their public display of affection.

A few minutes later she emerged from the restroom, head down in concentration. Without warning she was pulled back by her ponytail and slammed into the wall behind her. Before she could react a hand came around her neck in a chokehold and she got her first glimpse of her attacker. Her eyes widened in shock. "*Tommy!*" She gasped out.

"Hey Sweetness." Tommy said with a sadistic smile right before his lips came crashing down onto hers.

Chapter Twenty-Six

J ake, finally free of Tabby, was able to rejoin the guys and Maddey. Currently they were laughing at a story Maddey told from when she, Jordan, Sammy, and Skye were at NYU. He was taking in everything he could learn about Jordan so he could use it to his advantage.

As if he heard them talking about him, Sammy came running toward them. "Hey Sammy."

Taking in Sammy's panicked expression Maddey could tell something wasn't right. "Sammy what's wrong?"

"Where's Jordan?"

"Downstairs, why?" Ryan asked.

Jake watched Jase tense as if he got an unsettling feeling in his gut— something wasn't right. His friend turned to look over at the dance floor below but didn't see his sister.

"Okay, I know this is going to sound crazy and all," Sammy paused. "But I could have sworn I saw Tommy."

The group immediately came to attention.

"Are you sure?" Ryan asked.

"As sure as I can be. I've only ever seen pictures of the guy but still."

Ryan and Jase were already up and moving toward the

stairs as they spoke. "It's not good if he's here, he's supposed to be banned from the premises. We have to find Jordan before he does."

"We're coming to help," Jake said as he moved toward the stairs with Tucker.

"Me too." Maddey said.

Ryan whirled in Maddey's direction. "No, absolutely *not*."

"And why not?" Maddey placed her hands on her hips. "She's my best friend, and I know what this asshole did to her. I want to help."

Ryan's fierce expression softened at Maddey's explanation. He walked over to stand in front of her and lifted a hand to cup her cheek. "Babe, I need you to stay up here, please?"

"Why? I could be an extra set of eyes."

"I can't go looking for Jordan while I'm worried about something happening to you." He stopped her when she was about to interrupt. "You and Jordan look so much alike. What if he goes after you thinking you're her. I can't worry about that. *Please*, stay up here."

"He has a point," Jake added.

"Okay fine, but hurry up," Maddey relented.

"Thank you." Ryan breathed out a sigh of relief and with a quick kiss the guys headed down the stairs.

They decided to split up into two teams. Jake went with Ryan and Sammy. Jase and Tucker made up the other group. He was grateful Sammy joined in the search instead of going back to the DJ booth. It was always good to have a guy of his size on their side in a fight.

Jake's main objective was to find Jordan and make sure she was safe, once he did that then he could deal with Tommy Bradford.

He heart felt like it was going to beat right out of his chest from the adrenaline pumping through his system.

He had to find Jordan and make sure she was okay. She was his, whether or not she admitted it out loud, there was a bond between them and he'd be damned if he was going to let anything happen to her.

Jordan, where are you?

JORDAN STRUGGLED AGAINST the hold on her hair. Before she had time to react, she was slammed into the wall behind her, the breath knocked from her body. She tried to get her bearings. Once she was able to see who threw her into the wall her heart fell out of her stomach.

Tommy!

Oh shit how did he get in here?

After what happened two years ago Tommy was banned from Rookies, so his presence in the bar was not a good sign. Proven by the fact he now had her pinned against the wall and looked at her with an evil look in his eyes.

She struggled against Tommy's hold; he had her lower body pinned with his legs and his right hand around her throat. She fought against his attempts to shove his tongue down her throat.

Tommy was currently running his free hand over her torso painfully groping her. She tried to push him off of her but due to his size and her current lack of oxygen it was like trying to push a brick wall.

She needed to think and regroup. How did he get into Rookies? She was seriously in danger of passing out if she didn't get oxygen into her lungs ASAP. Trying to break his chokehold was unsuccessful, but if she could just get her mouth free… she bit down on his bottom lip with all her might and didn't let up until he pulled away and she could taste blood.

Her small triumph was quickly deflated when she caught the sadistic look lurking in his eyes. He touched his fingers to his lips to wipe away the blood. "Sweetness, if I knew you liked it rough like that, we could have had some fun."

He squeezed her left boob for emphasis and she cringed in pain.

She looked around for anyone who could help, but his tight hold on her throat barely allowed for breathing let alone screaming. She cursed Tommy's evil brilliance to attack her in one of the few blind spots in Rookies. A person would have to be actively looking around to find them.

She had one last fleeting thought and it was of Jake. Maybe if she'd had the courage to say something to her brothers and started dating Jake, she wouldn't be in this position. *Oh god Jake I'm so sorry I was an idiot.*

As if thinking of Jake summoned him, she could have sworn she saw him in the distance. Still struggling against Tommy's hold on her throat, she craned her head to the left to try and see better.

Jake! Oh my god it really is Jake.

She wondered why he wasn't coming over to help her and realized he couldn't see her around Tommy's assault. She made one last feeble attempt at pushing Tommy off and prayed Jake saw.

JAKE FRANTICALLY LOOKED around the bar for Jordan. The only blonde with a ponytail he saw was making out with a guy by the bathrooms and he knew that couldn't be her. He ran his gaze back over the dance floor hoping to catch a glimpse of her, but no such luck.

A flicker of movement by the bathrooms caught his eye and he could have sworn he saw the couple that was making out struggle. He looked over in their direction and almost had a heart attack.

The girl was Jordan.

Oh!

My!

God!

Her pleading, terrified eyes found his and instinctively he started in their direction. As a second thought he called to Ryan so he would have backup but didn't waste any time waiting for him to join before making his move.

The bastard had her by her throat while she struggled. He had to give the guy credit, the location he picked was perfect, shielding his assault from any onlookers.

With the walls forming a corner it created an alcove and the overhang from the VIP section upstairs cast shadows all around. Plus most people would think it was somewhere couples would go to have a little more privacy, like he himself originally assumed was going on.

As Jake made his approach, he weighed his chances against the guy one-on-one. They were around the same height and size, but Jake had the upper hand, this asshole was messing with Jordan, and no one messed with someone Jake loved.

Loved?

Well hell.

It was inevitable. Since the first night they met he had felt an instant connection to her so it was only a matter of time before his feelings followed. He was done waiting for her to come around, he was going to prove to Jordan that they belonged together, everyone else be damned.

He grabbed Tommy by the back of the neck and pulled him off Jordan. Instantly Jordan slumped down to the floor and Jake knelt in front of her.

"Jordan, are you okay?" He cupped her face in his left hand and stroked her cheek with his thumb.

With all of his attention focused on Jordan, he missed Tommy coming up behind him. He abruptly became aware of him when he was yanked back by the collar of his shirt. Caught off guard, Tommy was able to land a right hook to his face. He countered with his own left hook, dodged Tommy's next punch and shoved him backwards.

Before the other guys were able to arrive, Tommy was able to escape.

Ryan was the first to arrive on the scene. Jake pointed in the direction where Tommy fled. "Go after him, I've got her."

Ryan nodded in agreement and took off to find Tommy.

He turned his attention back to Jordan who was still slumped on the floor. He quickly took in her appearance; her shirt was askew, tears running down her cheeks, and her neck was red and swollen. *Are those fingerprints?* It took everything in him to stay with her and not go back to give Tommy a piece of his mind in the form of his fists.

Jordan still wouldn't talk to him. He needed to get her out of there. He was sure she would need to talk to someone, the police perhaps, about what happened here but for now she was in no shape to do so. He adjusted her shirt and slid an arm under her knees and one around her shoulders to pick her up off the floor.

Jordan relaxed into the cradle of his arms, resting her hand against his chest.

Normally he would be happy to hold her in his arms but all he was able to feel was fury at what had happened to her.

The rest of the guys arrived as he tended to Jordan.

"I'm taking her home." His tone brokered no room for argument.

Jordan needed to rest, there was no way he was letting her stay at the bar. If anyone wanted to talk to her they could do it tomorrow, not tonight.

To Jake's surprise Jase nodded. "Okay but take her to the hockey house just in case. We're gonna try and find him."

"Okay. Ryan took off earlier. It looked like Tommy was making a run for it."

The guys took off to join in the search for Tommy.

With that settled he strode through the bar with Jordan in his arms.

Chapter Twenty-Seven

J ake carried Jordan the whole way to his car. The rain
that started falling earlier in the evening had picked
up in to a steady downpour.

Jordan stared blankly out the window, the pouring
rain seemed to fit her mood perfectly. The rain was coming
down so hard by the time they made it to the car, her clothes
were already soaked through. She couldn't stop herself from
shaking but wasn't sure if it was from the cold or the terror.

Out of nowhere she flinched when Jake touched her with
a sweatshirt. She felt guilty about her reaction to his touch but
too much was bouncing around in her head for her to focus
on that now.

It was the first time she'd seen Tommy since what
happened two years ago. And things hadn't changed much,
that same crazed look was still in his eyes.

How did he get into Rookies?

JAKE CARRIED JORDAN the entire way to his Jeep. He
could feel the shivers raking her body as they were pelted
with rain. Once inside the car he reached into the backseat for

the sweatshirt he usually left there and handed it to her causing her to flinch.

Seeing her reaction to his touch had him reaching for the steering wheel to curb his anger. He needed it to ground himself so he didn't run off and join the search for Tommy Bradford. *She* was his priority.

He took in how extremely pale she was and watched as tremors coursed through her body. He was so angry by how scared that prick made her feel that he swore he could feel steam coming out of his ears. Forcibly pushing down his frustration and anger, he started the car. He watched as she pulled the sweatshirt over her arms and took a calming breath. He thought she still looked too pale and could see slight shivers flow through her body. He wanted to reach out and comfort her, but now was not the time or the place.

He pulled out of his parking spot, grateful he only drank two beers during the course of the night. The urgency to get her home and someplace safe coursed through his bloodstream. He made it back to the hockey house in record time, even with periodically checking the rearview mirror to make sure they weren't followed. Who knew where Tommy made off to when he ran away.

He pulled into the driveway and parked the car. He needed to get her inside and taken care of. After that however, they needed to talk. It was obvious from what just happened there was more to the story she had told him.

The biggest issue would be the amount of time he would have alone with her. He wasn't sure how long it would be until the guys arrived back at the house so his time to uncover the truth and rein in his own chaotic emotions could be vastly limited.

He was out of the Jeep and halfway to the front door before he realized she wasn't behind him. As he ran back to the Jeep he could feel the ice cold rain trickle down the back of his t-shirt, causing a shiver to run down his spine. When he opened the door for her she made no move to get out, obviously still in shock from the night's events. Instead of letting them get even more soaked by the rain by waiting for her to move, he scooped her back up into the cradle of his arms, again enjoying the feel of her there, and carried her into the house.

Once inside the house he placed her on the couch in the living room, not caring her clothes were wet from the rain. When he went to pull away she tightened her hold around his neck and pulled him closer to her.

"Jordan, sweetheart, it's okay. I'm just going to go upstairs and get us some dry clothes, we both got soaked in the downpour," he consoled her as he eased her arms from around his neck. It was harder than he thought it would be to let her go but he knew it wouldn't be good for them to sit around in wet clothes.

He took the stairs two at a time to get to Tucker's room where he left his duffle bag earlier. As he pulled out dry clothes, his cell phone rang, its music cutting into the eerie silence of the room. He wasn't going to answer but he saw Ryan's name on the caller ID.

"Hey man, what's happening?" He asked Ryan right away.

Ryan didn't waste any time on pleasantries. "Some of the guys are out looking for Tommy. Jase and I are going to try and figure out how he even got in. Everyone knows he's banned from the premises so it doesn't make any sense but..." he trailed off taking a deep breath to get his anger back under control. "How's Jordan doing?"

Jake was in the process of trading his wet jeans for dry basketball shorts so it took him a second to reply. "She's shaken up. We got soaked in the rain so I'm grabbing some dry clothes for her to change into and then I was going to talk to her."

"If you need any clothes just take some from one of my drawers."

"It's okay, I have an extra t-shirt and sweats in my bag so I have her covered. Hang on a sec." He put the phone down while he peeled his soaked t-shirt off and put on a dry one. He went into the bathroom to hang his wet clothes up to dry.

It was good Ryan called because now he could find out how much time he had with Jordan before the cavalry arrived. "So when do you guys think you're going to be getting back?"

He could hear Ryan talking to someone else in the background. "Actually we're not. Jase, Maddey, and I are going to go back to my parents' house. My mom is freaking out."

"She knows what happened?"

"Oh yeah my aunt called her after everything went down."

"Do you want me to bring Jordan home now?"

"No. Tommy doesn't know our parents moved and we want to keep it that way. It's one thing if he found the new hockey house but we can't compromise our home." Again Ryan broke to speak to someone else. "Plus Skye and Maddey think Jordan needs time to decompress on her own before everyone starts hurling questions at her. As much as Jase and I want to be there, I think they have a point."

"That's probably a good idea. She still seems a little bit in shock and keeps rubbing her left shoulder."

Ryan took a deep breath. "I was afraid of that." He paused. "There's Advil and Miracle Ice in the medicine cabinet downstairs, give her some and she should be okay. I'll keep you posted on what happens and call you in the morning... and Jake..."

"Yeah Ry?"

"Take care of her, okay?"

"You got it bro, no worries."

He ended the call and ran a towel over his hair. He headed

downstairs relieved to have the night with Jordan but still concerned about her. When he got back to the living room, she hadn't moved from the position he had left her in.

He bent down in front of her and placed his hands on her knees. She was trembling.

He reached out a hand to cup her jaw. "Hey." He waited until she looked at him. "I brought you a towel to dry off with and some dry clothes to change into."

"Thank you."

"Hey." He said to get her attention again. "You're safe now. You know that, right?"

"Yeah, I know."

"Okay, good. Now go change, you're making the couch all wet."

JORDAN SAT ON the couch unable to move. She wasn't sure how much time had passed when Jake placed his hands on her knees.

She was still trembling but at Jake's touch she uncurled her legs from underneath her and looked up into his green eyes. The concern she saw in them caused the fog of shock to clear a little.

He traced the line of her jaw with his thumb and the warmth that radiated from his touch felt great against her cold skin. He was so thoughtful and caring all the time, she wasn't sure how much longer she would be able to resist him. She couldn't take the worry she saw lingering in his gaze so she looked away again. "Thank you," she said as an afterthought, she didn't want to be rude.

"Hey." He said to get her attention again. "You're safe now. You know that, right?"

She tried to tell herself that she knew she was safe because she was at the hockey house and Tommy didn't know where this one was located but she knew that wasn't the complete truth. It was Jake's presence that made her feel safe. Back at Rookies, even with Tommy a few feet away, once Jake showed up she knew she would be safe.

"Yeah, I know."

"Okay good. Now go change you're making the couch all wet."

She got up from the couch and picked up the clothes he gave her. Before she went to change, she turned to face him again and placed her hand on his arm. "Thanks Jake, for rescuing me and… everything else."

She gave him a brief smile trying to convey her emotions.

"Don't look at me like that." His voice sounded pained.

"Like what?"

"Like you want me to kiss you."

"Maybe I do," she said on a breath.

"Damn it babe." He cursed before closing the distance between them. He reached out and pulled her in for a kiss.

One would think after being pinned and restrained by Tommy earlier in the night, having Jake holding her face would freak her out but it didn't. He was her safe place. She kissed him back with everything in her until he pulled away.

"Go change," he told her, his voice thick with emotion.

Still reeling from what had just happened it took her a moment to move. As soon as she got her bearings she turned on her heel and escaped to the safety of the bathroom. Once inside she threw the clothes and the towel on the floor and braced her hands on the sink. Putting her head down, she took a few deep breaths to regain her equilibrium and thought about what had happened.

She took in her appearance in the mirror taking note she was still a little pale. She pulled the ponytail holder from her hair. Picking up the towel she threw on the ground, she blotted her hair dry and then ran her fingers through it to make it look semi-presentable.

The sweats were clearly Jake's because they were too wide

and way too long. After pulling them on she had to tie the drawstring as tight as it would go and had to pull the ends of them up over her feet. The t-shirt wasn't any better but the well worn cotton material felt soft against her skin. She noticed that it had Jake's hockey number on it and smiled at her appearance. Dressed in too big sweats with a too large t-shirt with his number printed on it, she looked like how a girlfriend would look.

As quickly as her smile appeared it vanished. Any hope of broaching the subject of dating Jake with her brothers was shot to hell by Tommy's attack. She also knew the abridged version of her history was no longer going to fly. Jake was too smart to not think she left something out.

The main reason why she didn't want to tell Jake the whole story of what happened with Tommy was selfish. She loved the way he looked at her and she was afraid once he knew the truth, the look he gave her would become filled with pity instead.

Steeling herself for the conversation she knew she was about to have, she left the bathroom and went back to the living room. She found him lounging back on the couch looking way too sexy in basketball shorts and a white hockey t-shirt than should be legal. Taking another deep breath for fortification she went over to sit next to him on the couch.

WHILE JAKE WAITED for Jordan to finish changing, he opened the windows in the living room and the back door that led to the patio. He hoped the sound of the rain would be relaxing. He still wasn't sure how she was going to react to what had happened at the bar. Her wanting him to kiss her sure shocked the hell out of him.

Tommy assaulting Jordan at Rookies clued him in on the fact that there was more to what happened between them in the past than him just hitting her. He *needed* to know.

He heard her return from the bathroom but waited for her to sit down before he looked at her. She pulled her legs underneath her and tucked her feet underneath her butt. His clothes were swimming on her but he couldn't help but smile at how cute she looked. Her hair hung around her face half wet, half dry but she looked completely adorable. He personally liked the fact that she was wearing his hockey t-shirt looking for all the world like she was his girlfriend, which little did she know she soon would be.

He could see bruises forming on her neck where that bastard had grabbed her. He reached for the Advil and water bottle he left on the table and she took it without question.

He waited until after she swallowed the pills to speak. "I also grabbed Miracle Ice and an actual ice pack if you want to put it on your shoulder. I saw you rubbing it earlier."

"Thanks, I hit it when I was pushed against the wall."

His nostrils flared at the statement. "How's your neck?" He asked through gritted teeth.

She placed a hand on the side of her neck feeling how tender it was. "It's a little sore."

He knew she wasn't telling the whole truth. "It's starting to bruise pretty badly." He took an ice pack off the coffee table, smacked it against his leg to activate it, and held it out for her to take.

Taking the ice pack from him, she placed it against her neck and winced at the sudden coldness.

They sat in silence for a couple of minutes while they waited for the Advil to kick in. When she settled deeper into the couch he decided to speak.

"So now are you gonna tell me what really happened between you and that jackass, Tommy?"

When she went to pull away, he pulled her legs across his lap on the couch, hoping his touch would be soothing.

"Okay, fine, but you have to promise not to think differently of me. I don't want your pity."

"Jordan, I keep trying to tell you how I feel about you. How could you even think that I would see you differently because of something that asshole did to you?"

"Do you want to hear what happened or not?" She asked.

"You know I do."

"Okay then promise, no pity."

"Okay."

Chapter Twenty-Eight

J ordan sat up against the arm of the couch more, gearing up to tell him exactly what had happened that fateful night. There were only a handful of people who knew what actually happened that night and now she was about to let Jake fully into the fold. As much as she was afraid to have him look at her differently if he knew, she had to trust him with this.

"So I already told you I caught Tommy cheating on me."

He shook his head. "I still don't understand how someone could cheat on you."

"I also told you he hit me. But I may have underplayed the facts."

"Okay, keep going."

The hockey team was having the end of school year party. She was in the dining room playing beer pong with Jase like usual. The team was excited about gaining Jase as a member of the team in the fall so they were already trying to haze him.

The only thing that would have made the coming fall better was if she was attending Brighton Tynes. Instead, she and Skye were going to NYU. It was a bittersweet feeling. Sure she was super excited to go to NYU but by being in New York she wouldn't get to spend as much time with the team as she had been able to this past year.

In the current game of beer pong they were playing, all she had to do was hit the last cup and the game would be theirs. She lined up her shot and blocked out all the harassment she was receiving from the guys and sunk the cup.

"Yes! I love being your partner sis." Jase picked her up in a huge hug.

"Thank you, thank you," she said taking a bow.

"Come on JD, rematch, best two out of three?" Billy demanded while he gave her a noogie on top of her head.

"Dude watch the hair," she said as she pulled away. Glancing at her watch, she sighed as she noticed how long Tommy had been missing. "Sure, just give me a minute, I want to find Tommy. Somebody has to protect me from noogies because clearly my own brothers aren't up to the job." She sent a glare in Ryan's direction.

"Hey what did I do?" Ryan said holding his hands up in surrender.

"Nothing." She shook her head and went off in search of her missing boyfriend.

She didn't find Tommy in the kitchen or the living room so she decided to see if he was upstairs. Once upstairs she noticed the door to Tommy's room was cracked open, which was odd because the guys normally kept their doors closed during a party. She figured that's where he had to be.

As she pushed open the door she wasn't prepared for what she found. Tommy, on his bed shirtless, with his hand up some brunette puck bunny's skirt.

She was completely out of her element.

She stood there, jaw open, at a complete loss for words. She must have made a noise at some point because the brunette looked up and tapped Tommy until he looked in her direction.

Finally she came to her senses. "We're so over," she said as she turned to walk out of the room

Before she could make it anywhere Tommy grabbed her by the

arm and pushed her against the wall. The breath whooshed out of her lungs and her head bounced against the wall.

"What do you mean we're over?" Tommy screamed in her face.

She lifted a hand to her head, still trying to recover from the hit she took. After she checked to make sure there was no blood, she looked up into Tommy's eyes and gasped at how crazed he looked.

"It means," she paused to take a deep breath, "if you want to fool around with other girls, you're done fooling around with me." She pushed away from the wall and moved to get around him.

Abruptly Tommy backhanded her across the face and her head banged against the wall again. "We're done when I say we're done," he screamed in her face.

What the what?

It took a moment for her head to clear. She swallowed down the panic threatening to overwhelm her at how vulnerable she currently was. "That's not how it works Tommy. I'm not going to be with someone that cheats on me. I'm gonna be with a guy who treats me right and that clearly isn't you anymore so goodbye. *Now get your* fucking *hands off me."*

She jerked out of his hold and moved toward the stairs to head back down to her brothers but Tommy was quicker. He grabbed her by the back of her shirt and jerked her against his larger body.

"You don't get to leave me you little bitch. *If I can't have you no one can!" Tommy punctuated his statement by promptly shoving her down the stairs.*

She hit the middle of the staircase hard on her left shoulder causing it to dislocate. As she continued to tumble down the stairs, she smacked her head at the bottom before she crumpled to the floor.

The guys heard the commotion coming from the stairs and went to see what was going on. They weren't prepared for what they found. Jordan was hunched over on the floor and Tommy was standing at the top of the stairs. Automatically Jase ran to where she was lying on the floor.

Her twin knelt next to where she laid crumpled on the floor. He wasn't sure if he should touch her or not so he just let his hands hover above her. "Jordan, are you alright?" He asked, concern evident in his voice.

She struggled to sit up when Jase reached her side. She touched her right hand to the spot on her head just above her eye and when she pulled it back it came away with blood— a lot of blood. She looked from her hand to her brother's horrified expression. By this point Skye and Nick had also reached her side.

"Oh my god is that blood?"

"Are you hurt?"

"Is anything broken?"

"What happened?"

The questions all came at her once. She wasn't quite sure who asked what. She looked up the stairs at Tommy and shuddered when she realized he seriously just tried to kill her.

Ryan noticed Tommy still hadn't come to see if she was okay and when he saw the terrified look on her face he knew Tommy was responsible for her fall.

"Someone call the cops and an ambulance," he shouted as he ran up the stairs.

Some of the guys caught on to what Ryan had figured out and went to help him with Tommy.

"So I went to the hospital, got my eyebrow stitched up and my shoulder popped back into its socket. The cops came to take my statement. Tommy's dad is a big time lawyer so he only ended up having to pay a fine and got two years probation. When the school found out, coach kicked him off the team and the school expelled him." She concluded her story and waited for his reaction.

JAKE SAT THERE stunned. He couldn't even fathom what she had been through. Never in a million years would he have guessed it. He had assumed there was more to her story, but this, *hell* no.

After the initial shock wore off, he realized he still had to respond to her revelation. She sat with her arms folded across her chest, as if trying to hold herself together. She looked as if she were awaiting the arrival of the firing squad instead of waiting for his reaction. Her furrowed brow brought his attention to her eyes and part of what she told him suddenly clicked into place.

He reached out and ran the thumb of his right hand across her left eyebrow. "Is that how you got this scar?"

She nodded her head in answer.

His expression instantly hardened. "Son of a bitch," he growled. "That bastard is lucky I didn't know this earlier otherwise he wouldn't have made it out of the bar tonight."

He was relieved to see her smile at his statement. True, what had happened to her with Tommy was *terrible* but he didn't want her to use it as a barrier between them. He moved his hand from her face to the back of her neck and started to tug her toward him. "Come here."

She allowed him to pull her over to cuddle into the crook of his arm, letting out a sigh once she was in position.

He positioned her with her legs draped across his and the rest of her resting alongside his body.

He used his free hand to angle her face up to his. As he spoke he ran his thumb across her cheek. "Wow that was easier than I thought it would be." He smiled revealing his breathtaking dimples.

"What was?"

"Getting you into my arms."

"Oh." She looked down when she spoke.

He was having none of that. After the night's events and learning the truth of her breakup, he was done letting her push him away. He didn't care if they had to keep their relationship a secret or not, as long as they both knew they were together.

He pushed her chin back up with his finger and before she could stop him, he kissed her long and deep.

This kiss was different. Earlier when she asked him to kiss her, he was hesitant, not wanting to remind her of being attacked. But when she kissed him back, he cradled her head in his large hands and deepened the kiss.

"This is insane," she said when once she found her voice.

The left side of his mouth hitched up into smile. "What is?"

"That I'm making-out with you on a couch in the middle of the hockey house."

"It's awesome, right?"

"No." She paused to shove him in the chest. "It's not awesome... what if my brothers walked in while you had your tongue down my throat, then what?"

"I told you earlier they aren't coming back to the house?"

"You did?"

"Yeah. You must have really been out of it." His smile took on a devilish quality. "And if I'm not mistaken you were the one with their tongue down my throat."

"Details, details."

There was a long moment of silence. Eventually, Jake broached the subject he was nervous about. "So... where does all this leave us?"

"I have no idea." She sighed. "All I know is I can't keep my distance anymore."

"Finally!" He punctuated his statement with a quick kiss and then reached over and turned on the TV.

With a soft laugh she settled back against him and within a few minutes fell asleep.

Chapter Twenty-Nine

J ake was woken up by the ringing of a cell phone. He reached his arm behind him to grab his iPhone before it woke up Jordan. He wasn't going to answer it but when he saw Ryan's name on the caller ID he knew he should.

"Hello," he answered.

"Hey man, how's she doing?" Ryan asked right away.

He looked down toward the sleeping Jordan and smiled. They watched a little late night TV to unwind after the stressful events and eventually the two of them fell asleep right there on the couch. At some point in the night he pulled the throw blanket from on top of the couch over them. Currently Jordan's head rested on his chest and the rest of her was stretched out down his body. He should feel guilty for deceiving his friends but things between him and Jordan were too right for him to feel anything but happiness.

"Okay I guess... she's sleeping right now." He slid himself out from underneath Jordan's body and did his best not to disturb her. She stirred a little when he moved but she quickly settled into the pillow he vacated.

He stood there for a moment watching her sleep. Some of

her hair fell across her face when she shifted positions. He reached out to tuck it back behind her ear.

As he watched her sleep, he couldn't help but smile at the fact that she wasn't putting up any barriers between them anymore.

He made his way into the kitchen to finish his conversation with Ryan. "So what's happening?"

"My parents were planning on having a barbeque today so we're gonna have the guys from the team over. Also Maddey's parents will be there and her dad offered to be our liaison with the local police, so Jordan can give her statement to him instead of having to go down to the station."

"Sounds good. I'm sure Jordan will want to head home after she wakes up."

Ryan hesitated before he answered. "Well that's actually the reason I'm calling you this early." He paused again. "Jase and I realized after last night that we can't keep the rest of the guys in the dark about what happened between JD and Tommy, so we want them to come over before she gets here so we can fill them in. And then later on we can fill you in."

"There's no need, Jordan told me what happened last night after we got back."

"She did?" The shock was clearly evident in Ryan's voice.

"Yeah."

"Like everything?"

"Everything."

"Everything *everything*?"

"Yeah."

"Wow."

"No kidding." He rummaged through the fridge for something to drink. He settled on the orange juice and poured himself a glass. "But do you think it's a good idea to keep Jordan out of the loop in all of this?"

"Probably not but I don't want her to have to relive it all

over again, so for now we keep her out of it and we'll suffer the consequences later on."

"You're a braver man than I." He replied on a laugh.

"Yeah… Anyway I told the guys to be here for one o'clock so try and keep her there until two if you can."

He looked at the clock on the microwave to see what time it was. Luckily it was already after noon so he figured he could handle two more hours. "I should be able to handle that."

"Thanks, bro."

"No problem, see ya later, man." He closed the phone and turned to make a cup of coffee.

JORDAN AWOKE TO the sound of Jake's voice and the smell of coffee coming from the kitchen. The pillow she was on smelled like him and she snuggled deeper into it thinking about the night before. The horror of her encounter with Tommy was still fresh in her mind. What pissed her off the most about last night was that right when she thought her life was getting back to normal, Tommy came around and messed everything up again. A part of her knew she would never be able to forget the crazed look he had in his eyes.

But then those images faded away and ones of her on the couch with Jake filled her mind. Him holding her close as she told him the truth of her past with Tommy, him leaning in to kiss her and her not stopping him, all followed by falling asleep practically on top of him.

She reached up and touched her lips to check if they were bruised from kissing Jake. They felt fine but she couldn't stop the smile that spread across her face at the memories of the night before. It amazed her how quickly the sheer terror of Tommy's assault faded around Jake. That's what he did for her. He was her safe place.

She meant what she said when she told him she was done

keeping her distance from him. She'd been thinking of ways to approach her brothers with the knowledge of her feelings toward one of their teammates and thought maybe, *possibly*, she could ease them into the idea. But after last night's fiasco she knew they would be even more protective than ever. If that was even possible.

She released a frustrated sigh and sat up. First things first, she had to find out where they actually stood in this mess.

She made her way into the kitchen and found Jake leaning against the counter, ankles crossed in to front of him, sipping a cup of coffee. She smiled and started to make her way over to the coffeemaker next to him.

"Hey beautiful," he said when she looked him in the eye.

"Hey yourself."

"Come here." He placed his coffee cup on the counter and opened his arms for her.

She took her cue from him and walked into his open arms. He quickly enfolded her into a tight embrace, hugging her to his chest and resting his chin on top of her head.

"What I wouldn't give to start everyday off just like this," he admitted into her hair.

"Jake…" She looked up at him, uncertainty swimming in her eyes.

"Hey…" He reached up to cup the side of her face with his right hand, running his thumb across her cheek, like he did so often. "What's wrong?"

The feel of his hand caressing her face felt so good she wanted to stay like that forever but she had to know what was really happening between them. She had never been a coward before, not even when facing Tommy, so she wasn't going to start now. This, whatever *this* was, was too important to chicken out of now. Swallowing past the lump in her throat, she looked into Jake's warm green eyes and asked the question she was afraid to ask.

"I was just trying to figure out what exactly is going on between us."

She felt his body exhale before he relaxed against the counter more. "We're together now, babe."

"But what does that mean?" She started worrying the corner of her lower lip.

"It means…" He broke off and pulled her into a kiss.

The kiss started off gentle but as Jake traced the seam of her lips, she opened up to him and once she did he deepened the kiss. After she was thoroughly kissed, he pulled away and finished what he was saying.

"That we're together now. I'm tired of people coming between us."

She was still reeling from his passionate kiss so it took a moment for her to answer. "But, Jake, my brothers weren't going to be thrilled to begin with that I like a member of the team, now after what happened last night with Tommy I'm sure they are going to be even more set against it."

"Jordan, baby, I have waited too long for you to let me in to let a little thing like your brothers stand in the way of me being with you now."

"But…"

He cut her off before she could finish. "No more buts. We are together now, in layman's terms, you're my girlfriend, I'm your boyfriend, that's all that matters. The rest are just details we'll figure out as we go along."

She could hear the determination in his voice and knew he was right. Since the moment they met she had been drawn to him. It felt right whenever she was with him so she knew he was worth the risk. But there was still one thing they had to clear up.

"We have to keep us a secret though until we figure out what to do about Ry and Jase."

"As long as I know you're mine, that's all that matters. The rest is just semantics."

Chapter Thirty

I t was after two o'clock when they pulled up in front of their houses. The block was lined with cars up and down both sides of it. Jordan climbed out of Jake's Jeep and looked at the activity going on at her house and leaned back against the passenger door.

"Why do I feel like I missed something really important?"

Jake couldn't help but laugh at the perplexed expression on her face. "Ryan called me this morning and said your parents were having a barbeque so they invited the team over as well."

"That explains all the cars." They made their way up to her front door. As they walked up the driveway she recognized a familiar car. "Looks like you're gonna meet my godfather today," she said pointing to the tricked out Viper parked behind her father's car.

Jake's smile was so big it looked like it was splitting his face in two. "I guess today is my lucky day. I get to wake up with my girl and meet my favorite goalie of all time. Does life get any better?"

She quickly turned around and swatted him in the chest.

"*Shhh,*" she hissed through her teeth. "Be careful with the whole 'my girl' stuff, the enemy is around."

He was too quick for her. Before she could pull her hand back, he grabbed her wrist and ran his thumb across the palm of her hand before letting go. As he released her hand he gave her a little wink.

Her only reaction was to roll her eyes and shake her head as she turned to open the front door.

As she made her way through the house she noticed the doors to the den were shut. Normally she would have checked out why they were closed but she had more important things to take care of first. She took a deep breath as she made her way toward the sliding glass doors in the back of the house. She could hear laughter and Aerosmith's *Mama Kin* coming from outside so she knew that's where she could find her parents.

Robert and Ruth Donnelly's summertime barbeques were legendary. They would handle all the usual holidays like Memorial Day, Fourth of July, and Labor Day, but they were also known for throwing random ones when they knew Rick was going to be around. But why of all days did they have to have one while she had bruises on her body?

Abruptly she stopped and turned around causing Jake to bump into her. He tilted his head in question for why she suddenly turned around.

"Tell me the truth. How bad is it?" She asked running her hand over her throat.

He removed her hand and replaced it with his. "It's noticeable but it's not as bad as you think."

"Promise?"

He ran his fingers across her neck one more time because he could. "Promise." Almost reluctantly he let his hand drop.

She walked to the back doors and went to see her parents. She expected the backyard to be packed with the amount of cars she saw parked on the street, but there was only about a dozen people. Including her parents, Jake's parents, her godfather and his wife, Sean and Carlee, Maddey's parents, and Skye's parents.

She said hello to everyone and made introductions for Jake. She saved her godfather for last.

"Hey, Uncle Rick," she said as she gave him a big hug.

"If it isn't my favorite goddaughter. How's it going Pumpkin?"

She laughed at Rick's greeting. "I'm your only goddaughter you fool, but I can't complain."

She looked behind her for Jake. "There's someone I want you to meet," she told Rick.

Pulling Jake by the arm she directed him to stand next to her. "Uncle Rick, this is Jake, Jake, I'd like you to meet my godfather, Rick."

"Nice to meet you sir," Jake said as he reached out to shake Rick's hand.

"Breathe," she whispered to Jake.

"Same here," Rick said returning the hand shake then turned to look at his goddaughter. "Is this the guy you said is going to break all of my records one day?"

"Yeah." She smiled as she watched the shocked expression that crossed Jake's face.

Sure, to him Rick Schelios was a world famous All-Star goalie, but to her he was just her godfather, and they talked all the time. So what if she mentioned Jake in their conversations, it wasn't a big deal. *Yeah, right.*

Jake looked down at her. "I thought you said I was just okay?"

She laughed and shook her head at Jake. "Well I couldn't have you getting an even bigger ego, now could I?"

"No we couldn't have that," he responded with a laugh.

"Even if she never said anything, the stories I've heard from your teammates were enough to spark my interests. I think I'm going to have to come to a few games this season and check you out myself."

"Oh? I'm surprised Ryan and Jase told you highlights about other people other than themselves, *shocking*," she said with a laugh.

"It wasn't just your brothers. Billy and Nick told some good ones and then that Tucker kid sure had me going with some of their antics."

Rick's statement brought her up short. "When did you talk to all of them?"

"A little while ago, before they went inside for a team meeting."

Uh oh.

Jake watched Jordan's entire expression change.

This was not going to be good.

"You knew, didn't you?" She asked with accusation and hurt in her voice.

"Yes. Ryan called me this morning. But listen—"

He didn't get to finish because she quickly turned on her heel and stormed off in the direction of the house. She knew where they were. This secret meeting of theirs was the reason why the doors to the den were closed. Her gut told her something was fishy when she saw them closed but she ignored it. It would be just like her brothers to try and "protect" her and have a meeting about her without her.

She stomped her way down the hall. She could hear Jake behind her trying to keep up. She reached the pocket doors to the den and shoved them open with as much force as she could muster.

The sound of the den's doors being practically thrown open caused everyone to turn around and look. On the other side of the doors stood Jordan practically vibrating with anger.

Ryan and Jase stood in front of the couch leading the meeting. She stared daggers at them.

"*WHAT. THE. HELL?*" Jordan bit out.

Ryan looked past her to Jake and saw the same "oh shit" expression mirrored on his face. She didn't miss the exchange.

"*Don't* look at him for help." She strode through the room purposely toward her brothers. "He's in enough trouble now for helping you guys."

She took in everyone else in the room. The team all had nervous expressions on their faces. It was almost comical.

Almost.

"Clearly, you guys are talking about me, so can you please tell me why you decided to have this conversation without me?" she asked the room at large.

Ryan was the one brave enough to answer. "We didn't want you to have to relive it again."

She looked at her older brother dumbfounded. "Do you *really* think that after last night I'm *not* reliving everything already?"

When nobody had anything to say to that, she pressed on.

"To be honest, it's almost a relief. Now everyone knows and we don't have to be all secretive about why I stopped coming around... Yes, this whole thing sucks, but I'm done running away from it. We tried that and it didn't work. For two years I've been waiting for the other shoe to drop.

"I've had nightmares about that night and what would happen if I ever ran into him again. Now we know."

She sucked in a lung full of air. "What makes me angry, though, is that you decided to talk about it without me. I'm *not* a child... you *seriously* need to stop treating me like one."

The room went completely quiet. It was obvious the new guys weren't sure how to react.

Tommy almost killed her that night at the hockey house. It was an absolute miracle she didn't get hurt more seriously from her tumble down the stairs. She could only imagine how her brothers told the tale.

"Jordan," Skye called out to her.

Skye waited for her full attention before she asked the question everyone needed the answer to.

"What happened last night?"

Jordan wasn't sure she would have been able to answer that question if anyone else had asked, except Skye. Belatedly she realized she didn't even tell Jake everything that had happened the night before. They were more focused on *other* things. The memory made her blush.

She turned to face the room at large.

"I guess it's safe to assume you all now know the details of my breakup with Tommy?"

She watched as everyone nodded and then continued.

"He pushed me against the wall hard enough to knock the wind out of me. Then, grabbing me by the throat, he pinned my body with his and shoved his tongue down my throat. I couldn't breathe. All I kept thinking about was I needed to find a way to breathe or I would pass out. The only time he paused his attack was to tell me I was his and I needed to remember that."

What happened next was too embarrassing to tell.

Now came the hard part.

"For the past few weeks I've been getting these weird phone calls and texts from an unknown number. I guess now it's safe to assume they were all from him. Because this morning I had these messages in my voicemail."

She took her phone out of her pocket and hit play.

Noise from Rookies could be heard playing in the background.

"Oh Sweetness, you look good. Two years is too long to go without seeing you. Now all you need to do is get it through that thick, pretty skull of yours that you're mine. Eventually your brothers will leave you alone long enough for me to remind you of that."

There was a long stretch of silence, and by silence, only the sounds of Rookies could be heard before he spoke again. His voice even more menacing than before.

"If that asshole doesn't learn to keep his hands to himself I'm going to break them."

Jordan looked to Jake while the last part of the message played. They both knew who Tommy was referring to. A part of her was grateful she didn't let Jake listen to the messages until he was in a room full of people. She wasn't sure how he would have reacted otherwise.

"The bastard."

"He's twisted."

"I should have killed him when I had the chance."

Ryan, Jase, and Jake all spoke at once.

Surprisingly she couldn't help but laugh. It was shocking how much Jake was like her brothers. She just hoped they wouldn't turn against him when they found out he was now dating their sister.

"That wasn't the only message he left," she told the group.

"Play them," Ryan said.

"You're really trying my patience, Sweetness. You need to stop hiding from me in your ivory tower."

"And this is the last one," she said as she hit play for the third time.

"If you think your little lookalike will keep you from me you are surely mistaken."

"The fucker was watching you the whole night," Tucker said before anyone else.

All of a sudden Jordan felt completely, emotionally drained.

"Okay then. Now that everyone knows everything, I'm going to go change and then I'm going to try and forget it ever happened."

She quickly made her way out of the room and up the stairs to her room.

· · ·

·

JAKE LISTENED TO Jordan's voicemails with the rest of the group. He caught her worried look when Tommy obviously spoke of him. Fortunately everyone was more focused on the broader scope of what was said.

As he listened to the creep talk like he owned her, it made him wish he kicked his ass the night before. But Jordan came first.

The room fell silent again with Jordan's departure.

Billy was first to break the silence. "Holy shit did you *see* her neck?"

"What kind of bastard would do that to a girl?" Tucker asked.

"And I thought what happened that night at the hockey house was bad, but this is on a whole other level," Nick commented.

The room fell back into a strained silence. Jake badly wanted to go after Jordan but he knew it was important to be with the team to develop a plan of action.

"So what's the plan you guys have come up with so far?" He asked the room at large.

"First things first, we have to figure out how Tommy got into Rookies," Ryan said.

Skye spoke up from her seat. "Actually, Aunt Ei found that out last night. With turnover and everything, not all the bouncers knew of Tommy. I guess after so much time has passed…" Skye trailed off.

"That's ridiculous. How could they be so irresponsible?" Ryan said.

"Ryan…" Jase said turning to his brother. "It's been two years since everything happened. We haven't even heard anything from Tommy in all that time. Mom and Dad moved, we changed hockey houses, Jordan went off to school. It's understandable everyone relaxed."

The tension in Ryan's shoulders eased at his brother's logic. He was right.

"There is something that worries me though," Jake mused.

"What's that?" Jase asked.

"He was all about taunting her before he attacked her. Why no voicemails after he got away?"

"The fucker is clearly unhinged," Tucker said as if reading his mind.

"The important thing now is keeping her safe. I guess we'll have to make sure someone from the team is with her at all times in case Tommy decides to make another appearance," Ryan stated.

Maddey stood up from her seat so fast she practically jumped out of it. "No. *Absolutely* not!"

Ryan shot his girlfriend a puzzled look. "What do you mean no?"

"Just as it sounds, no." She crossed her arms over her chest and stood her ground. "You *cannot* do that to your sister. It will drive her crazy and then you know what, she'll kill you."

"Babe, listen…"

"No, you listen!" Maddey cut him off and walked over to poke him in the chest. "Now I know the situations aren't exactly the same, but it's the best example I can think of." She took a deep breath before continuing. "My brothers tried to play that game with me. They can go off into god forsaken places and do god knows what no matter how dangerous it is but god forbid their baby sister wants to go to school in the city. It drove me nuts and almost drove a wedge between us. If you do this, Jordan may never forgive you."

Ryan tried to interrupt her spiel but she wouldn't let him. She put up her hand to stop him.

"I do agree there should be something done at least when we all go out to make sure he's not out there stalking her, but… if you try and do any of those things behind her back it will *not* be good."

"You're right."

"I know," she said with a smile.

Ryan couldn't help but laugh at Maddey. "God you are just as stubborn as my sister." He reached out to put his arm around her shoulders and pulled her close to his side.

"Well, I love her so I'll take that as a compliment."

"So how are we going to make this work?"

"It's actually going to be easier than you think," Skye said from her seat in the back of the room.

"After what happened with Tommy the first time, she didn't really want to be by herself much. So getting her to be with people isn't going to be a challenge."

"It's all in how you go about asking or telling her what you want to do." Maddey finished Skye's thought.

Nobody spoke for a few minutes.

Jake had a sudden burst of inspiration. Ever since Jordan agreed to be with him, as long as it was a secret, he had been thinking of ways he could be with her without raising suspicion. This was the perfect opportunity.

"I have a suggestion."

"Go ahead Jake, I've got nothing," Jase replied.

"Ever since she started teaching the kids their swim lessons we have been splitting the driving. So it's real easy for me to check on her at the pool. Plus I can have her help me watch Carlee and Sean to keep her busy some days." He held his breath while he waited for Ryan and Jase's reactions.

"Actually, that's a pretty good idea," Ryan replied.

"Also, she has been spending a lot of time at my house because it's the summer. There's no way for Tommy to know where I live because you guys didn't even know me back then," Maddey stated.

"And now that you and Maddey are dating you have more of a reason to be around us," Skye told Ryan.

"Ry," Billy said to get his attention, "Jordan has been like a sister to all of us on the team since then and I'm sure the new guys feel the same way. I mean, come on, she's a pretty cool chick."

All around the team nodded in agreement.

"So we will just make sure we do a lot of things as a team and make sure we keep Jordan involved."

"Yeah, Tommy's crazy, not suicidal. It would be nuts to make a move with the whole team around. He's gotta know after what he pulled last night we would close ranks," Nick added.

"I agree. He's lost the element of surprise now. We're all going to be on the lookout for him now," Wade said.

"Bro, they're right," Jase faced his brother. "By keeping Jordan in the loop, it saves us all sorts of drama. Just look at how angry she was that she wasn't included in the meeting."

"I agree."

"Plus Jake's right. With him living right next door he can keep an eye on her without her feeling suffocated."

Jake couldn't believe his good fortune. He had the perfect way to be with Jordan on a regular basis and it didn't even have to be hidden from his friends.

Now what they were actually doing during their time together was a whole other story.

Jordan practically ran to her room and shut the door. She went over to her dresser that had bathing suits in it and braced her arms on it.

When she looked up and caught sight of her reflection in the mirror above the dresser, she let out a startled gasp.

Her neck looked *terrible*. She gently lifted her fingers up to run along the bruises and cringed at how bad they looked. She was surprised her mom didn't freak when she saw her earlier.

It was time to stop thinking of the negative and focus on

the positive. She changed into her zebra print bikini, pulled on a pair of jean shorts and a loose fitting t-shirt.

She opted to leave her hair down to help cover some of the bruising and went to leave her room to go back outside.

When she opened the door she saw Sean and Carlee down the hall and called them over. She bent down to be eye level with her little brother.

"Hey buddy."

"Hi," Sean sulked.

She reached to fluff his hair. "So I heard a funny story last night."

"About what?" He asked sullenly.

"Well, it turns out Mom was playing a joke on our older brothers and *you* got caught in the cross fire."

"What do you mean?" He looked up at her confused.

"Well… you know that boy Tyler that was here the other day?"

"Yeah." He looked down and pouted.

She couldn't help but laugh at Sean's upset expression. "He's just a friend." She paused. "Actually he's Maddey's brother. We went out together to plan her surprise birthday party."

That got Sean's attention and he looked back up at her.

"But Mom said you guys were on a date."

"Oh, honey," she reached out and fluffed his hair again, "she was just telling Ry and Jase that to freak them out."

"Oh." At first Sean looked confused and then he smiled and looked her right in the eye. "So he's not your boyfriend?"

She laughed at how happy Sean sounded about that. "No honey, Tyler is not my boyfriend."

"Good."

She shook her head at her younger brother. He was so much like their older brothers at times it was scary.

"So does that mean Jake is still your boyfriend?" Carlee asked.

Jordan was flabbergasted. How these two pint-size things of trouble could have figured them out so fast was beyond her. She was about to do some damage control when all of Carlee's question registered, she said *still*.

"Carlee sweetie, what do you mean?"

"You guys were sleeping outside and took us to swim lessons and now you're not."

"And then that Tyler guy came over and you left with him and we thought you and Jake got in a fight and broke up."

"And we didn't tell anybody about you guys sleeping outside or anything."

"And I like Jake, you should date him not that Tyler guy."

Carlee and Sean were talking so fast and right after each other that Jordan felt like she was watching a tennis match by the way they were going back and forth.

They certainly were observant five years olds, that was for sure.

Jordan wasn't sure how to respond. She was relieved when she saw

Jake on his way up.

JAKE LEFT THE den to find Jordan and fill her in on the plan. He couldn't help but smile at how he worked it out for them to spend time together without causing suspicion.

He was halfway up the staircase when he caught sight of Sean and Carlee with Jordan. He could hear them peppering her with questions and laughed when he realized they were asking her about him.

Jordan looked up and caught his eye. The relief that flooded her expression when she saw him was enough to make him go right over instead of making her suffer on her own.

"Hey kids, what's up?" He gave his sister a hug and Sean a pound.

The two didn't hesitate with their questioning for him.

"Don't you like Jordan?"

"Yeah you told Mom she was pretty."

"I like you better than Tyler."

"Did you guys have a fight?"

"Why aren't you her boyfriend yet?"

Jake laughed and looked at Jordan. "Have they been like this the whole time?"

"Oh yeah." She smiled at him.

He knelt down in front of Sean and Carlee with Jordan. He looked at her before he answered. At her nod of encouragement he answered the little pip-squeaks.

"I will answer your questions if you can keep the answers secret." He looked first Sean and then Carlee in the eyes.

The kids looked at each other and then back to Jake and Jordan and nodded vigorously.

"Yes, I do like Jordan, and I do think she is very pretty."

He watched her blush at the compliment.

"But the problem is Ryan and Jase don't want her to date one of their teammates, so I'm not supposed to be her boyfriend."

"Why not?" Sean asked.

"Why?" Carlee echoed.

"Do you remember Tommy?" Jordan asked.

Sean made a face at her question. "Yeah I don't like him."

"No one likes him now sweetie, but everyone did at first."

"I didn't." Sean made a face.

"What do you mean? You used to come places with us all the time."

"I just didn't." Sean paused to look at Carlee. "You know… Jake is always very nice to me and he takes me and Carlee places and plays with us."

Sean was relentless in his campaign for Jake. He was flattered.

"I know, buddy, it's one of the things I like most about him."

Jake smiled with pride at Jordan's statement.

"So why isn't he your boyfriend?"

"Do you remember how Ry and Jase acted when Mom told them I was on a date with Tyler?"

"Yeah they were *sooooo* mad."

"Well they would be a million times madder if I was on a date with a teammate."

"Why?"

Jake felt like she was playing a game of twenty questions.

"Because of what happened with Tommy."

"That's stupid."

He let out a deep belly laugh at Sean's statement. The kid took the words right out of his mouth.

"That's exactly what I told your sister," he said to Sean. He turned to take Jordan's hand in his.

"That's why we decided that we are going to date anyway. *But…*" He waited until he had both kids' attention. "We have to keep it a secret from Ryan and Jase."

"So does that mean Jordan is your girlfriend now?" Carlee asked.

"Yes it does."

"YES!" Sean punched his hand in the air in victory.

"It took you *long* enough," Carlee said to both of them.

"Yes it did," Jake agreed. He hoped that the decision to tell them the truth wouldn't come back to bite them in the ass, they were only five after all.

"But we mean it." Jordan looked pointedly at her brother. "We can't let Jase and Ryan know."

"Okay, deal." Sean nodded his head enthusiastically.

"Now go outside and play. We'll be out in a little bit and we can play in the pool together." Jake said this to the kids to get rid of them. He came upstairs to talk to Jordan and he didn't want to do it in front of the rug rats.

"Okay." Sean took Carlee's hand and the two of them ran down the stairs together.

"Do you think they can keep a secret?" He asked Jordan.

"Maybe. I feel like it's going to take a lot of bribery though."

Once the kids were safely out of sight, Jake stood up from his crouch and helped Jordan stand as well. He gently guided her back into her bedroom.

He kicked the door shut with his heel and kept walking Jordan back until they hit the wall. He hooked an arm around her waist, his other hand sinking into her hair, holding her in place.

God she was beautiful.

She simply took his breath away. He stood there a moment, drinking in the sight of her.

He still couldn't fathom that, after constantly keeping him at arm's length, she was allowing him to do all of this without pushing him away. He leaned in and closed the distance between them.

He placed his lips against hers and took a moment to breathe her in. He used the hand in her hair to tip her head back.

His tongue stroked along the seam of her lips until she opened herself to him. Once she did, he leisurely explored the depths of her mouth.

He put everything he felt into this one kiss. All the frustration from her keeping her distance, the fear he felt last night before he found her, and the joy from her agreeing to be his girlfriend. *All* of it.

Eventually they broke apart, both of them breathing heavy.

"Okay, I'm going to go downstairs now before we get ourselves in trouble," he said and made his way out of the room.

· · ·

JORDAN COULDN'T HELP but notice that for the second time in as many days, she was pushed against a wall by a guy.

However, the way Jake held her against the wall was so different from how Tommy did. It was almost *unfair* to consider it the same action.

Where Tommy's actions were painful and scary, Jake's were gentle and comforting. Where Tommy's gaze was brutal and menacing, Jake's was kind and reassuring.

She could get lost in Jake's deep green gaze. His eyes were bright and glowing with the feelings naked for her to see.

It all combined to simply take her breath away. And when he leaned in to kiss her, she felt as if she had died and gone to heaven.

This kiss was utterly different from any of the other kisses they had shared previously. In the past when Jake kissed her it was urgent and almost demanding.

But this kiss.

There.

Were.

No.

Words.

She kissed him back with as much passion as he did her. She let out a contented purr in the back of her throat.

She reached her arms up around his neck reaching for purchase. She pulled him even closer and thought she never wanted this kiss to end.

Eventually they broke apart, both of them breathing heavy.

"Okay, I'm going to go downstairs now before we get ourselves in trouble," Jake said and made his way out of the room.

She used the time in her room to collect herself. Her emotions were all over the place. Between what happened with Tommy and her decision to go for it with Jake, she was a little thrown. She didn't regret her choice to see where things led with Jake but she wasn't going to lie to herself either, the whole situation wouldn't be easy.

She didn't like to keep secrets from her brothers, especially Jase, but she knew how they would react. If the night before never happened, she might have had a chance at changing their minds but after another incident with Tommy she knew they would be even more set in their decision that she not date another member of the team.

When she reached the bottom of the stairs, she noticed the den was empty. She was hoping with their decision to be together Jake would fill her in later, so she wouldn't be left in the dark.

Chapter Thirty-One

J ordan made her way into the backyard and went to join her dad and godfather. She didn't get to talk to them very long.

"Excuse us," Maddey said to both Rick and Mr. D as she and Skye pulled her away by the arm and back toward the house.

The girls stopped just outside the glass sliding doors that led into the house. Maddey and Skye faced her and at the same time said, "Okay spill."

She looked back and forth between her two best friends. "I already told you everything that happened last night."

"That's *not* what we're talking about and you know it," Maddey replied and gave her a knowing look.

When she still didn't respond Skye chimed in. "We are talking about what's going on with you and Jake, because it is obvious things are different between you guys."

A panicked look crossed over her face. "Oh my god!" Her hand went up to her face. "Do Ryan and Jase know?"

Maddey laughed. "Those two?" She looked over to where Jordan's two brothers were hanging out in the pool. "No they are just as clueless as ever."

"We picked up on the change because we're female and we pay attention."

Skye's reply made the three girls laugh.

She relaxed and knew she would eventually be telling her friends what was going on with her and Jake, with everyone preoccupied she figured now was as good a time as any. She filled them in on everything that happened the night before when they got back to the hockey house. From her falling apart and telling Jake everything that happened with Tommy two years ago, to the incredible kiss they shared on the couch and her decision to be with Jake even if it was going to be in secret.

"I can't explain it, but the way he makes me feel when I'm with him, there's just this pull that I can't seem to break. It's like I *need* to be near him."

Her friends showed their compassion and support for the situation she was now in. They filled her in on what the guys decided after she left the den and she was relieved to hear Jake came up with the perfect way for them to spend time together without raising suspicion.

"Hey you guys," Tucker shouted at them from the pool.

"What?" Skye yelled back.

"We're gonna play some pool volleyball, so get over here and join us."

The girls laughed and made their way over to the pool. As she made her way into the pool, Sean ran over to the edge to talk to her. "Hey, Jordan, can Carlee and I play too?"

She looked around the packed pool and noticed a bunch of the guys on the team were set up to play and was nervous about things getting out of hand. She bent down to talk to her brother. "How about you and Carlee referee the game for us, make sure no one tries to cheat?" She gave him a wink.

Sean smiled ear-to-ear. He liked the suggestion and ran off to get Carlee.

She walked down the steps into the pool and went to

stand next to Jake. Since she and Maddey were so short they chose to play on the team in the shallow end of the pool. It would be Jake, Ryan, Billy, Tucker, and Seth with them and Jase, Skye, Sammy, Nick, Pat, Wade, and Chris against them.

She wasn't surprised to see her brothers called their closest alumni friends for their "team meeting."

Jake slid up next to her. "You are really good with them you know?" He nodded his head in Sean and Carlee's direction.

She smiled at the compliment. "Thanks, but they make it easy."

She turned her attention to Tucker. "So we're gonna be on the same team?"

"Yeah I don't think his ego can take another loss to you sis," Ryan said on a laugh.

"Yeah, yeah, yeah… whatever you say. Let's play some volleyball." Tucker brushed off the ribbing he was getting from his teammates.

The game was intense and a lot of fun and was not lacking in trash talk. The score was tied for most of the game but in the end Skye was able to score the winning point.

By the time the game was over the next round of food was out and everyone got out to eat. Jordan claimed one of the lounge chairs around the pool as her seat to eat.

"So I heard you had some good ideas for us to be together without anyone thinking anything of it."

"Well, at first your brothers were plotting to keep you protected without you knowing what the plan was but then Maddey got up in Ryan's face and told them you had to be involved."

"*Really*?"

"Yeah. She really put him in his place too, it was kind of impressive."

She smiled. "I *freaking* love that girl." She bit the corner of her lip while she thought of what to say next and didn't miss the flare of heat in Jake's eyes at the motion. Her smile broadened.

She gave him a knowing look. "I told the girls about us. Sammy's not too far behind."

"I told Tuck."

"BB3 is probably the only 'brother' of mine to take the news well. But I guess having all our besties on our side can't hurt."

"Exactly," he said with a wink that sent a shiver down her spine.

"Brilliant," she said as she bumped her shoulder into his.

They both sat there and laughed because considering how messed up the circumstances were, it gave them the perfect opportunity to spend time together without having to keep it a secret.

Jake and his parents stayed behind after the other guests left to help with the cleanup. He watched Jordan head inside to work on the stuff in the kitchen and went to check if she needed any help.

As he entered the kitchen he found her rubbing her bruised shoulder. He made his way over to her and replaced her hand with his own. She was startled at first by his presence but after a moment she relaxed against him.

"Does it hurt badly?" He asked her.

She shook her head in response. "Not really, just a little sore. Ever since I dislocated it, I sometimes get a twinge in the muscle. Banging it last night didn't help but I should be fine in a few days."

He bent down and kissed the top of head. "Do you have anything you can put on it?"

"Yeah there should be some Miracle Ice in the downstairs bathroom, it always seems to help. I'll go get it."

"No stay here, I'll get it."

He made his way to the bathroom by the front door. He looked in the medicine cabinet to no avail, but found the Miracle Ice underneath the sink. She was still standing by the sink when he returned to the kitchen and he took a moment to take in everything about her. So much had changed between them in the past twenty-four hours, their old relationship was almost unrecognizable. "God you're beautiful," he blurted out.

She blushed slightly at the compliment and he wondered when she would get used to them. "What was that for?"

"No reason, just happy I can tell you what I think without you running in the opposite direction." He smiled. "Now turn around."

She did as he asked. He unscrewed the top on the Miracle Ice and took a glob out. He rubbed it between his hands for a few seconds and then reached out and started to massage the Miracle Ice into her shoulder. He moved the strap of the tank top she put on earlier down her arm so he could treat her entire shoulder. He was careful not to exert too much pressure on where she was bruised. Seeing the large purplish, blue bruise made him want to pound Tommy's face in all over again.

"I like this," she said on a sigh.

"I know, this stuff is my salvation during the season."

She laughed. "I wasn't talking about the Miracle Ice." She turned around and looped her arms around his neck. "I was referring to you taking care of me, it's nice."

He smiled and leaned in for a quick kiss. "I'll take care of you as long as you'll let me."

"Is that so?"

"Yup." He looked toward the backyard and figured it was time for him to go back out and finish helping with the cleanup. "Okay time for me to go back to work." And with another quick kiss he walked out of the sliding doors.

Later that night Jordan sat on her bed and rubbed more Miracle Ice on her shoulder after a nice hot soak in the tub to help ease the ache. She turned on Nick at Nite and laid back on the bed with Navy to watch a few *Friends* reruns. A little while later there was a knock on the door.

"Mind if I come in?" Her mother asked.

"Not at all, Mom."

Her mom closed the door behind her, which she thought was odd, and made her way over to sit on the opposite side of the bed. Her mom didn't speak automatically which earned her a questioning look from her. Eventually though she broached the difficult topics she came in to talk about.

"So how are you holding up, really?"

"Honestly… pretty good. I know I didn't do anything wrong, Tommy is just crazy. I'm not going to let him affect my life anymore. I've wasted too much time letting what he's done to me rule my life and I'm over it."

"Good. That makes me so happy to hear." She reached out and squeezed her daughter's hand. "So what's going on with Jake? Things seem like they have changed between you two."

"Oh, *Mom*. I don't even know where to begin."

"It's okay, start from the beginning, that usually helps."

Jordan laughed. "I don't know, I feel like everything is happening so fast but not, if that makes any sense?"

When her mom nodded in agreement she continued. "It's like when Tommy attacked me last night, the only thing I was thinking about was why didn't I tell Jake how I feel. I was trying to hold on hoping someone would find and help me and then there he was. He got Tommy off of me and instead of kicking his ass like I *know* he wanted to, he took care of me.

"Then when we got back to the hockey house he made sure I was comfortable and he never pressed me to talk about it, he just let me say what I wanted to say when I wanted to say it. And after I told him everything that happened with Tommy two years ago you know what he did?"

She looked to her mom and when she said nothing she continued.

"He kissed me and proceeded to tell me he doesn't care what Ryan or Jase say, he wants to be with me and he is going to be and he's not going to let them get in his way." She wasn't sure how her mom would react, but like always she didn't disappoint.

"I knew I liked him." They shared a knowing smile. "I can tell by the way he looks at you that he cares about you, and now we know he's smarter than your brothers. I mean, don't get me wrong, I love them dearly but sometimes they can be so thick-headed I want to slap them."

"Mom!"

"What?" Her mom gave her an innocent look. "You know it's true. But that's not the point. The point is, if you and Jake are going to be together, which I'm happy you are by the way, what are you going to do about your brothers when they find out?"

"To be honest, I'm not really sure, but for now we are going to keep the truth about our relationship a secret."

"Okay."

"Really?"

"Really. I just want you to be happy and when I see you with Jake, you are. The only thing we have to figure out is how to get Sean to keep the secret, because you know there's no way to keep it from him since he lives here, but I'll worry about that. You just worry about being happy."

"I am. I can't explain it but when I'm with Jake, I can't *not* be happy. It's so different."

"Then that's all that matters." With that her mom got up from the bed and made her way to leave her bedroom. "Goodnight honey."

"Goodnight Mom."

Chapter Thirty-Two

The next few weeks were complete heaven. The agreement with her brothers allowed Jordan to spend time with Jake without them getting suspicious. The more time she spent with Jake, the more she realized how completely different he was from Tommy. Jake always tried to compliment her and genuinely cared about her opinions. They didn't have to do anything special to have a good time and he always kept her laughing. She was hoping that with time her brothers would be able to see that Jake wasn't the same as Tommy and would be able to accept their relationship.

One could only hope.

Because she had fallen for him. Hard.

Surprisingly, it was very easy to convince the little ones to keep their secret. To them it was like a game of secret agents. They loved to help come up with reasons for why both Jake and Jordan had to be together.

"Hey babe, you ready?" Jake called from downstairs.

"Yeah, I'll be down in a sec."

Tonight was Maddey's surprise birthday party so they

were headed down together. Jordan grabbed her overnight bag to stay at Maddey's for the night and headed down to meet Jake.

"Damn, you look *hot*," Jake exclaimed as she made her way down the stairs.

Jordan couldn't stop the blush from creeping up her neck at his compliment. She still wasn't used to how he would give her compliments whenever the thought crossed his mind. She didn't think there was anything special about her yellow tube top, daisy dukes, and flip flops. But damn was he good for her ego.

"You don't look so bad yourself," she said as she took in his khaki cargo shorts, white pumas, and maroon t-shirt. Since they weren't going too fancy for the night, they were able to dress down. The things his shoulders did to a t-shirt should be illegal.

She stopped on the bottom step as she leaned in to give him a kiss hello. As per usual her short kiss hello quickly morphed into a more heated embrace.

Jake put one arm around her waist and a hand behind her head and pulled her tighter against him. His actions made her lose her position on the step she stood on and caused her body to line up flush against his. She braced her hands against his hard chest as he plundered her mouth.

Eventually reality settled back in and she broke the kiss.

"What was that for?"

He pushed an errant hair behind her ear. "Well I figured I'm going to have to behave tonight so I wanted to get *that* out of my system now."

Her smile was all satisfaction as she leaned into his touch. "I'm glad you did. Keeping my distance from you will be the hardest part about tonight."

"I know what you mean." He reached down for the bag she brought down with her. "Is this all you need?"

"Yeah everything else is already at Maddey's parents' house."

She called goodbye to her parents and the two headed out to Jake's Jeep.

Chapter Thirty-Three

The birthday festivities continued the next day. Jordan, Skye, Sammy, Jake, Jase, Ryan, and Tucker spent the night at Maddey's and the eight of them, along with Maddey's brothers and Dex decided to spend the day at the beach. It was perfect. The girls laid out sunbathing while the guys tossed around a football down by the water.

"So…" Maddey turned to face Jordan. "What's been going on with you and Jake?"

She couldn't stop the smile from spreading across her face. She pulled her sunglasses down to cover her eyes as she leaned up on her elbows to look out at the guys playing football in the water. Her gaze instantly found Jake in all his bronzed glory. He really was a sight to behold.

"It's been amazing." She sighed as she rolled over to face her friends. "I've completely fallen for him."

"We know," Maddey said.

"It's obvious to us," Skye confirmed.

"Well *shit*," Jordan let out.

The three girls burst out laughing.

"So how are things going with my brother?" She asked Maddey.

"He's amazing. I can't wait until you don't have to keep Jake a secret and we can double."

Jordan sighed. "One day."

The girls flipped over to keep their tans even.

"So are we gonna talk about the elephant in the room or not?" Jordan asked Maddey.

"And that would be?" Maddey played dumb.

"Dex."

"What *about* him?"

"Are you okay seeing him?"

"Yup."

"Are you sure?"

"Nope."

"Okay then." Jordan paused. "Let's drink."

"And this is why we are friends."

The girls laughed and reached for the cooler that had the beer.

Maddey's brothers were awesome. They fit in with their group seamlessly. Maddey had been so surprised to see them that she cried.

Ryan was holding his own but Jake had a feeling the SEALs weren't through with their 'inspection'.

"So Ryan, what are your intentions with our sister?"

Ryan almost dropped the football Tucker tossed him, he was so startled by Tyler's question.

"We've been dating for a little over a month. I think it's been going good." He paused. "I really like her."

"Just so you know, you hurt her we hurt you," Connor deadpanned.

"I figured as much. But to be perfectly honest, I'm more afraid of my sister than the three, I mean four, of you." He pointed to Maddey's brothers and their best friend. "I'm pretty sure her exact words were, and I quote, you break Maddey's heart and I'll break your legs, even if it ruins your chances in the pros."

"That sounds like Blondie alright," Tucker said catching the football from Sammy.

Ryan shook his head at the memory. "The scariest part is I don't doubt her for a second."

"I knew I liked your sister when I met her," Tyler said on a laugh and tossed the football to Connor.

"Yeah she may be tiny, but she can be vicious and completely loyal," Jase interjected.

"But all kidding aside, I've fallen for your sister. I have every intention to *never* hurt her."

"Good enough for us," Justin stated.

The guys tossed the football around for a few more minutes before they broached the other sensitive subject.

"So what's been going on with Jordan's situation with her ex?" Justin asked.

"After the night Tommy attacked her at Rookies, it's been complete radio silence," Jase answered.

"We've been trying to make sure she isn't really alone too much, at least when she goes out places. The guys on the team have helped to look out for her and with Jake living next door to our parents he's been using the little ones as good excuses to hang around," Ryan added.

"Dude. That was one of the scariest nights of my life and I didn't even know the whole story then. I swear it took ten years off my life," Jake stated. He looked over to where the girls were sunbathing on the beach and shuddered at the thought of what could have happened that night if they hadn't gotten to Jordan when they did.

"She hasn't had any more phone calls or texts from him, has she?" Tucker asked.

"She hasn't said anything," Jake said.

Conner tucked the football under his arm after he caught it. "I don't know about you guys but I could use a beer."

"Agreed," Tucker responded.

The guys made their way out of the surf and back up the beach to where the girls laid out on the blankets they had set up to claim space on the crowded beach.

The girls were laying on their stomachs talking and didn't hear the guys approach. So the guys took the opportunity to shake off near the girls and shock them with cold water.

"What the hell!" Maddey yelled.

"That's cold," Skye commented.

"Payback's a bitch," Jordan stated calmly and smiled at the "oh shit" expression on their faces.

Ryan caught Tyler's gaze. "See, I told you she's vicious."

The guys all settled into the beach chairs around the blanket. Tucker reached into the cooler to pass out beers to the rest of the guys.

The conversation flowed and jokes were flying. Jordan could see how happy it made Maddey to have her family home.

"How long are you guys home for?" Maddey asked her brothers.

"We have to report back in two more days," Dex answered.

"But we didn't make any plans for our time off so we get to spend it all with you," Justin added.

"Do you think you can handle the pressure of having us around?" Conner taunted Ryan.

"Yeah I think I can handle it," Ryan said with a wink to Maddey.

The guys talked sports with a lot of trash talk going around. Jordan was laughing over Tucker's comments as she got up to get a bottle of water out of one of the coolers. She knew she could have had one of the guys pass her the water but she had an ulterior motive for getting up.

Luckily for her when she opened the cooler there was only one bottle left. She uncapped the bottle and took a deep drink before placing it in the sand. Then she picked up the open cooler and threw the ice and water over the guys as payback from earlier.

They let out yells of surprise and Jake, Tucker, Jase, and Conner stood up to get the ice off.

Jake raised his eyebrows at her while he brushed the rest of the ice off his body. Jordan shivered at the look in his eyes.

"Oh shit," she whispered.

"I'd run if I were you," he stated calmly.

She took off down the beach with the four guys following close behind. Jake was first to reach her and threw her over his shoulder in a fireman's carry.

She let out a squeal when he picked her up. She tried to wiggle out of his grasp but her efforts proved futile. He carried her into the ocean and sent her flying in the air.

She came up spitting water and shoved her hair out of her face. In the time it took her to surface, everyone else had joined them in the water.

"Asshole," she said as she splashed him.

"You started it," he countered.

A full on splash war commenced. Tucker snuck up behind Skye to dunk her and the two of them battled it out.

Jordan followed Tucker's actions and tried to dunk Jake. She swam out to where he was treading water and pushed down on his shoulders while using him to prop herself up.

She quickly had to swim away when she caught Jase closing in on her.

By the time everyone made it out of the water they were exhausted. They packed everything up to head back to the McClain's house for dinner.

Chapter Thirty-Four

I t was around nine o'clock by the time Jordan and Jake
got home that night, luckily everyone showered and
changed at the McClains.

Ryan was staying the weekend with Maddey, and Jase and
Tucker went back to the hockey house.

While they were at the beach, her mom had sent her a text
saying they were going to her Uncle Rick's for a barbeque and
would be staying the night. The best part was that the Dono-
vans went with them and now she had the whole night alone
with Jake.

Grabbing a bowl of popcorn, she made her way to where
he was on the couch.

Since he was laying on the oversized chaise portion, she
was able to snuggle up right alongside him. She tangled her
legs between his, wrapped her arms around his waist, and
rested her head on his chest right beneath his chin.

Jake tightened his arms around her and stroked his hands
up and down her back. She let out a contented sigh and felt
him smile at the sound. He kissed the top of her head and
rubbed at the knots in her lower back.

"Why are you so tense, babe?"

"It's nothing really. It's just getting really hard to be with you but not *with* you when we're around other people. I'm so happy we are together that I just want to shout it for all the world to hear, but I can't."

He continued to run his hands along her back in a soothing manner.

"I know exactly how you feel, babe."

God how she loved when they were alone and he used pet names for her.

"It's getting harder to keep living a lie. I think if my friends didn't know, I would be going completely out of my mind."

She was quiet for a moment before she continued.

"The other day Jase and I were out to lunch and he kept looking at me funny. I was becoming a nervous wreck.

"I feel like he knows something is going on with me but he's just not quite sure what exactly. I'm used to telling him everything. He's my other half and it kills me to keep this from him."

She had been spilling her guts into his chest. He put his finger under her chin and lifted her face up to his.

"So then let's tell them the truth."

"I'm scared," she whispered and bit her bottom lip.

"Baby," he whispered back. He cupped the back of her head and brushed his lips against hers in a soft kiss.

At the touch of his lips she instantly relaxed and melted against his body. She loved that no matter what was going on around them, Jake had a way to calm her.

With a sigh of contentment she settled back into the crook of his arms to watch the movie they decided to rent for the night.

Jake loved the feel of Jordan in his arms, it was like she was made for him.

Throughout the movie he continued to run his hands up

and down her back. Every now and then he could feel her body give a little shiver.

At some point toward the end of the movie Jordan's hands found their way under the hem of Jake's t-shirt to caress his back in return. Every so often her hands would sneak around to the front to trace the ridges of his abs. She felt the muscles in his abs quiver under her touch. She couldn't keep her hands off of him. He was so warm and strong and she couldn't get enough.

Being with him when her brothers were around was a true testament to her self-control. Not touching him was harder than it looked.

She nuzzled in closer, rubbing her nose against his neck breathing in his clean scent. She heard an appreciative growl come from the back of his throat.

The way Jordan was kissing his neck was driving him crazy. He gripped her chin between his thumb and forefinger to tilt her face up for a kiss.

This kiss was the complete opposite of the one earlier in the evening. It was pure need that drove it.

Jordan's mouth parted to allow his tongue to enter. As the kiss deepened Jake hooked his arm around her waist and shifted her so her body was fully beneath him.

Since they'd started dating, they'd had some pretty heavy make-out sessions and even fooled around a little, but they had yet to go all the way. Something about this time was different. Maybe it was the build up leading to this or maybe it was their growing feelings for each other. Either way, they could both tell their relationship was about to take the next step.

Jordan slid her hands under Jake's t-shirt and started to pull it up his back. When she reached his head they finally broke their kiss so they could remove the shirt. Once that was taken care of they went back to kissing.

Jake pulled her head back with a gentle tug on her hair to

expose her neck for better access. He trailed his lips across her cheek and jaw down to her neck. He bit the soft spot where her neck and shoulder met.

Jordan let out a moan when he bit down on her neck, her back arching up in response.

Tingles shot down her body as he ran his hand down her arm to the hem of her cami. Hyper aware of the sensations wracking her body, the soft cotton material felt like it was abrading her skin as he lifted it over her head.

Once settled again, Jake took a moment to take her all in. Her face was flushed and her lips swollen from his kisses. He ran a hand between her breasts, tracing the cups of her bra while her chest rose and fell quickly with her increased breathing.

Leaning on one elbow he slowly began to draw the straps of her bra down her arms. When they reached her elbow, he reached underneath her body to unhook the clasp at the back. After the straps cleared her arms he dropped the garment on the floor.

"God you're beautiful," he said reverently.

Jordan blushed at Jake's exclamation. But what took her breath away was the look of love shining deep in his eyes.

She had no words to express the emotions coursing through her at that moment. So she threw her arms around his neck and kissed him for all she was worth.

Hooking a leg over his hip she ground herself against him. Her hands ran down his back, tracing the muscles as she went. When they reached the waistband of the sweats he was wearing, her fingers dipped inside to squeeze his butt.

Jake growled at her advances. "*Baby,* if you're not careful, things aren't going to stop."

She smiled up at him and leaned into his ear to whisper, "I don't want it to stop." She punctuated the statement by biting down on his earlobe and pulling it into her mouth.

She felt him shudder at her words and actions. Encouraged by his response, she slipped her hands further down his sweatpants, starting to tug them down. Once they were taken care of, she let her hands have free rein over his body.

And what a body it was.

All hard muscles and sexy ridges.

He was big without being overly bulky. She ran her tongue from his ear to his collarbone, which she grazed lightly with her teeth. Her hands continued to roam and when she got to his erection she wanted to swoon.

Hard steel wrapped in warm velvet. They had been taking things slow but at this moment slow was the furthest thing from her mind.

Jordan was already more than half way in love with him. Nothing was holding her back.

"*Fuck,* babe, if you don't stop that I'm going to end up taking you right here on this couch."

"Oh *god* yes!" She moaned in response.

With a strangled curse he divested her body of her pants and panties in one swoop. Once he was settled back in place he lovingly caressed her face and tilted it up for another passionate kiss.

When he pulled back, he stared deep into her eyes. "I wanted to make this special for you but you are making it really hard."

Jordan could see the torment in his eyes and knew he meant every word he said.

"Jake being with you is what makes it special, not the location." She kissed him softly on the lips. "Please make love to me now."

Jake ran his hand down her body to the juncture between her legs to test her readiness. When he discovered her wetness he eased her leg higher up his hip. He took her mouth in a devastating kiss, mimicking what they would soon be doing with their bodies. Slowly he eased his way inside her.

Jordan gasped as Jake entered her. The feeling of fullness was unlike anything she had ever felt before. After he was fully seated inside her, they started moving together in perfect sync.

Jake grabbed her butt and tilted her body up to meet his thrust. Jordan ran her nails down his back. He knew he would wear her marks and loved the thought.

They were both covered in a sheen of sweat as things started building between them. Their breaths became more labored and their movements more urgent. Jordan came and Jake tumbled over with her.

They laid there kissing while waiting for their heart rates to return to normal. Jake pushed some hair out of Jordan's face while he looked deep into her eyes. Never had anything felt so right as it did being with her at this moment. He kissed her deeply, with all the emotion he was feeling.

They laid on the couch for a little while longer. Eventually they made their way upstairs to her bedroom to sleep for the night. They slept tangled up together, waking to make love one more time during the night.

Chapter Thirty-Five

A few days later Jordan and Skye headed to Maddey's. The four roommates were going out with other friends from college. It was a rare occurrence, as Ryan and Jase already had separate plans, so she took a chance on inviting Jake out with them. So far she hadn't heard from him but she was hopeful.

They made their way into Maddey's room. After a round of hugs and kisses they plopped down on the bed to relax. The girls chatted about nothing in particular, laughing and having a good time.

Maddey noticed Jordan looked a little different. Something about her just seemed to glow. "Okay spill."

Jordan looked up startled. "Spill what?"

Skye looked at her best friend closely, her eyes squinting in concentration. "OH MY GOD!"

"What?" Jordan jumped at Skye's outburst.

"You and Jake *totally* did it."

"Oh my god that is so it. You got *laid*," Maddey exclaimed.

Jordan went scarlet red. She planned on telling her best friends about what happened with Jake but knowing they could read her so well was a little embarrassing. She *really* had to work on her poker face.

She pushed her face into Maddey's comforter. "Yes I did."

"OH MY GOD!" Skye and Maddey shouted in unison.

"Details."

"Now."

They both demanded.

She had to laugh. She knew her besties wouldn't make this easy on her. She went on in detail about her night with Jake. Her friends were swooning at the tale.

"I love him," she admitted.

"Have you told him that?" Maddey asked.

"No, I'm too afraid. There's too much at stake right now. Our whole relationship is a secret, what if my telling him I'm in love with him finally pushes him over the edge."

"That doesn't make any sense. He was the one that pushed for the relationship. He even suggested dating in secret. I seriously think you are overthinking things," Maddey said.

"He's different with you. I got to see what he was like before he met you. It's easy to see how much you mean to him," Skye added.

"Thanks that means a lot to me." Jordan squeezed Skye's hand in return.

She rolled over onto her back, frustrated. "I just wish I could be with him in public and not have to worry about keeping our relationship a secret."

"Well at least tonight you don't have to keep quiet. He *is* coming right?" Maddey asked.

"I hope so. When you told me this morning that Ryan wasn't coming, I went over to ask him but he wasn't home. I didn't want to risk texting him, so I wrote a note and asked Carlee to give it to him. I hope he comes."

The girls continued to talk and joke around for a while.

They turned up some music and decided to get the party started while they got ready for the night.

"What's everyone wearing?" She asked her friends.

Skye unzipped her bag and pulled out a Kelly Green bandage dress.

"Ooo *that's* going to look so good with your red hair." Maddey nodded her approval. "Shoes?"

The girls all swooned when she showed them a killer pair of strappy sandals. "What about you Madz?" Skye asked.

"I was thinking this hot pink, scoop necked halter top, with a black lace, ruffled mini skirt, and these," she bent in her closet before standing, "hot pink FMPs."

"Yup, *totally* going to have to borrow those someday," Jordan informed her friend.

"So jealous you guys can share shoes," Skye complained.

"The one perk of us being vertically challenged," Maddey said. "What about you, Jor?"

"Lets see." She bent to her duffle on the floor. "I have this black corset top, makes the ladies look real good, white short shorts, and these killer black lace up booties."

"Oh yeah we are definitely swapping shoes soon." Maddey looked at Jordan's shoes like she would look at chocolate cake.

Jake returned home from his lunch with Tucker. They went out to have burgers and watch the afternoon Yankees game. It was nice to hang out with his bud. As he started walking up the stairs, Carlee ran from the kitchen calling his name.

"Jakey! Jakey!" She bounded up to him.

"What is it, cupcake?" He walked back down toward his sister.

She was holding a piece of paper in her sticky little hand.

"Jordan note." She lowered her voice. "Secret message," she said on a giggle.

Carlee and Sean were really into their secret spy roles in keeping his relationship with Jordan clandestine. He ruffled her hair as he took the note from her.

> Hey babe! We're going out with a bunch of
>
> friends from college tonight.
>
> Ryan was supposed to come but he can't.
>
> I would love it if you would come.
>
> There's a car service that will
>
> pick you up at 9 if you want to come.
>
> Hopefully I see you later
>
> <3

Jake smiled down at Jordan's girly handwriting. He thought it was cute she was nervous about him wanting to come out with them at the last minute.

If only she knew how quickly he would jump at the chance to spend time with her. Especially when he didn't have to keep his feelings to himself. He looked down at his phone to check the time. He still had a few hours to kill before the car service arrived.

He sent a text to Tucker.

THE BRICK WALL (Jake): Hey man any plans tonight?

WANNA TUCK (Tucker): Nothing special. Was thinking of hitting up Rookies wanna join? I could use a wingman

THE BRICK WALL: Better idea… let's go to the city

WANNA TUCK: The city?

THE BRICK WALL: Yeah Jordan and her friends are going to some club.

WANNA TUCK: Sweet, fresh meat

THE BRICK WALL: Perv

WANNA TUCK: *middle finger emoji* I'm in. What time?

THE BRICK WALL: Car service will be here at 9

WANNA TUCK: Car service?

THE BRICK WALL: Yup no need to DD tonight

WANNA TUCK: I knew I liked Blondie.

THE BRICK WALL: Hands off

WANNA TUCK: Yeah I know. Be over soon

Jake headed upstairs to shower, his night just got a whole lot better.

Chapter Thirty-Six

J ake and Tucker made their way into the nightclub looking for the girls. The bouncer at the door told them the VIP section was upstairs on the left. They found the staircase without a problem. Looking up he tried to take the entire scene in.

What he found standing at the top took his breath away. Jordan leaned over the railing dangling a beer bottle between her fingers. He took the opportunity to study her without her knowledge.

"Man my girlfriend is *hot*."

"Yeah she is," Tucker agreed. Jake wasn't aware he spoke his thoughts out loud.

Jordan looked down and saw them standing there. She motioned for them to come up. They showed their wristbands to the bouncer at the bottom of the stairs and made their way up.

She met them at the top of the stairs. He couldn't resist picking her up and planting a deep kiss on her lips. Eventually he put her down and released her lips.

"Wow," she said as she removed her arms from around his neck.

"Wow is right." Her hair was curled down her back instead of the usual straight style and her lips were a glossy red.

Damn, she was fine.

He loved the heated look in her eyes as she took in his appearance. He was happy to note he seemed to do it for her as much as she did it for him.

Since they didn't have to worry about keeping their relationship secret here, he reached out and pulled her into another kiss. Like most of their kisses that weren't during stolen moments, this one started out on a simmer and quickly reached boiling.

They finally broke apart when they heard their friends catcalling behind them.

"Damn, Blondie, it's a good thing Ry and Jase aren't here. I think they would have a heart attack at your outfit," Tucker said as he gave her a kiss on the cheek.

"Do we have a problem BB3?"

"Not at all. I like what I'm seeing."

"Dude, seriously. Stop hitting on my girlfriend." Jake punched Tuck in the arm.

"What, afraid she'll finally come to her senses and leave you for me?"

"Please."

"Children." Jordan rolled her eyes beside them.

As they broke apart she trailed a hand down his arm, copped a feel along the way, obviously liking what she had. She grabbed his hand and led him over to where their friends were sitting. Both him and Tucker hugged Maddey and Skye hello and did a slap handshake with Sammy as he was handed a beer.

"Man, I thought you were going to set off the sprinklers with that kiss. If you go long enough without seeing me, will you greet me like that Jake?" Sammy joked with him.

Sammy had a twisted sense of humor sometimes. "I don't

know, Jordan seems to have a possessive personality. I don't see her letting *that* fly."

The group all laughed.

He grabbed a beer from the bucket on the table and sat down next to Sammy. Jordan went to sit on his other side but he reached out and pulled her to sit in his lap.

"What are you doing?" She asked on a laugh.

He nuzzled her behind her ear. "Hey, I don't get to do this when we usually hang out. I'm going to enjoy every opportunity tonight." He finished his statement with a nip to her earlobe causing her to shudder in his arms.

She let loose a blinding smile and settled deeper into his arms.

"Not that I'm not enjoying being able to act normal with my girlfriend, but where's Ryan tonight?" He asked Maddey.

"He had plans with the other seniors on the team. So it worked out perfect for this little covert operation that is your relationship with my best friend.

"When I told him we were going out he was going to reschedule with the guys but I told him it was cool, that I was going out with the girls and everything would be fine." She took a swig of her beer.

"It doesn't bother you that I'm here turning it into a lie?"

"I didn't lie." She paused and looked over at Jordan to share a secret smile. "I came here with the girls, well and Sammy, but he's considered one of the girls. I can't help it if you showed up after us. *Of course* we would let you hang out with us. We *are* friends after all," she said with a wink.

"Well I'm really glad you decided to use your evil powers to help me." He reached out to clink his beer bottle against hers.

"So how did you guys manage to get the VIP section here?" Jake asked.

"Sammy is dating one of the promoters," Maddey answered.

"Yeah and he's super hot too," Skye added with a smile.

"Hotter than me?" Tucker asked.

"Please Tuck, *we've* been over for a while. Don't even try it," Skye said, nonchalant.

Jake looked over to Sammy to see him smiling like the cat that ate the canary. "What can I say, I know how to pick em."

The gang hung out for a while in the VIP section reminiscing about some of their crazy days at NYU. Some of the antics the girls got into would send Ryan and Jase into an early grave if they ever heard them.

Everyone made their way down to the main level to dance. Even with hundreds of people around Jake and Jordan were in their own little world.

JORDAN LOVED THAT she was finally able to dance with Jake how she wished she could when they were at Rookies. And boy could he move. He made it easy to follow her hips against his.

She watched him and liked everything she saw, from his black leather shoes, to his muscular legs encased in dark faded denim, topped by a dark gray t-shirt. He smiled deep showing off his gorgeous dimples as she finished taking in his messy styled hair.

It was everything she ever dreamed of being able to do, what she wanted to do at Rookies but wasn't allowed. The group laughed while they danced and sang along to the 90's hits the DJ was playing. Jake's eyes were locked on the movement of Jordan's hips and he pulled her in closer.

Turning around to face him, she wrapped her arms around his neck and couldn't stop the smile from spreading across her face.

Jake's arms wrapped around her waist and closed the rest of the gap between their bodies. She loved the feel of his body moving in tandem with hers.

"What are you smiling at?" He asked loudly to be heard over the music.

"Just this," she answered with a shrug.

His green eyes sparkled in response. "It is great, isn't it?" Without waiting for a response he pulled her in for a kiss.

"I love the way you move," he bent down a little to say in her ear, so she could hear him better.

"I was *just* thinking the same thing about you," she responded with a laugh.

"I love watching you dance at Rookies but hate that I can't be the one dancing with you. You have no idea how many times I came close to cutting in when I would see some guys trying to push up on you," he punctuated possessively.

"Ha! Half the time I go down to dance it's because I can't stand to watch the puck bunnies throw themselves at you." The sadness was evident on her face.

"Hey." He bent and put a finger under her chin to lift it up to place a whisper soft kiss across her lips. "Soon it won't be an issue anymore. This whole situation with your brothers won't last forever," he continued once he had her full attention.

Tightening her arms around his neck she pulled him in closer.

"I know and this whole thing is entirely my fault. I don't even know why you put up with it," she murmured against his neck.

He took one hand off her hip and raised it to the back of her head, while leaving the other to rest on her hip just under the edge of her shirt. He kissed her with all the feeling and emotion that he'd been keeping in check.

She responded instantly by tightening her arms around his neck and going on her tiptoes so their bodies were flush together. When she felt his tongue trace the seam of her lips, she opened to grant him access.

Time stood still as they made out in the middle of the dance floor. *Nothing* else mattered except the two of them.

When the need for air became too great Jake pulled back and held her face in between his two large hands.

"Baby, I'd put up with anything for you. I love you."

He watched as shock and pure joy exploded in her hazel eyes. The gold flecks practically sparkled. Her jaw dropped down in amazement.

Jordan's heart skipped a beat and she froze, not sure she had heard him correctly over the loud music.

"Are you *serious*?" She croaked.

If it wasn't for the pure happiness radiating off her body in waves he would have been nervous. But he could feel the love she had for him in every look she gave him and her every touch. He grinned like a Cheshire cat.

"As a heart attack."

"Oh my god," she whispered. She stared him right in the eyes and could see the laughter dancing in those emerald pools.

Reacting instinctively, she crushed her lips against his in a kiss that could have melted the leather of his shoes. Then she said the words he too had been longing to hear.

"I love you too Jake."

Chapter Thirty-Seven

As the final weeks of the summer went by, Ryan and Jase were still blissfully unaware of Jake and Jordan's relationship. Sure keeping things a secret made things a little convoluted but in the end everything seemed to work out.

The more time they spent together, the more in love Jordan felt. She was still trying to figure out the best way to tell her brothers and had committed herself to telling them before the start of school and the hockey season. She was hopeful this would be possible since all had been quiet on the Tommy front since that fateful night at Rookies.

With that resolve in mind she planned on dropping the bomb after the end of summer party the team was throwing that night at the hockey house. Now she needed Maddey to arrive so she could bounce the idea off someone else.

As if on cue she heard the front door open.

"Jor, where you at?" Maddey shouted after she let herself in like usual.

"Upstairs," she yelled back.

"Hey girl." Maddey said as she entered the room, dropping her overnight bag on the bed before giving her best friend a hug.

She paused in packing her own overnight bag to return her friend's hug.

"Hey I'm so happy you came to hang out with me before heading over to the hockey house."

Maddey regarded her knowingly. "Uh oh. I can tell by your face you have something going on in that pretty head of yours. Spill."

Jordan took a deep breath and let it out in a rush.

"I was thinking of telling Ryan and Jase about me and Jake after the party tonight."

"Wow," Maddey said, stunned into silence.

"Yup."

"That's a big move."

"Yup."

"Are you sure you're ready for this?"

"Nope."

"Did you talk to Jake about it?"

"Nope."

"Okay, enough with the monosyllabic answers," Maddey scolded.

"Sorry, I'm just nervous." She sat down on the bed with a thunk as the enormity of what she was considering hit her.

Maddey sat down next to her and curled her legs under her to get comfortable.

"I think the first thing you have to do is talk to Jake and see what he thinks."

She laughed and waved her hand in the air in a dismissive manner. "*Please*, he's been wanting to tell them since the beginning."

The girls looked at each other and fell into a fit of giggles.

"Well this weekend certainly won't be boring that's for sure," Maddey concluded.

"Yeah potential homicide has that effect," Jordan deadpanned.

"Okay time to focus on something else." Maddey rose from the bed and went into Jordan's closet. "What are you wearing tonight?"

Some of the guys unloaded the cars from their trips to Costco and the liquor store for the evening's party, while the rest of the team set things up around the house.

It was only noon and they had the majority of what needed to be done complete. The backyard had cornhole, Kan Jam, ladderball, and horseshoes set up in different areas. They even put the volleyball net up in the pool.

Tucker and Jake got the kegs situated in their coolers with ice, while Jase and Ryan took care of tables and chairs.

"Do we have enough wood for the fire pit?" Jase asked.

"Yeah, I went out yesterday and picked up a few more cords just in case," Tucker confirmed.

"Okay, good. What else do we need to prep food wise?" Jake asked as he tapped the last keg.

"We just have to put out the chips and stuff but we'll wait until closer to the party for that. The girls are bringing potato and pasta salad, as well as stuff to make s'mores," Ryan supplied.

"And we bought enough burgers, dogs, chicken, and steak to feed an army," Jase added.

The guys shared a laugh as they made their way inside the house.

"What time is Sammy coming to set up?" Jake asked.

It was a nice perk to be friends with a DJ when they had parties. Sammy really knew how to keep a party going strong.

Ryan checked the time on his phone. "He'll probably be here in an hour or so. He said he would come early in case we needed any additional help setting up."

"Any idea how many people are coming to this thing?" Jase asked from where he sat down on the couch turning the TV to a baseball game.

"The Facebook event said about a hundred of us, though that is including most of the team. But you know how these things go, anyone could show up." Jake shook his head at the memories of some of their more epic parties in the past that came to mind.

As planned, Jordan and Maddey arrived at the hockey house a few hours early to help with food and to hang before everything got hectic. Skye was due to join them once she got off her lifeguard shift at the pool.

Ryan currently had Maddey pinned against the counter in the kitchen. He ran his nose down the side of her ear and placed a kiss to the sensitive spot behind it.

"Oh how I've missed you babe," he whispered.

"I've missed you too." She tilted her face up for a proper kiss.

"If the two of you weren't so cute together, I think I would be sick," Jordan grumbled as she put away food in the fridge.

"The thing that sucks about school starting back up is now I'm going to see you even less when you move back into the city," Ryan told Maddey.

"Are you actually pouting Ry?" Jordan shook her head at the sight. "Damn, you've gone soft."

"Bite me," Ryan told his sister.

"*Careful...* You know I would," she said with an evil laugh.

Maddey threaded her arms around Ryan's neck. "Don't worry. I'll come spend as many of my off days here as I can. Plus your sister is so excited to be able to go to your games again that I won't miss many. It'll be easier having company to watch the games with anyway."

He let out a short laugh. "Oh man, you have no idea what you are getting yourself into going to the games with her. She's intense."

"Good I'll have someone to teach me what is going on."

"You know I will. You'll be an expert by the time I'm through with you." Jordan reached out to bump fists with her friend.

"Well, hopefully you'll still be attracted to me after. She can be pretty brutal in her critique," Ryan worried.

Maddey smiled. "I'm sure your manly prowess is safe." She placed a quick kiss on his lips.

"I can't wait to see you wearing my jersey. It will never look so good," he said with a hint of possessiveness in his tone.

When her brother lifted her friend onto the counter to make-out Jordan knew it was time to high tail it out of there. With her older brother now occupied in the kitchen with her best friend and Jase off elsewhere, she used this rare moment alone to talk to Jake without prying eyes or ears. Under the guise of watching the Yankees game on TV she sat down next to him on the big couch in the living room.

Turning to him, she smiled. "Hi."

"Hi." Jake returned her smile.

"I wanted to talk to you about something."

"Okay, shoot."

She was nervous. Jake, always able to read her like a book, picked up on it instantly. He took a quick look around to make sure they were still alone and reached for her hand to give it a reassuring squeeze.

"Babe, you know you can talk to me about anything."

"Well I was thinking." She paused again and bit her lip. She decided to bite the bullet. "I'm thinking about telling my brothers about us after the party."

Jake's eyes widened in surprise. Of all the things she could have brought up, this was not one he expected. Sure he wanted to come clean with the guys right away but she knew he understood why she wanted to keep her brothers in the dark. He knew eventually their relationship would be able to be out in the open and that all that really mattered was he had her as his girl.

"Wow." He was still speechless from shock.

After a minute he continued. "What changed your mind?"

"I'm sick of sneaking around and having to watch other girls around you without being able to lay claim. Like tonight will suck, I'm sure." She made a face thinking of the puck bunnies that would be at the party later that evening. "I mean you do a good job of pushing them away but it's still not the same as me telling a bitch to *back* off."

Jake laughed at the look of disgust on her face. He liked the jealous side of her.

"Babe, you know those girls have *nothing* on you. You are the *hottest* girl I know."

That got him a smile from her.

"So, let's tell them now," he offered as a solution.

After thinking about his suggestion for a moment she shook her head. "No. I don't want there to be anything that could ruin the party. It's not fair for the rest of the team."

He nodded at that. "Okay so what's the plan?"

"I don't know," she said sheepishly.

He laughed. "Okay, well what should we say? Should we tell them we've been together most of the summer?"

"I don't know that either." Jordan paused to look him deep in his gorgeous bright green eyes. "I just know that we *will* tell them *tonight* no matter what. *Nothing* will keep us apart anymore. I'm just done with it all."

"Whatever you want, babe, I'll just follow your lead." He ran a finger down the side of her face in a loving caress.

Chapter Thirty-Eight

The party had been in full swing for a few hours and Jordan was doing her best to not grind down her molars to dust in frustration from watching the puck bunnies make passes at Jake. Just like always, Tabby had been particularly attentive to him all night.

Trying to get her mind off of what was going on in the other room, she had spent the past hour playing beer pong with Jase.

"What, is there no one out there that can take us on?" Jase taunted the room at large. "We've been running the table for over an hour and have had barely anything to drink. I'm *thirsty*."

She rolled her eyes at her twin. He was such a *guy* at times.

"We *can* retire you know," she cast him a look. "I *would* like to spend time somewhere other than the dining room."

Jase looked down at her and smirked. "You know I think that's an *awesome* idea."

He turned to face the room at large. With a slight bow he said, "Well it's been an honor to play for our fans but my sister and I will be retiring for the night. Good luck to you future competitors."

She pushed her brother on the back to get him moving toward the sliding back doors. "Okay, Wayne Gretzky. Will you just go, it's beer pong for *Christ's* sake."

"Oh, but you know you love me." He laughed as he let her manhandle him outside where they joined Ryan, Maddey, and Skye by the fire pit.

"Only because I shared a womb with you," she muttered.

"Did you guys finally lose?" Ryan looked up from the Adirondack chair he sat in with Maddey snuggled on his lap.

"No. I was finally able to convince hot shot over here,"— she hooked her thumb in her twin's direction— "we should retire so we could experience the rest of the party." She rolled her eyes in the direction of her twin.

"I swear the way he left, you would think he was retiring from the NHL and not a beer pong game."

She settled into the empty chair next to Ryan and murmured her thanks to Jase as he handed her one of the beers he poured from the keg.

"Hey, I went two years without having a decent partner. It's nice to finally have someone I can kick Jake and Tucker's asses with." Jase tapped his solo cup against hers.

"Why are we talking about my ass? Because if you wanted to grab it you know you don't have to ask ladies," Tucker said with a wink as he joined the group.

"Please," Skye answered with an exaggerated eye roll. "If I'm grabbing anyone's ass it isn't going to be yours."

Maddey choked on her beer at Skye's response.

"Oh, darlin' you know you love my ass." Tucker waggled his eyebrows at Skye. The sexual tension between the two crackled like always.

"Seriously I think you guys need to start sleeping together again. The sexual tension is so thick between you two I feel like I need to take a shower after I'm with you," Jordan suggested.

"Blondie, you are so smart. I think that is an *excellent* suggestion." Tucker saluted her with his beer.

"*Hey*. I thought you were my BFF?" Skye asked.

"Oh I am."

"How is you helping Tuck get his dick wet helping me?"

Jordan sputtered into her beer. Leave it to Skye to be blunt as usual. "Well *you* also get laid in the scenario."

"Good point." Tucker sent Skye a hopeful look.

"Not gonna happen."

The group laughed at Tucker's rejection.

After a while more people joined the group around the fire including Sammy and Jake. Jordan was happy to note Tabby was on the other side of the backyard at the moment.

Skye had gone into the house to get all the supplies to make s'mores earlier. And the whole crew had a blast making them.

"Oh, this is the best campfire treat ever." Jordan exclaimed while licking the last remnants of melted marshmallow off her fingers.

She looked up and caught Jake's heated stare across the fire as he watched her tongue clean her fingers and smiled. Sending him a quick wink she hoped no one noticed. She was happy to note Jake adjusted his shorts, clearly not unaffected by her.

He was so hot sitting there in his green Ninja Turtle t-shirt and khaki cargo shorts and she longed to go over and curl up in his lap as Maddey was in Ryan's. She checked the time on her phone and realized it was already after midnight. The party would be winding down soon and the moment would come soon enough for her to bite the bullet and reveal the truth of her relationship for all the world to know.

Jake noticed the anxious look on her face and sent her a

reassuring smile. He mouthed the word *soon* to her and she returned his smile.

The next hour flew by with good conversation and tons of joking around. Tucker was always there to tell a joke or an outrageous story. The backyard was finally emptying out of the extra partygoers and those who would be staying overnight at the house started to make their way inside.

To Jordan's dismay some of the remaining people were a few puck bunnies, including Tabby. Deciding to shake it off, she started to help clean up in the dining room. Soon it would all be a moot point. Her brothers would know about her and Jake and puck bunnies would become the least of her worries.

As she finished wiping the last of the beer residue off the table, she went to check the time on her phone and noticed it wasn't in her back pocket. She could have sworn she had it with her when she came inside.

"Has anyone seen my phone?" She asked the room at large.

"I thought I saw a phone outside on one of the fire pit chairs earlier," Tabby answered, pausing in her blatant attempt at flirting with Jake while he cleaned up the garbage in the kitchen.

Still slightly miffed at Tabby's presence in general, she muttered a soft thanks and opened the sliding glass doors to go out back.

There was nothing on the chair she had been sitting in. She double checked the whole area around the fire pit but no phone. Deciding to check the other areas she was earlier, she checked around the cornhole game and the horse shoe area and still no dice.

She headed over to the pool to see if maybe it fell out while she was helping referee the end of the overly competitive water volleyball game and again came up empty. She figured she'd have to go inside and grab someone's phone to call herself to find it. She was getting ready to do that when a voice startled her.

"Whatcha lookin' for, Sweetness?"

She froze where she was, panicked. That was *not* Jake's voice. No, that cold, calculating, satisfied voice belonged to Tommy. A million questions flittered across her brain including how he found out where the hockey house was.

Her fight or flight instinct kicked in and she went to turn to run back to the house when his hand reached out and roughly grabbed her around her upper arm and pulled her to face him. She could feel the bruises forming already.

A very evil, Grinch like smile spread across Tommy's face as she felt her whole body seize in pure terror. He pulled her body flush against his and reached down to grab her ass.

"Did you miss me Sweetness?" He couldn't keep the smile out of the sound of his voice.

Jordan was still in a state of shock and it took a few seconds for the moment to catch up with itself and comprehend what was happening. When it all clicked into place she began to struggle in earnest.

Bringing her hands and elbows together she wedged them between her body and his and pushed with all her strength, silently cursing her small stature.

Tommy laughed at her feeble attempts at escape. "Where are you trying to go, Sweetness? You are right where you *belong*." He bent down and covered her mouth with his own, digging his thumb into her chin when he knew she would try to bite him. He knew her tricks now.

"What the hell do you think you are *doing*? GET. OFF. ME!" She growled after she was finally able to break free of Tommy's slobbering mouth.

He enjoyed feeling her struggle against him and kept her pinned to his body as much as he could. "I love when you play hard to get."

She didn't know how she was going to get away from Tommy but she wasn't going to give up without a fight.

Then she remembered she wasn't alone. There was a house full of people in it but a few yards away. She wasn't sure if anyone would hear her but she had to try. She knew she needed reinforcements.

"JAKE!" She screamed. "HELP! JAKE!"

He was always the first person she thought about.

Tommy laughed in her face. "What you think lover boy will come to your rescue?"

Her back went ramrod straight at how Tommy referred to Jake and she stopped struggling for a moment with surprise.

"What? You thought I didn't know about you and that asshole? I've seen you guys together. How *dare* he touch what is *mine*. But regardless he's probably busy with Tabby. I know you've seen the way she is with him, it is only a matter of time until they get together."

"*Tabby*?" Her brain was still struggling to keep up with the turn of conversation.

"Yes Tabby. The stupid little puck bunny will do *anything* for someone who gives her the slightest bit of attention." He stroked her along the side of her face.

"I acted all sympathetic to how she wanted Jake but couldn't get his attention. I offered her my help if she helped me with you. It should be illegal how easy it was to manipulate her."

"That's *sick*," she said venomously.

She wasn't any closer to getting away from Tommy and when he tried to kiss her again she made another attempt in getting help.

"JAAAAAAAAAKE!"

She was still fighting against Tommy as he pulled her in for a kiss by her hair. All her struggles caused them to move closer to the edge of the pool and suddenly she felt her feet lose their footing and she toppled into the pool with Tommy in tow.

JAKE PLACED THE dining room table's chairs back around it once he finished cleaning off the rest of the evidence of the beer pong games that were played on it. Tabby was still trying to hang off him as she had been doing all night. Usually he was able to shake her attempts at getting too close, but she was being especially clingy tonight.

After extracting his arm from her grip, *again*, he looked up because he could have sworn he heard someone call his name.

"Did someone say my name?" he asked the room at large.

"I didn't hear anything," Tabby answered as she glanced over at the patio doors apprehensively.

He shrugged it off and continued in the final cleanup process. But then he heard the noise again and swore for sure he heard his name. He saw Maddey nearby and caught her attention.

"Where's Jordan?" He asked.

"I think she's still outside looking for her phone," she answered on her way down the hall with a full garbage bag.

"Thanks. I'll go see if she needs a flashlight to help find it."

On his way to the door he noticed Tabby tried to block his way out but was able to get around her. He cast a quick look around the backyard and didn't see her anywhere which was odd. Then at a closer look he heard noise coming from the pool and his gut could tell something was wrong with this picture. He turned back to yell through the door he left open for Ryan and Jase as he ran toward the pool.

The sight that greeted him chilled his blood. Jordan was wrapped in the volleyball net that used to be up across the pool, while a figure was trying to push her under the water. On instinct he jumped in after her to help.

Upon closer inspection he noticed Jordan's attacker was none other than Tommy. He pulled him off of a flailing Jordan and punched him squarely in the face. That was when Ryan and Jase jumped in and dragged Tommy to the edge of the pool.

Jordan was trapped in the volleyball net like a dolphin in a fisherman's net. Tommy's advances had made it nearly impossible for her to break the water's surface. Jake had to get to her before she ran out of air.

With Ryan and Jase fighting with Tommy, Jake was free to go to Jordan. He saw her battling with the net under the water and swam the short distance to where she was. He placed his arms under her body and lifted her up as he pulled the net from where it was tangled around her body. He could hear her gasping for air as she clung to his neck as soon as she was free.

He supported her against his body with an arm under her knees and the other behind her back. He trudged his way through the water to the stairs at the end of the pool.

With all the commotion going on outside, everyone that was in the house had made their way out into the backyard and couldn't believe the scene that was unfolding. Reading the situation correctly, Sammy already had his phone to his ear calling the police, while the rest of the guys helped bring an unconscious Tommy out of the pool.

He set her down on the patio next to the pool and knelt in front of her. He held her face in his hands and tilted it up to his. "Baby, are you okay? Did he hurt you?" His voice was anxious as he asked.

She shook her head. "I'm fine. He didn't hurt me," she answered around gulping breaths as she tried to make up for the oxygen she was deprived of.

"Are you *sure*?" He stroked her cheeks with his thumbs.

"Yes I promise. I'm more messed up from being tangled in the net and not being able to get air, but I feel fine now."

As the panic from what transpired started to wear off, she wound her arms around his neck and the two of them crashed together in a fierce kiss simultaneously, both trying to reaffirm that they were real and whole.

With the chaos of everything, they forgot they weren't alone and realized their mistake at Ryan's venomous voice.

"Uh, does *anyone* want to tell me what the *hell* is going on here?" Ryan stared down at where one of his best friends was kissing his sister.

Jake and Jordan broke apart quickly and Jake rested his forehead against hers.

"Well I guess it's time to face the music," he said to her.

"This wasn't exactly how I envisioned this going," she said.

"Cats out of the bag now."

"Time to bite the bullet."

"Seriously what the *fuck* is going on?" Ryan asked, utterly confused.

Jordan rose to stand with his help. "Umm, well you see… Jake and I have been dating."

"*What*?" Ryan asked not sure he heard her correctly.

"We've been going out for most of the summer."

"What?"

Jordan shook her head at her older brother. "Ry, you heard me, now *hear* me."

Ryan's face contorted. "What the hell JD. Did you *not* learn your lesson the first time dating someone on the team?" He pointed to Tommy. "I mean do you need more proof than that?"

Jordan went toe-to-toe with her big brother. She wouldn't let him manipulate the situation. "Ry, he *isn't* like Tommy."

"How do you know? We didn't know Tommy was like this until it happened."

"It's different."

"How?"

"I *love* him," she said with conviction.

Ryan was clearly struggling to find the words to say. Jake wasn't sure which event, Jordan's relationship status or her attack, was harder to grasp. She gave him a minute to process and turned to her twin. "Seriously. *Come on,* Jase. You guys know Jake. You are so much closer to him than you ever were to Tommy. Do you *honestly* think he would ever hurt me?"

"No," Jase reluctantly agreed. "But why all the secrecy?"

"I know how you guys are. I mean look at you both now. Jake just helped save my life for lack of a better word, not for the first time, but the *second*, and you still want me to have nothing to do with him. We liked each other and wanted to see where things went before we broached the subject of us dating with you.

"I love you both so much and didn't want to upset you or your friendship with Jake, but it got to the point where I had to do what I wanted. I don't need your permission, but I would like your acceptance."

Ryan and Jase shared a knowing look and turned to Jake as a unit. He stood his ground.

"Well she told us how she feels, what about you?" Ryan asked Jake.

"I love her too," he declared.

After a tense moment Jordan's brothers relaxed and pulled him in for a man hug.

"Well, I say between that and the fact that you *did* fight this asshole twice for her, I can get behind that." Ryan said with a dismissive wave at Tommy.

"The cops should be here shortly," Sammy informed them.

Jordan snuggled into Jake's embrace. "As much as I'm not looking forward to dealing with all this,"— she waved a hand in Tommy's direction— "I just want this to all be over already."

"You're not alone in that babe. We'll all be here to help you get through this," Jake said into the top of her head.

"Plus, now the cops will finally have enough to lock him up," Maddey said.

"Yeah even his dad can't get him out of this, since his dumbass couldn't stay away," Jase added.

The group shared a laugh and they knew everything would work out. Now all they needed was for the cops to come to take out the trash.

Epilogue

J ake looked around the hotel suite and couldn't believe he was actually there. Sure, it was every athlete's dream to play their sport professionally, but knowing he was there for the NHL draft was still hard to fathom.

Being there with Jordan and their families brought back memories of the prior year when everyone gathered for when Ryan entered the draft. Ryan's situation was a little less stressful since they had an idea beforehand where he would end up playing but for Jake they had no idea.

Ryan was drafted as the number one overall pick and went to play for the New Jersey Blizzards who won the first pick in the draft lottery. It was awesome he was playing locally.

Since the BTU team had won the NCAA National Championships the three years Jake was the starting goalie, they had more guys entering the draft than ever before. Jase and Tucker were also entering the draft with him.

Jake's biggest worry over not knowing where he was going to be drafted to, was what it would mean for his relationship with Jordan. He rubbed his hand over where the ring box rested in the inside pocket of his suit jacket.

These past two years together had been amazing, even when you considered their rocky start. Having Jordan cheer him and her brothers on at every game had been the best part.

He looked out to where she was standing on the balcony observing the city below and smiled.

God, he loved the hell out of her.

JORDAN GRIPPED THE bar in front of her as she took a deep breath to calm her nerves. She couldn't say she was surprised to be at the draft for Jake. His playing only got better with every game he played. The draft itself wasn't what had her nerves jumping around like Mexican jumping beans, but the uncertainty of what it meant for their relationship.

Ryan and Maddey had managed to make their relationship work this past year with him in the pros, so she hoped it was a sign that she and Jake could also make it work. Not knowing where he would end up playing was what scared her the most.

She let out a sigh. Running a hand through her hair, she let out a small laugh. They made it through the Tommy situation and having to date in secret and were still together. She should be so lucky to have their biggest obstacle to date be the city Jake would have to earn a multi-million dollar salary in, first world problems and all that.

Please, if they could get through all that crap at the beginning of their relationship, they could get through anything.

The sliding glass doors to the balcony slid open behind her and Jake's arms came around her body shortly after, pulling her back to lean against the solid wall of his chest.

She felt him smile when she relaxed against him automatically. Things between them were so natural and easy. He rested his cheek against the top of her head inhaling deeply.

"What's going on inside that gorgeous head of yours?" he asked.

"Why do you think I have anything going on in my head?"

"You've been unusually quiet since we left our families to come upstairs." He reached out to turn her around to face him. He cupped her cheek in his hand and brushed his thumb along the corner of her mouth.

"Plus, I can see where you've chewed off your lipstick from biting your lower lip. You usually do that when *something* is on your mind."

She leaned into his touch and smiled at how well he knew her. She was hesitant to tell him what she was thinking about. This time was supposed to be about him and she wanted him to enjoy every second of it.

"It's stupid really." She tried to turn away but his grip on her tightened.

"Baby, if it's bothering you it's not stupid. You know you can tell me *anything*, right?"

"I know but it just feels selfish of me."

He pulled her into him and hugged her close against his chest. He had a feeling he knew what she was thinking about since the same was on his mind. He wasn't one hundred percent sure how he was going to ask her to marry him but he decided now was as good of a time as any.

Drawing back, he tucked a stray strand of hair behind her right ear and cupped her cheek in his hand again. She always seemed to relax when he did so. Reaching down to thread the fingers of his right hand with those on her left, he lifted their joined hands to rest over his heart.

"I know you're worried about the draft."

He cut her off before she could utter the protest he knew she would.

"But baby, you don't have to be. No matter where I get drafted, we will make it work."

He rubbed his thumb across the knuckles of her hand.

"We've dealt with our Romeo and Juliet relationship, no problem. Plus we handled the drama of Tommy. Do you honestly think we can't handle a little thing like *geography*?"

That got a small smile out of her. He took that moment to kiss her deeply.

He pulled back and slid down to one knee.

Jordan let out a small gasp when she realized what was happening.

Jake looked a little nervous as he met her gaze. "Jordan, baby, I love you with all my heart. You keep me grounded and make me happier than I ever thought possible." He paused to take the ring box out of his pocket to open it.

"Wherever I go, I want you to go. Will you make me the happiest guy in the world and spend the rest of your life with me?"

She felt tears run down her cheeks. Without answering she threw her arms around Jake's neck and kissed him, knocking them over onto the floor of the balcony.

After a few minutes Jake rolled them over so he was on top and pulled back from the kiss. He looked her deep in her eyes.

"Well?" He asked.

"Well *what*?"

"Are you going to give me an answer or what?"

"Oh." She paused. "I thought it was obvious. Of course!"

"Thank *God*!"

They went back to making out for a few more minutes, the ring box lay forgotten on the balcony floor until Jordan rolled over it with her shoulder.

She looked at the ring and then back at the man she loved with all her heart.

"Well *fucking* put it on me already!"

Jake laughed at her impatient command. Slowly he took the ring out of the box and slid it onto her finger. Seeing his ring on her finger did it for him as much as seeing her wearing his jersey.

"*God*, I love you so much, baby."

"I love you too Jake."

"No regrets?"

"None. Where you go, I go."

They sealed the deal with another kiss.

Want more BTU Alumni? *All your Power Play favorites are back and joined by a new cast of characters in BTU2- Tap Out.*

Want to know what happens during Ryan's last Frozen Four? Or find out how The Coven gets their name? *Sign up for my newsletter to get your exclusive bonus content. *Psst you might also get your a peak at those joining in the fun in Tap Out.**

>*Sign up @ www.alleyciz.com*

Reviews are the life blood of an indie author. *So if you're one of the cool kids who writes them here are the links to Amazon, Goodreads, and BookBub. Smothering toddler hugs and sloppy puppy kisses!!!*

Alley

Playlist

Justin Timberlake: "FutureSex/LoveSound"
Lauv/Julia Michaels: "There's No Way"
Bruno Mars: "That's What I Like"
Nick Jonas: "Jealous"
Aerosmith: "Rag Doll"
Bruno Mars (feat Cardi B): "Finesse Remix"
Britney Spears: "Toxic"
8-Bit Arcade: "Katy Perry & Zedd Emulation"
Lady Antebellum: "Just A Kiss"
Ed Sheeran: "Kiss Me"
John Mayer: "Slow Dancing in a Burning Room"
Rayvon Owen: "Can't Fight It (Stripped)"
Rihanna/Calvin Harris: "We Found Love"
John Legend: "You & I (Nobody in the World)"
Spotify Playlist

Randomness For My Readers

Hello new friends!

I hope you enjoyed hanging out with Jake and Jordan and getting to know all their crazy friends. Did you know, when I first started writing *Power Play* I had zero intention of publishing it. I know, I know… What?! Well it's true.

So how did *Power Play* come to be you ask? Well lets see…

Ever have one of those dreams you can't shake? The kind that you have over and over no matter how many nights in a row, you either repeat it or it picks up where it left off the night before? Well that's what *Power Play* was to me. Jake and Jordan just had to tell me their story and one day I decided to write it down.

Then chapter by chapter I sent it off to my two book junkie cousins to read and eight years later I finally finished the rough draft. Eight Years?! I know forever. Luckily for you, now that I decided "Hey maybe I should do this thing," I write a hell of a lot faster.

Even with it done, I still didn't know if I was going to publish it and release it out in the world. Then with my Hubs and family giving me a push and my parents paying for my first editor I decided to give it a go.

Then thanks to fangirling all over Maria Luis and R. Linda in their reader groups, I made them become my internet besties *one day we will hang out in person* and picked their brains on how to turn this dream of being an author a reality and now you have *Power Play* in your hands. Still can't believe this is real life.

So thank you so much for giving *Power Play* a shot *see what I did there* as well as taking a chance on me by reading my debut. If you want to go for the hat trick, make sure you pick up *Tap Out* when it comes out in September. *See told you I write faster than one book every eight years.*

So now for a little bullet style fun facts:

- Like Jordan I was a competitive swimmer. I didn't swim in college but I was a 4 years Varsity swimmer in high school and summer club team member for years.
- My Hubs did play hockey growing up, but sadly by the time I met him he know longer played.
- A Corvette is my *dream* car
- I love the Transformers
- *Friends* and *How I Met Your Mother* are on constantly repeat in my house. I even have my toddlers trained to ask to put it on TV *major parental accomplishment right there*
- The Hubs and I were reigning beer pong champs back in the day
- I worked in a bar during college, even have my bartending license. *Did you know you can go to school to be a bartender?*
- The story of how Jordan and Skye met? That's how really met one of my besties.
- My main squad is huge like the BTU crew and most of us have been friends since high school or sooner.

If my rambling hasn't turned you off and you are like "This chick is my kind of crazy," feel free to reach out!

Lots of Love,
Alley

For A Good Time Call

Did you have fun with J&J's Squad? Do you want to stay up-to-date on releases, be the first to see cover reveals, excerpts from upcoming books, deleted scenes, sales, freebies, and all sorts of insider information you can't get anywhere else?

If you're like "Duh! Come on Alley." Make sure you sign up for my newsletter.

>Sign up @ www.alleyciz.com

Ask yourself this:

* Are you a Romance Junkie?

* Do you like book boyfriends and book besties? (yes this is a thing)

* Is your GIF game strong?

* Want to get inside the crazy world of Alley Ciz?

If any of your answers are yes, maybe you should join my Facebook reader group, Romance Junkie's Coven

>Join the Coven @

www.facebook.com/groups/AlleyCizReaderGroup

Stalk Alley

* All links can be found @ www.alleyciz.com

Facebook Reader Group

Newsletter Sign up

Like Alley on Facebook

Follow Alley on Instagram

Hang with Alley on Goodreads

Follow Alley on Amazon

Follow Alley on BookBub

Subscribe on YouTube for Book Trailers

Follow Alley's inspiration boards on Pinterest

Acknowledgments

I can't even being to express how thankful I am for each and every person who helped make this dream of mine a reality. Now I know how actors feel trying to give their Oscar speeches, hopefully I don't miss anyone. If I need I'm sorry and I still love you, just you know, mommy brain.

I'll start with the Hubs who has to deal with my lack of sleep, putting off laundry *because... laundry* and helping to hold the fort down with our three crazy mini royals. You truly are my best friend. Also, I'm sure he would want me to make sure I say thanks for all the hero inspiration, but it is true. Keep that wink game strong.

For my parents for supporting me and helping make it possible to follow my dream.

Like I said before for Maria and Renee for letting me badger them with endless questions while I tried to learn and navigate my way through this self-pub thing.

For my cousins Megan and Melanie for sticking with me and pushing me to write more, even when it was months or years before they got new words from me. Jake and Jordan's story never would have been told without you both.

To my Beta Bitches, my OG Coven: Gemma, Jenny, Megan, Caitie, Sarah, Nova, Andi, and Dana. Our group chat gives me life.

To Jenny (again) my PA, without her I wouldn't be organized enough for any of my releases to happen. Seriously girl thank you so much for everything you do. Plus I'm so honored to have the trailer queen on my team.

For LJ Shen for *unknowingly* being the catalyst to me finding most of my Beta Bitches and my PA thanks to a group chat formed from her reader group. Bow down to the Queen.

For Ben my editor for helping me learn how to be a better writer and helping me come up with some of my favorite changes to *Power Play's* story.

To Gemma (again) for going from my proofreader to fangirl and being so invested in my characters stories to threaten my life *lovingly of course*

To Dawn for giving *Power Play* it's final spit shine.

To my real life squad for giving me the memories and constant source of inspiration needed to throw a fictional twist on.

To Michelle and my street team for being the best pimps ever.

To every blogger and bookstagrammer that took a chance on a new author and read my words and wrote about them. Without you only like 10 people would know about *Power Play* or me.

Thank you to all the authors in the indie community for your support and answering ALL of the questions I had and will continue to have. Without you all this wouldn't have happened.

To my fellow Romance Junkies in my Coven, for coming on this journey with me before even reading a word I wrote, you are the real MVPs.

And, of course, to you my fabulous reader, for picking up

my book and giving me a chance. Without you I wouldn't be able to live my dream of bringing to life the stories the voices in my head tell me.

Lots of Love,

Alley

Also by Alley Ciz

BTU Alumni Series

Power Play (Jake and Jordan)

Musical Mayhem (Sammy and Jamie) BTU Novella

Tap Out (Gage and Rocky)

Sweet Victory (Vince and Holly)

Puck Performance (Jase and Melody)

Writing Dirty (Maddey and Dex)

Scoring Beauty- BTU6 Preorder, Releasing September 2021

#UofJ Series

Cut Above The Rest (Prequel)- Freebie

Looking To Score

Game Changer

Playing For Keeps

Off The Bench- #UofJ4 Preorder, Releasing December 2021

The Royalty Crew (A #UofJ Spin-Off)

Savage Queen- Preorder, Releasing April 2021

Ruthless Noble- Preorder, Releasing June 2021

About the Author

Alley Ciz is an internationally bestselling indie author of sassy heroines and the alpha men that fall on their knees for them. She is a romance junkie whose love for books turned into her telling the stories of the crazies who live in her head...even if they don't know how to stay in their lane.

This Potterhead can typically be found in the wild wearing a funny T-shirt, connected to an IV drip of coffee, stuffing her face with pizza and tacos, chasing behind her 3 minis, all while her 95lb yellow lab—the best behaved child—watches on in amusement.

facebook.com/AlleyCizAuthor
instagram.com/alley.ciz
pinterest.com/alleyciz
goodreads.com/alleyciz